Fall

a ROCK SOLID romance

KARINA BLISS

FALL
Copyright © 2016 Karina Bliss

ALL RIGHTS RESERVED

Print Edition 1.1
ISBN: 9780994116574
Publisher: Karina Bliss
www.karinabliss.com

Cover Design: www.okaycreations.com
Editor: Wanda Ottewell
Proofreader: Serena Clarke
Interior Formatting: Author E.M.S.

Published in the United States of America.

Keep Rage together at all costs…

Powerhouse PA Dimity Graham is off her game. Her career is everything to her and she never lets anything personal mess that up.

So how can she explain getting busy between the sheets with Rage's nice-guy drummer Seth Curran?

She's supposed to be keeping this band out of trouble, not getting into it.

But before she can put everything back where it belongs, Seth needs her help.

♪ ♫ ♩

Faking a relationship seemed like a good idea that night, right before they fell into bed together.

But standing on New Zealand soil, facing the people he disappointed to pursue his dream, Seth doubts he and Dimity will convince anyone they're hot and crazy for each other.

To his surprise, Dimity is working her magic on everyone and they're all convinced this is the real deal.

The problem is, he's almost convinced, too.

CHAPTER 1

THE DAY HER MOTHER REMARRIED in the Bahamas, Dimity Graham decided to celebrate her freedom by getting laid in Los Angeles.

No more sending money for another surgical procedure Helena was sure would convince Dimity's father to leave the bitch he'd ditched them for, and come home.

No more obligatory visits struggling to breathe because her self-absorbed mother sucked all the oxygen from the room.

Over the past sixteen years—until Helena had given up hope and succumbed to Floyd, her besotted dentist—her mom had tried to speed Steven Graham's repentance and return. She began with helplessness, "Honey, you know I'm hopeless with money"; moved onto guilt, "We're losing the house because I've missed too many payments"; and peaked with emotional blackmail, "I've told our only child to decide whose side she's on."

At eleven years old, Dimity had chosen to support her mother because—as she'd regretfully told her father over Aegean salmon and a lollipop tree for two at Bloomingdale's—*someone* had to. A diplomat with a keen sense of self-preservation, he'd accepted her decision with relief and abandoned her to Helena's ravaging dependency.

Dimity wished she'd inherited his selfishness. Unfortunately, she'd picked up a conscience by way of a defective gene—her great-aunt had been a nun. Certainly, Dimity had been living like one lately, and that would change tonight. She was finally free to divert her mental energy into meeting her own needs—once she figured them out. Sex seemed a good start.

But work came first. Plonking her glass of champagne on the ivory escritoire that held her two laptops, she phoned her rock-star boss in New Zealand.

Zander answered with a groan. "Fuck, woman, it's six a.m."

"And you're still in bed?" She didn't cloak the disgust in her tone. On tour they regularly survived on four hours sleep.

"I'm recuperating from vocal surgery, remember? Can't this wait until a civilized hour?"

"No. Your realtor has an offer of ten million on the New York penthouse but I think we should stall until *Entertainment Tonight* runs their celebrity crib feature on Thursday." Offering an exclusive viewing to the show had been her brainchild. The publicity would increase the number of potential buyers.

"The next payment on the lawyers' retainer is due when?" he asked. They were suing the insurers of the tour, who were claiming Zander's vocal polyps fell under a pre-existing condition and were refusing to pay out millions of dollars of cancellation insurance. If the insurers won, he'd go bankrupt.

"Tuesday. But the proceeds from your Barbados property will cover it." She looked around her pretty office in Zander's French Provençal manor in Calabasas. The sale of this one would break her heart. It was the only real home she'd ever had.

"You know I trust you to make the best decision. What's this middle-of-the-night call really about?"

Loneliness. She and Zander had worked eighteen-hour days for close to three years and she missed her mentor.

"Dimity?" The reason for Zee's plunge into a balanced life must have grabbed the phone. "Is anything wrong?" Elizabeth Winston was an emotional divining rod, exasperating and lovable in equal measure. Ever since she'd found Dimity weeping in a utility closet during the tour she'd acted like an interfering big sister—when Dimity wasn't acting like hers.

"I'm *fine.* Better than fine. Mom got re-married today and I'm finally free." *All long-term prisoners feel a little panicky stepping outside the cell.*

"That's wonder—" Elizabeth began to say before Zander's voice came on.

"So go celebrate."

"I fully intend to go on a sexual rampage." Dimity wasn't going to let a little panic stop her from embracing freedom.

"Now there's a thought…since you woke us anyway." The rough tenderness in his voice suggested he was looking at Elizabeth.

"Zee, no lurrrve stuff during a business call."

"This isn't a business call, you're bored and restless. Here's a challenge. Go flirt with my head of security, he's got a crush on you…Ow, why did Doc just hit me?" Doc was his nickname for his PhD love.

"Because she knows I'm trouble," Dimity explained patiently. "Best leave the good men out of it." Growing up in a dysfunctional household had given her a realistic view of where she sat on the evolutionary scale when it came to sustaining healthy relationships. Idly, she wondered if Bam Bam Rubble from The Flintstones had ever grown up. Her true calling lay in this job.

"You can't avoid that conversation with Luther forever." Zander didn't believe in tiptoeing around an issue when he could stomp. "You two will be working closely again when Elizabeth goes on her book tour next year."

In Bed With A Rock God. There was no one less likely to write a tell-all memoir than a Pulitzer Prize-winning biographer, which was probably why it was the most hotly anticipated book of the year.

"I have no problem avoiding him for another five days until I fly to New Zealand," Dimity said. This house was large enough to hide from a clan the size of the Kardashians. "But enough about me. Any update on your vocals?" The band's future was in limbo until Zander learned whether surgery had repaired his singing voice.

"Hang on," he said. She heard the sound of muffled conversation and tried not to read too much into it. The only drawback of her mother's unexpected remarriage was the time it freed up to worry more about her—the band's—future.

Zander came back on the line. "I'll have news when I see you down under."

Her fingers tightened on her cell. "Good news?" It had been seven weeks since Zander's surgery and they'd hoped for a result after six. But the operation hadn't been straightforward because he'd done more damage when he persisted in performing, against medical advice. He'd said he'd give his vocals plenty of time to heal before testing his vocals. Given the years she'd spent trying to rein in his recklessness, his sensible, conservative approach should have delighted her.

"Dimity, we make our own luck," he reminded her.

It was one of the many things she'd learned from rock's king of reinvention. "Damn right," she said, grateful for the reminder. "And on that note, I'd best finish up here so I can go make some lucky bastard's night."

"Leave him alive."

"I'll consider it. Goodbye."

"Dimity?"

About to hang up, she paused. "Yeah?"

"I miss you, too."

"Zee, you're embarrassing yourself," she said coolly, but she was smiling as she cut the connection. At least there was one person she could rely on. Helena was still punishing her with coolness for not making the wedding. Dimity's smile faded as she replaced the handset.

Zander Freedman was recognized as one of rock's greatest vocalists, and the king of reinvention. He'd brought his mega band, Rage, back from the dead by re-populating it with musicians he'd handpicked through a smash-hit reality show, immediately followed by a sell-out world tour.

He also had a deserved reputation as the most selfish egomaniac in rock 'n' roll. Meeting Elizabeth had changed him for the better. As long as his killer instinct was still intact, because they'd never needed it more.

To protect the livelihoods of the many people dependent on the tour's success he'd pushed his voice to the max, even lip-syncing the national anthem in front of the President at a war vets' fundraiser two months ago.

When the news broke, his haters had delighted in attacking him when he was literally voiceless, unable to use his considerable powers of chutzpah and charm to fight back. Combined with the lawsuit, her boss was in one of the darkest periods of his twenty-year career, the future of Rage in doubt. But, with Dimity's help, he'd risen from the ashes before and they could do it again.

What if his singing voice never comes back?

She caught herself nervously tugging at her false eyelashes and forced herself to pick up her task list. Why worry about worst-case scenarios when she could keep things running smoothly pending his triumphant return?

The rumble of Luther's Hummer distracted her ten minutes later, and she crossed to the window in time to catch the glow of the taillights disappearing into the six-car garage.

Ever since Zander had drunkenly let slip that his bodyguard had a thing for her a few months earlier, she'd avoided being alone with Luther. Particularly since he'd returned from New Zealand a couple of days ago, after reviewing Zander's security there. With all other staff on leave, the two of them were rattling around the mansion by themselves. Part of her was flattered by his crush. Inspiring such an upright, honorable man to carry a torch made her feel…validated.

Ugh. She'd been contaminated by Zander and Elizabeth's love cooties.

The motorized whine of the garage door made her draw back from the window.

You can't avoid that conversation with Luther forever. Zander had a point. Pausing to remember where the bodyguard would be at any given time felt like a weakness. And Dimity abhorred weakness in herself. Her mother lived to dodge personal responsibility, and her daughter was never taking that path. Besides, if Zander had noticed her wimpiness, other people would, too.

To hell with it. She powered down her laptop, resolved on telling him she wasn't in the market for a relationship. Then she'd have cleared her entire emotional in-tray and could focus on being slutty. And if she hurt his feelings…no, she wouldn't let those qualms stop her again.

Seizing her tote, she gave her appearance the obligatory check as she passed the hand-carved baroque mirror next to the door. In the music industry, image was everything, and she had her brand down to a fine art—an uptown girl dressed in Salvatore Ferragamo cut-out pumps the exact shade and softness of her tan leather jacket.

In a nod to rock 'n' roll she'd teamed her cream jeans with a glitzy belt, a tiger-patterned silk blouse and chunky gold jewelry. She didn't freshen her makeup—that would make the coming conversation too important—only raked a hand through the shoulder-length hair she paid her hairdresser a fortune to differentiate from every other faux blonde in this town. She'd touch up her war paint in the taxi en route to the club.

It took four minutes to stride from her office, down the grand staircase, through the entrance hall and conservatory and along the corridor in the sprawling left wing of the house to Luther's private apartments, plenty of time to decide on her approach. Really, she had three styles of delivering unpleasant truths—the jab, the hook, and the uppercut. Luther was man enough for the uppercut.

She had to knock twice before he opened the door—a rugby game blared excited commentary on the big-screen TV beyond him.

His dark gaze sharpened as he looked down at her. "Something up with Zander?"

"No. This is personal. Can I come in?"

Nothing changed in his expression but she sensed an immediate wariness. "Sure." He gestured her inside. "The test is on, All Blacks versus—"

"I'm not here to watch the game." Unlike the French Provençal opulence of the rest of the house, the furniture in his suite was both modern and sparse. A monster couch and armchair faced the TV. Between the two, a coffee table held a bowl of guacamole and nachos, a nearly empty bottle of tequila and a full shot glass. She hadn't pegged Luther as a solitary drinker. It made him more accessible…and maybe easier to hurt? But she couldn't chicken out now.

"Remember when Zee was drunk and said you had feelings for me and—"

"This isn't something we should talk about right now."

"It won't take long." Grabbing the remote from his hand, she hit pause to silence the overexcited commentator. "You know I think you're a great guy—" in the dead air, her voice rang like a clarion and she softened her tone "—but you and I? It's not going to happen."

He looked pained. Oh God, she *had* hurt him. "Dimity—"

"It's okay," she soothed. "I'm sure it's just a proximity thing…two attractive people working together. I don't even mind admitting I'm tempted. But you're the type of guy who'd want to put a ring on it, and I'm married to my career so—"

"Dimity." Luther held her gaze, waiting until he had her full attention. "Zander was wrong."

She looked at him blankly.

"I am in love with someone. It's not you."

"Oh." For the first time in forever she felt a blush heat her cheeks, starting warm and rocketing in temperature until her face flamed. She *never* revealed a want without first ascertaining if she could have it. She opened her mouth, scrambling for a joke, an insult, anything to mitigate the damage, but even her survival instinct had ducked for cover.

She could only stare helplessly as her blush leaped across the few feet separating them and spread across Luther's normally impassive face.

"Which is not to say," he said, with the delicacy of a man tiptoeing around a land mine, "that I don't find you attractive."

Her whole body broke into a sweat. He should be pretending he didn't know how humiliating this was for her, not staring into her soul with awful, insightful compassion. *Kill. Me. Now.*

"So, mate." Seth's voice made her jump. "If it's not Dimity, then who?"

Rage's Kiwi drummer rose from the sofa and stretched lazily. His crumpled plaid shirt rode up, revealing a lean, taut belly. Judging by the tangles in his tawny hair, the lint on his shirt and the red-gold stubble on his jaw, he'd been lost down the back of the sofa for several days. He looked at Luther. "Who's your mystery woman?"

The bodyguard's gaze finally shifted, and she could breathe.

"None of your business," he growled. "Forget everything you just heard."

Seth's broad shoulders rose in a sigh. "I wish I could." Astute blue eyes met hers. "Dammit, woman. I thought *I* was the only guy you brushed off."

"Exactly why I'm spreading the rejection around." He was throwing her a lifeline and she was desperate enough to take it. "I don't want you thinking you're special."

"Of course not," Luther said kindly.

Now she had to get out of here before she killed *him*. "I'll let you two get back to watching your barbaric national game."

"That's okay, it's finished." Reaching over the sofa, Seth took the remote from her and absently wiped her palm-sweat dry on his jeans, before switching off the screen.

The first time she'd met Seth after the reality show auditions to repopulate the band, she'd been amazed that Zander had shortlisted him. "He's *waaaay* too straight for rock 'n' roll."

"Wait 'til you see him perform," Zander had said.

Behind a drum kit, Seth metamorphosed into a beast. "Like Animal off *The Muppet Show*," Dimity told Seth, trying to shame him into a makeover. Working with rock stars was like taming tigers—both jobs required fearlessness and the ability to assert immediate dominance.

He'd laughed at her.

Given most people were intimidated by her take-no-prisoners approach, she'd been startled by that. Worse, he'd encouraged the other new band members to tease her, too, and over the following months the whole tour family had degenerated into the Brady Bunch. Their relationship had settled into pretend-flirting on his part and scathing put-downs on hers.

Though he remained stubbornly resistant to getting a stylist, they'd become friends—and she didn't have many who could handle her abrasiveness.

Even desperate to make her escape, she noticed a tightness to his movements as he dropped the remote on the coffee table. "Are you okay?" In five days he was flying to New Zealand with her to visit his family. Nobody wanted to be ill facing a twelve-hour flight—or contagious. "You look awful."

Luther cleared his throat warningly, but Seth only shrugged. "Mel got engaged." Picking up the shot glass on the coffee table, he downed the contents.

"The screamer you picked up a few weeks ago?" She knew damn well he was talking about his ex-girlfriend Mel, and not his rebound fuck, but the reminder served its purpose. His devastated expression eased into a wry grin.

"You're never going to let me forget that, are you?"

She'd been delivering documents to the house Seth shared with Moss, the lead guitarist, when she'd heard blood-curdling shrieks and moans. Kicking off her heels, she'd raced to the backyard, grabbing a garden rake as a weapon en route, only to see a naked woman reclining on the pool steps, half in, half out of the water. Head flung back, her bare breasts thrust skyward, she screamed her release as Seth screwed her, naked but for her thighs wrapped around his waist.

Dimity had fled, but the bright, sunlit image was still seared into her brain. Blue sky reflected in the shimmering water, droplets beading on Seth's bare torso.

She knew he'd lifted his self-imposed celibacy after a mourning period post-breakup, but the look in his eyes—pagan, primal—had shocked her. Seth was the poster child for a nice guy. He was Tom Sawyer grown-up—friendly, mischievous, playful, a lovable scamp with muscle. Not this Viking barbarian.

"I thought someone was being murdered." Later, she'd discovered the woman was an actress. Clearly, not a good one. Worst faked orgasm she'd ever heard.

"Well, she keeps phoning for a repeat performance." Seth poured the dregs from the tequila bottle into his shot glass. "At least I'm irresistible to *some* women."

For over a year Dimity had watched this man try to maintain a long-distance relationship with his childhood sweetheart. Then for several months she'd watched him suffer stoically after being dumped. *Why the hell couldn't Mel have delayed announcing her engagement until the wound had scabbed over?*

"I'm trespassing on bro time, so I'll go." Dimity was lousy at expressing sympathy—painful emotions made her uncomfortable if she couldn't provide a fix, and she wasn't one for empty platitudes. Seth was in good hands with Luther. Embarrassment still buzzing under her skin, she forced herself to meet the bodyguard's eyes. "I'm relieved your crush on me was only in Zander's imagination. I wanted to clear the air because I'm heading out to a bar and will be bringing a hook-up home."

"Perfect." Gulping the last mouthful of tequila, Seth handed the empty shot glass to Luther. "I'm in the mood to keep drinking and since you're the only person in the world who doesn't feel sorry for me right now, I'm coming with you."

She owed him for this rescue, and tough love she could do. "As long as you don't cramp my style."

"Jesus, Dimity," Luther mumbled.

But Seth laughed.

"I'll even help you make a short list."

"I'll drive," said Luther.

Dimity froze. *Oh yeah, I really want to spend the evening with the guy who just humiliated me.*

"Forget it, we'll catch a cab." Seth shrugged on a leather jacket. "I won't scare off other guys, but you sure as hell will."

"He's right," she told Luther, relieved. "You'll frighten the fish." Before following the drummer to the door, she murmured, "Don't worry, I'll look out for Seth." Luther waited until their charge had stepped into the hall.

"So…we're okay?"

She met his gaze squarely. "Absolutely." She went out, closed the door on him, and leaned against it. *I'm never, ever exposing myself like that again.*

Seth offered her his arm.

Scowling, she pushed away from the door. "You'd better not be feeling sorry for me."

He looked pained. "I just lost the love of my life. Can we please remember the real victim here?"

"That's all right then." Mollified, she tucked her arm through his.

"God," he said. "You are so what I need right now. Let's get drunk."

CHAPTER 2

As Dimity had hoped, Seth spent the drive to the bar bonding with the cab driver, which gave her the chance to repair her makeup and the hairline fracture in her composure. By the time they'd arrived she could pretend the whole emotional exposure thing had never happened.

The bouncer recognized them both, shook her hand and gave Seth a hug. "Hey, buddy, it's been a while."

Everyone liked Seth. He could transition from playing pool with roadies to discussing economics with financiers—he even loved kids. Dimity had even seen him kiss a dog once. There was no creature, walking or crawling, he couldn't make a connection with.

Which made it even sadder, she thought, as he opened the door for her, that he'd been rejected by the only person he desperately wanted.

They stepped inside. The bar was called The Comfort Zone, ironic given its undercurrent of suppressed violence and the fact that its patrons—a melting pot of intellectuals, drag queens, celebs, bikers and musos—were distinguished by their willingness to push boundaries.

Stylishly under-lit, it was a place where people who felt too much could get numb, and those desensitized by excess could still find something to fear. Drugs and kinky sex weren't sold, but they were definitely bartered.

Unsurprisingly, it was a favorite haunt of Moss, Rage's lead guitarist, and his was the face Dimity searched for as they weaved their way through to the bar. She wouldn't abandon Seth for a hook-up without leaving him in the hands of a caretaker. It was her job to watch over the band in Zee's absence. They needed to be battle-ready when he returned.

Moss saw them immediately, but then he noticed most things, despite his jaded vibe. His hooded gaze even held a hint of concern as he nodded to Seth, who muttered, "Fuck, no babysitters," and steered her in the opposite direction.

Over her shoulder, she glanced at Moss, who shrugged and returned to his conversation.

At the bar, Seth pulled out his wallet. "What will you have?"

"Champagne."

"A bottle of Moët and a tequila shot, thanks." He flipped the barman his credit card, then pulled out a tall barstool for Dimity. "And keep the shots coming."

"I guess I should offer a listening ear," she said reluctantly.

"Nothing to tell. I loved someone. I set her free."

Dimity forgot empathy. "What kind of defeatist attitude is that?"

"Says the woman who just surrendered the field to Luther's mysterious crush."

"If you'll recall," she said tartly, watching the barman pop the cork on the champagne bottle and pour the fizzing liquid into a flute. "I went there to make it clear I *wasn't* interested. I didn't want his feelings hurt when I arrived home with another guy. Mom re-married overseas today and sex is how I intend celebrating."

"Wow." Seth handed her the brimming glass. "That's not weird at all."

She smiled. "Shut up. It's an emancipation fuck because my last financial dependent has flown the nest."

He moved the ice bucket holding the champagne to her side of the bar and took his seat. "I've never heard you talk about your mother."

"And you won't now." She raised her champagne.

"Cheers." Seth picked up his tequila. "To small talk." Knocking back his shot, he swung to face the crowd. "So what kind of guy are we looking for?"

"No one high maintenance. I work with rock stars." The champagne was icy-cold on her tongue. "But I'm shallow," she added, "so looks, obviously."

"Obviously." He smiled. "Anything else?"

Thoughtfully, she sipped her champagne. "Someone who won't be intimidated by a smart woman—or threatened either. I'm not interested in a pissing contest with some alphahole needing to prove balls beat ovaries. But he needs to have *some* intelligence." She scanned the room for prospects. The trouble with working around charismatic, beautiful, pain-in-the-ass creatives was that other men seemed dull in comparison.

On a small stage to their left, roadies were setting up instruments. Bands at The Comfort Room performed by invitation only. The owner made his selection solely on talent, which left a lot of successful acts out in the cold. When Zander was rebuilding Rage's profile, the band had played here twice. "And no one in the industry either," she added. "Too often they see me as a way to Zee."

Seth eyed her thoughtfully. "I thought you'd be spoiled for choice, now I'm surprised you ever have sex. It's not easy being you, is it?"

She waved away his empathy. "I love my life."

"How *did* you first start working for Zander?"

"I went to a party to pick him up."

"Naturally you succeeded."

She appreciated his certainty, but wasn't so sure about his amusement. "I left to get my coat and when I returned Zee had experienced an epiphany. He said he was sorry, but he'd just remembered a prior appointment to save his career. And then *I* had an epiphany and said, 'Let me help you with that.'" Her fangirl crush wasn't lust; it was a burning desire to learn from the master of reinvention.

"Mutual epiphanies," Seth nodded solemnly. "Sexy."

"It *is* sexy." She'd recognized in Zander the embodiment of her own philosophy. He was unapologetic about who he was. If he made the wrong move, he simply changed tactics. There was no time to mourn lost opportunities or sink into self-pity. He was exactly what she wanted to be—indomitable. "Know what my favorite thing to do is?"

"You've just told me it's not sex." Seth lifted his empty glass to attract the attention of the bartender. "Torturing baby rock stars?"

"I machinate."

"As do we all."

She rolled her eyes. "Scheme, plot, intrigue, devise, strategize, maneuver, conspire. Win. It's my thing." She paused while the barman refilled Seth's shot glass. "As Zee's girlfriend I would have lasted two minutes. As his right-hand woman we're coming up for our third anniversary."

"Maybe three minutes," Seth said. "Let's give Zander some credit."

She giggled. And she never giggled.

Seth looked as surprised as she felt, then he grinned. "One of those minutes would be arguing about who got to be on top."

"Stop!" She smothered another giggle. "He's like my older brother now and the idea's gross." She sipped her champagne. "But for the record, *I'd* be on top."

"Is that right?" His gaze flicked over her, and for an instant she glimpsed the marauder he'd been at the pool before he returned to scanning the crowd. "How about that guy?" He pointed to a blond in leathers. "He's been checking you out since we got here. Worth putting on your short list?"

"What short list?" Moss asked as he joined them. Dimity explained and a speculative gleam lit his green eyes.

"I suppose I can sacrifice myself for the cause." He draped an arm around her shoulder.

She shrugged it off. "Thanks, but I know where you've been. Plus, you're even more dysfunctional than I am." The lead guitarist came from poverty and was embracing hedonism with death-wish fervor.

"You'd probably kill me after sex anyway," he said lazily. "Like a female grasshopper."

"You're thinking of a praying mantis," said Seth.

"And I don't need to kill my lovers. They die of happiness, their lives fulfilled."

"Tell me the drugs you're on," said Moss. "I want some." He glanced at his bandmate's shot glass. "Or are we drowning our sorrows?"

"Drowning," Seth said. He drank the contents, grimaced and gave his empty glass to Moss. "Thanks."

With his roomie around to keep an eye on him, Dimity excused herself and went to the bathroom. When she returned, Moss had disappeared and a skimpily-clad woman had taken her seat and clamped a hand on Seth's knee.

For a moment, Dimity hesitated—maybe he wanted this—but then she saw the strain behind his smile. Normally Houdini-like in his ability to escape over-zealous advances, tonight he emanated a little-boy-lost vibe that would be blood in the water to any man-eater. As she drew nearer, she heard him say, "Sorry, Tania, but I'm with a friend tonight."

"I'm the friend," Dimity said pleasantly, "and you're in my seat."

The woman didn't even glance at her. "So that means you're free to take my number."

Deftly, he loosened her grip on his knee. "Your offer is flattering, but—"

"Let's cut this short, Tania," Dimity cut in. "He's too nice to tell you you're wasting your time. More importantly, you're wasting *my* time. And you're still in my seat." The brunette finally looked at her.

"What bug got up your ass?"

"Good point." Opened her purse, Dimity pulled out a packet of wet wipes. "You're wearing a G-string, if you're wearing panties at all." Removing one, she waited expectantly.

Seth choked. "What my friend—"

"Don't bother." The brunette slid off the stool. "Bitch."

"Thank you for noticing." As Dimity reclaimed her stool, she said to Seth, "Where the hell is Moss? I left him as your wing man."

"Yeah, we figured. He said, 'Buddy, you okay?' I said, 'Mate, I'm fine. Buy me a drink and fuck off.' And he did." He pinned her with a hard stare. "Start feeling sorry for me, and I'll have to ditch you."

♪ ♫ ♩

Seth held Dimity's gaze, making sure she'd received his message loud and clear. *I will not tolerate a babysitter.*

A good mate? Yes. A drinking buddy? Absolutely. Mama Bear? No way.

She was the first to look away, redirecting her stunning—and cunning—Bahama-blue gaze to the tow-haired guy he'd pointed out earlier as a likely hook-up. "He won't do," she said calmly. "I want honest muscle, not a steroid-abusing pretty boy." Circling one manicured fingertip around the rim of her champagne glass, she smiled at Seth. "You know, there is a major benefit to being single that you haven't considered."

He didn't return her smile, which he recognized as strategic. "What's that?"

"You're eligible for my list."

"Yeah?" He compressed his lips, but she must have seen the twitch of amusement because her shoulders relaxed. Damn her, she could always disarm him with humor. If there wasn't pity lurking in her offer somewhere, he would have been flattered. Hell, if he wasn't such a heartbroken mess, he might even have taken her on. She could wither the toughest guys' balls with one cold stare, but his ego wasn't built on machismo. And he enjoyed making guerrilla attacks on her misplaced belief that he was harmless.

"Being a nice guy works against you." She sat back and crossed her long legs. "But on the plus side, you're still in love with your ex, which makes you emotionally unavailable. According to my shrink, that's my type."

Seth blinked, unable to imagine her ever giving anyone access to her private thoughts, which he imagined alphabetized and locked away. "You see a psychiatrist?"

"Of course, I live in California now." She put her empty glass on the bar and he reached for the champagne bottle to refill it. "She told me I had abandonment issues. Oh, please. I've been paying Mom to abandon me for years and she simply wouldn't go." She brightened. "Until now."

Normally, he'd have followed up such an intriguing comment, but he needed to concentrate on keeping a steady hand as he refilled the narrow-necked flute. Maybe he should pull back on the shots.

"I could give you my therapist's number," she added.

"No." The liquor fizzed up, then subsided without spilling over the rim—a small win on a shit day. "I'm a Kiwi bloke. We suffer stoically, and die of heart disease brought on by repressed feelings." Replacing the bottle in the ice bucket, he passed her the flute. "And as much as I appreciate your offer, I'm not interested in being a pity fuck." He tried and failed to keep bitterness out of his voice.

"Pity only gets you *added* to the list. You still have to *earn* my sexual favors."

Even heartbroken, he had to laugh, which he suspected was her goal. He'd always thought Dimity kind. Never by word—the woman was a verbal wrecking ball—but by deed she was one of the kindest people he knew, always looking out for members of the Rage family. But you had to earn her loyalty. He still wasn't sure when his own membership had been approved. That was the thing with Dimity. You only discovered how much she liked you when you were in serious trouble.

And he was—gutted, heartbroken, lost, angry…hurting. But that was his problem to solve, not hers. She wouldn't go man-hunting if he didn't at least pretend to be okay, and he had no intention of ruining her plans. So he got with the program.

"At the risk of jeopardizing my nice guy status, you're a little too skinny for my tastes."

"That's okay, you're too ginga for mine."

"In your press releases you call my hair *auburn*," he reminded her.

She widened her eyes. "Do I?"

"You are so full of shit," he said affectionately. "Do you believe half the things you say?"

"I don't have to—I just have to make other people believe them. But I can take constructive criticism." She batted her fake eyelashes. "Tell me again I'm too skinny."

Chuckling, he shook his head. "I'm not encouraging female self-loathing." She had to know how beautiful she was.

"It's our industry, Seth. Every woman hungry, every man beautified."

"What?" he taunted. "You think because I'm having a weak moment, I'm suggestible?" She never gave up hope of talking him into a makeover. He deliberately repeated the phrase that drove her crazy. "I've told you before, I'm happy as I am."

She gave an exasperated snort. "No one's happy as they are, and tonight you're the most miserable bastard on the planet. Spit it out, what went wrong with Mel? Was it the long distance thing?"

He hesitated, reluctant to open that can of worms. "No. Mel's been traveling to overseas comps for years."

"Comps?"

"Competitions. She's a swimmer."

"How good?"

"One bronze and a silver in the last Paralympics." The ache in his chest became a gnaw, and he fed it with a shot of fiery tequila.

"That explains why you're in such great shape, you've got a lot to live up to."

He appreciated that she didn't ask what made Mel eligible, but identified what made her extraordinary—her accomplishments.

Cunning returned to her expression. "Now if you just let someone style your—" The rest of her sentence was drowned out by a burst of music.

"Saved by the band," Seth mouthed, grateful for the distraction. Thinking about Mel being extraordinary without him made him want to curl up into a ball and howl. He'd tried so hard to keep their long-distance relationship alive over the past fifteen months; tried so hard to have it all.

Clearly, he hadn't tried hard enough.

With an effort, he refocused on the stage. *Suck it up. You accepted the risks when you chose your career over her.* He recognized the band, an emerging indie rock group called The Box Cutters who'd featured in a music festival Rage had headlined last summer.

It was always interesting to see who Jack—the bar owner—was promoting, particularly when Seth might be starting from scratch again, if Zander's voice didn't recover and they were forced to start a new band. He'd had weeks to reconcile himself to the possibility, and still the idea hit him like a gut-punch, forcing all the air out of him.

But he wasn't going to consider worst-case scenarios in his career tonight, not when he was already dealing with Armageddon in his love life. As the musicians hit their stride he closed his eyes and let the belting melodies pulse through him, tapping out the drum beat on his thighs. *Yes, soothe me, move me, remind me* why *I risked it all.*

When the first song finished, Dimity leaned closer. His senses heightened, he caught the faintest scent of summer, berries, and flowers, so at odds with her ice queen persona. "Are you missing performing?" she called over the applause.

"Moss, Jared, and I jam every day." Jared was Rage's bass player and a brilliant songwriter, the only one of them married with kids. "But I miss that magical connection you get with an audience." Understatement. He'd changed his whole life for it, pawned his whole future. And now it was time to pay up. Maybe he did need another drink.

She nodded and sat back, excusing herself a couple of minutes through the third number. He watched her walk away. No sway to the hips for this warrior-princess, yet every free man she passed—and a few with dates—did a double take. She *was* too hung up about what she ate, but no diet could destroy her apple-cheeked ass, which was truly a wonder. Small pleasures. With a sigh, he signaled the bartender and ordered another shot.

Not only would he have to watch Mel being happy with some other guy when he returned to New Zealand for a couple of weeks, he'd have to confront his dad, who hadn't spoken more than a few words to him since he'd left to join the reality show.

With the band in hiatus through Zander's recovery, Seth finally had time to remedy that, face to face.

Unfortunately, the scandal also made it highly likely that Frank saw Seth's peace-making trip as his son crawling home with his tail between his legs to admit what a foolish, silly boy he'd been to ever leave his comfortable life.

And tonight, mourning Mel's engagement to another guy, he couldn't think of one damn thing that proved his father wrong.

CHAPTER 3

Dimity hunted Moss and found him sitting in a booth with a bunch of admirers.

"A word?" she said, and received glares from the two women hanging off him. "Down, girls. I'm not here to take your boner."

Moss stood and grinned at her. He was high on something—his dilated pupils suggested coke. "Too late to change your mind, snow queen, I've made other arrangements."

"Forget about that. If I arrange for you to jam with the band, will their instruments work for you?"

"Jesus, Dimity, take the night off."

"Seth needs this," she said.

He was silent a moment, then turned toward the stage, his gaze assessing. "Yeah, we could make do. Assuming they're prepared to share. I'll talk to them at the end of the set."

"No Rage numbers…we're still too controversial. Maybe one of Jared's?" The bass player had penned some original compositions, which had proved popular through the last tour leg. "Kayla's Song," written for his wife, was a bona fide chart-topper.

"This is a nice thing you're doing," Moss said.

She wasn't comfortable with warmth, didn't know what to do with it, so she deflected. "And good publicity."

He shook his head. "Are you *ever* off duty?"

"Never."

She slipped away to have a word with the manager. Zander hadn't told anyone about his lip-syncing, including her—which still made Dimity sore—and when the story broke, had played up his role as Machiavellian mentor to protect his younger band members from fallout.

His band had responded by announcing their support. It could have gone horribly wrong. But still enamored of the guys from the audition reality show that had plucked them from obscurity, the public had read their loyalty as adorable naivety.

Zander might be a pariah, but the other guys in Rage could do no wrong. Particularly Seth.

Manager Antonio immediately saw the benefit and made a quick call to the owner, who backed his decision. Business taken care of, Antonio kissed Dimity on both cheeks. "I've been thinking about you, bella." His dark eyes caressed her. "Have you been thinking about me?"

She looked at him blankly, then the penny dropped. Antonio was the last guy she'd sex with. "Every damn day," she purred.

He stroked her arm, and she remembered he was competent. "Later?" he suggested.

The buzz of organizing an impromptu gig had eased her restlessness and she needed to keep an eye on Seth. "Unfortunately, tonight I'm working." She kissed him with enough heat to keep him interested. "Another time?"

"I look forward to it."

The bartender had given Seth another drink. And he needed to stay in the ballpark of sober for the performance. She picked up the shot glass and sculled it. Ugh. She hated tequila.

"I'm guessing my services are no longer required," he commented, and when she looked at him watery-eyed, added, "Antonio?"

"I took a rain check." She glanced over to Moss, who gave her the thumbs up. "It's more fun getting drunk with you."

"Okay, then. Order us another round." He left for the bathroom and as he returned the band stopped playing mid-song. "We've got some talent in the house tonight. Reality stars and Rage musicians Seth Curran and Moss McFadden. Get your asses up here, guys, and jam with us."

A whoop went up from the crowd. If only she could bottle that goodwill and spray it on Zander. On stage, the bassist handed Moss a spare guitar and the drummer relinquished his place to a delighted Seth. Dimity made a mental note to send the band a thank-you gift. Around her, phones were being pulled out to capture the action. Guerrilla marketing via social media. Perfect.

Seth unbuttoned his shirt and shrugged it off. Underneath he wore a loose-fitting gray tank, the arm holes cut low to reveal pecs and ribs. He had a body like a dancer's—graceful, loose-limbed, and honed to muscle. Cells flashed as women in the crowd snapped photos.

If you think that's good, ladies, come to a Rage concert.

Midway through a ninety-minute gig, he invariably stripped off the shirt and played bare-chested. Like the Hulk, no clothing could contain him when he was in the throes of metamorphosis. And that was his fascination for her, professionally.

The two Rage bandmates conferred, then Moss plucked the first chord of a power number, his mouth curving in a feral grin that promised the crowd a wild ride. The lead guitarist was sexy and dangerous off-stage and sexy and dangerous on it, his charisma all about I'm-broken-fix-me-if-you-dare brooding.

Seth was the enigma, the curiosity, the surprise.

He was good-looking but accessibly so, with an open face. Parents would instinctively trust him to bring their little girl home safe from the prom, with her virginity still intact. Put him behind a drum kit and he became mesmerizing, insanely compelling. Savage. There was the moment of change now, Seth's grin sharpening and his nice-guy veneer falling away as his energy crystallized and his whole body exploded into performance.

She always made sure his publicity shots were taken at live shows when his hair and skin glowed the same copper-gold as the cymbals and his magnetism was on display—arms stretching, muscles bunching, and his hands on the drumsticks moving in a blur of speed. Tearing her gaze away, Dimity scanned the crowd. Yes, they were captivated, their attention darting between Moss's original-sin genius and Seth's bright kinetic-ism.

One song led to another, and at the end of the set they were mobbed as they left the stage, the normally cool crowd demanding selfies and autographs. Dimity sat back on her bar stool and sipped her champagne, enjoying a private moment of achievement. It wasn't sex she'd needed, it was this. Reassurance that Rage could rise again. That her will and determination could make it happen. *That we make our own luck.*

Moss escaped quickly to his groupies but Seth continued to chat patiently with the public. After Zee, he got the most fan mail of all the band members, an approachable everyman with universal appeal. Female fans either wanted to marry him or corrupt him, but until Mel had dumped him, he'd never looked at another woman with anything other than friendship. In these turbulent times, he gave the band what it desperately needed—credibility.

When he rejoined her, he was still glowing, his dark-red hair dampened from his exertions. He'd shrugged on his shirt, but left it unbuttoned.

For no reason at all, Dimity moistened her lips.

"Thank you," he said, accepting a glass of water from her. "I needed that." Moss must have told him it was her idea. "How about we find you what you need?"

"Me?" Maybe it was the heat radiating off him, or the time lapse since she'd last seen him perform, but his sex appeal was off the charts tonight. For his sake, she hoped someone posted footage on YouTube, and his idiot ex saw what she'd given up. "Oh, the pick-up. No, still happy to get drunk with you instead. What time is it?"

He glanced at his cell. "Eleven forty-five p.m. Huh, I missed a message." His expression darkened. "Mel. Eight hours ago. Hoping I'm okay."

"What a stupid question."

"Of course we still care about each other. We started dating when we were sixteen."

"Next you'll be telling me you'll hang out when you're home."

"Our families have been friends a long time," he said, defensive. "And it's not like I'm the innocent party here. I knew when I left how hard the separation would be on her."

"Oh boy." Never mind that it was equally hard on him. The calls he'd made at ungodly hours, because God forbid Mel forgo her beauty sleep by getting up outside her time zone; the air tickets he'd offered to send.

She'd heard him one night in LA trying to talk Mel into meeting him in Hawaii for a long weekend. "Five hours' flight for me, nine for you...isn't any time together worth jetlag?"

When he'd mentioned later that they'd decided jetlag would "affect her training too much," Dimity felt a stab of anger on his behalf. *You mean, Mel had decided.* Some people needed protecting and Seth was one of those—a kind, decent guy who wore his heart on his sleeve. "Pass your cell."

"Why?"

"We're sending Mel a selfie of you and me to show her just how okay you are."

"It's early morning in New Zealand."

"Even better."

She went to take his phone, and he resisted. "I've never played games with Mel and I'm not going to start now."

"Don't think of it as playing games, think of it as helping her to respect boundaries."

"Fine." He handed it over. "But I approve anything before you send it."

"Agreed." Pinning a sex-kittenish smile on her face, she flung his arm around her shoulders and leaned in close. "Raise your glass and say machin-*ate*."

Seth laughed and she pressed the shutter, then tapped a message to go with it.

All good. Dimity and I toasting your happiness.

She showed it to him. He sobered, looking at their picture. "And they say the camera never lies. Looks like we couldn't be happier."

"Send it?"

He shrugged as he re-buttoned his shirt. "Go ahead. But don't expect a reply. Mel doesn't think that way."

"Like a woman?" Dimity said dryly. She suspected Saint Mel wanted to have her cake and eat it too. "Trust me, we're all territorial."

Five minutes later, his cell beeped an incoming message. She read it over his shoulder.

Hey, you woke me up. So glad you're coming to terms with this. I'd hate to lose your friendship. BTW, is that the honey badger?

The trail of crumbs was definitely leading to a cake hogger. "Honey badger?"

"The honey who badgers me," he said. "Like your namesake, you're fierce, carnivorous and have a deep ominous growl. The honey badger drops stink bombs—you drop truth bombs."

"I like it. May I?"

Taking his cell, she tapped in a response and showed it to him.

Yes, the honey badger. Dimity's been helping me through this. One door closes, another opens. Maybe you'll meet her in NZ."

Seth frowned. "I don't think—"

"Oops, fingers slipped."

"Give me that." He confiscated his cell. But he'd barely returned it to his pocket when it chimed an incoming text. They looked at each other as he retrieved it. Mel.

Kinda crazy coming from me, but don't rush into anything. I only want you to be happy.

Dimity smirked. "I rest my case."

He re-read the text and frowned. "What am I missing?"

"No one *only* wants someone to be happy. There are always conditions. And the 'don't rush into anything' comment. Clearly, she's not ready to let you go."

"I'm not ready to let her go, either." His stubble glinted gold as he rubbed his jaw. "I'm too loaded to know if you're talking sense or not, but I need to believe you. Okay, screw it. What do we say next?"

"Nothing." Taking his phone, she slid it into the back pocket of his jeans, fleetingly aware of the tautness of his butt. "Stop being so accessible. If Mel's chosen someone else's bed, let her lie in it." He winced and she added gently, "She doesn't have a right to your business anymore."

"I'm nowhere near drunk enough to handle the truth." He was lifting his hand to signal the bartender, when a young guy tapped him on the shoulder.

"I hope you don't think this is too pushy, but I'm a drummer and I'd love to learn how you do the drum fill on 'Summer Daze'."

"Sure." But she noticed Seth struggled to find his friendly smile.

The muso finally moved on ten minutes later.

"You'll get no peace now you've performed." She should have considered that earlier. "Come home to Zee's and we'll finish the wake in private."

♪ ♫ ♩

As they left the club, fresh air hit Dimity like a tranquilizer dart and she swayed on her feet. Seth grabbed her elbow to steady her. "You're a cheap drunk, Ms. Graham."

It was that shot of tequila, she suspected, on top of two flutes of champagne—three if you counted the one at her desk earlier. Which was why she rarely let loose—she disliked the loss of control. "How are you not falling over? You've drunk a lot more than I have."

"Cast-iron stomach." He patted his abdomen.

He isn't wrong there.

"But trust me." He hooked a supportive arm around her waist. "I'm feeling it."

They caught a cab to the mansion. As Dimity keyed in a security code to disable the alarm system, Luther glanced out from his window and she gave him a friendly wave. There, that wasn't so hard. He saw Seth and gave her an approving nod—*good job, keeping him in one piece*—and closed the blind. She tried not to let his commendation matter.

In the kitchen, she kicked off her pumps, while Seth opened the freezer compartment of the industrial-size fridge. With Zander abroad, Consuela the cook was on leave, but she'd prepared a dozen pre-cooked meals for Dimity and "my boys," as she collectively called Luther and the band.

"Who do you think Luther's secret love is?" Reaching past Seth, she retrieved the bottle of champagne she'd uncorked earlier. "Hey, maybe *that's* why he's spending his vacation in LA instead of New Zealand with his family. Because she's an American."

"Here's my theory." Removing a pack from the freezer, he shoved it into the microwave. "If he wanted us to know, he would have told us."

"I forgot, I'm talking to a man," she said, disgusted. "Aren't you the least bit curious?"

"I'm more interested in finding the tequila."

"Pantry on the right." Clearly, she'd have to do her own investigation. She found a shot glass and champagne flute, then settled on a stool in front of one of two marble-topped islands in the enormous kitchen.

Seth exited the pantry with a bottle of El Tesoro Reposado. Positioning it next to the shot glass, he pulled out his wallet, removed sixty dollars and laid it on the counter, then wandered over to check the microwave, which was emanating scents of tomato, cilantro and garlic.

Dimity appreciated his gesture, having always disliked the entitlement mentality that many people adopted around the wealthy. With Zee in dispute with insurers, he could potentially lose everything. He was already cashing out to meet litigation costs and pay outstanding tour bills. There were so many *ifs* and *buts* to Rage's future, and too many elements outside her control. She popped the pressurized stopper on the champagne bottle. Bubbles foamed over the neck, and she pressed her mouth to the top to stem the overflow.

"I don't think I've ever seen you so rock 'n' roll." Seth commented as he returned with the reheated food—a spicy chicken chili.

Dimity wiped her mouth with the back of her hand. "What happens in the kitchen, stays in the kitchen." She was safe here, with this man.

"Deal." He broke the seal on the tequila and poured a finger into the shot glass. "To getting messy."

She lifted the bottle. "To messy."

Solemnly, they tapped shot glass against champagne bottle, and drank. Seth returned to his food prep, while she refreshed their drinks. Five minutes later, he placed a piled plate of chili in front of her, garnished with a dollop of sour cream.

"Trying to fatten me up?" she challenged.

"When did you last eat?"

"I had a spinach salad for lunch."

"No wonder you're feeling the alcohol."

She'd been about to push the plate away—nobody fussed over her without push-back—but that made her hesitate. She didn't want a hangover. And it did smell so good.

"Fine." She accepted cutlery and a napkin, and they ate in companionable silence for a while, except for the chink of cutlery on china. The cat came in, drawn by the smell of food, and Seth leaned down to pat her. "Sorry, kitty, this is too spicy for you."

Rising, Dimity found the dry food and poured some into Diamanté's dish, making effusive apologies to her pet for not feeding her earlier. Because she traveled so much, Dimity shared ownership of the tabby with the cook. One day she hoped to own a whole one. When she returned to her seat, Seth was grinning. "What?"

"Nothing." He dished himself a second helping, almost as big as the first.

She picked up her fork. "When did *you* last eat?"

"Not since Mel phoned to break the news at six a.m. She wanted me to be the first to know."

Wanting to be there at the death, you mean. The bright overhead halogens accentuated the dark circles under his eyes. "Don't you think that's weird?"

"We have a lot of mutual friends. She didn't want me hearing it from anyone else."

Thoughtfully, Dimity chewed the last morsel of chicken. The last thing she wanted to do was raise false hopes, but what kind of friend would she be *not* to point out that Mel was sending mixed messages? The question she couldn't answer—was his ex toying with him, or genuinely torn? Dimity knew nothing about true lurve, other than it never ran smoothly.

She swallowed her mouthful. "She's conflicted, Seth, she has to be." Bottom line? No woman in her right mind would lightly relinquish the love of a man so loyal, faithful, and downright lovable. He'd probably been a Labrador in his last life. "You should be exploiting those tender feelings and making her reconsider."

He shook his head. "Mel's a grown woman. She's made her choice."

"Even if she's choosing the wrong guy? Being understanding, wanting Mel to be happy, is bullshit if you think she's making a mistake. And if you love her, you should be *fighting* for her."

Seth put down his fork without comment. He looked broody and mad and tortured and unhappy.

"Your strategy's screwed, too." Now she'd decided to challenge him, Dimity was remorseless. "As long as you're patient and pining she'll relegate you to her back-up plan."

"Mel knows I've started dating again."

"Oh, please. You've been doing the 'I'll show her' with a few one-nighters. You think she'll take groupies seriously?"

His jaw set. "Make your point."

"A man's cock is rarely discriminatory, but his heart…that's something Mel probably still considers hers. So that's where you test her conviction. You need a girlfriend."

"Rent a relationship? She'll see through that in a second."

"Not if it's someone you've been around constantly for months. Someone you've already talked and tweeted about, someone who is in New Zealand the same time you are. I need an additional project now Mom's off my plate and Zee's temporarily off grid."

Come to think of it, Seth was just the type to retreat to some backwoods cabin with his broken heart and a gallon of whiskey. God knows, he was already dressed for it. And no *way* was she going to risk him leaving the band.

"Won't you have enough to do while you're there, organizing Elizabeth's book tour, and strategizing Zander's next move? The moment he releases his prognosis—whichever way it goes—the press will be all over him again."

She waved a dismissive hand. "Spare time is for wimps." A*nd for those with families*. To all intents and purposes, she was now an orphan.

Until Helena needed something that her new husband couldn't provide, Dimity doubted she'd even get a phone call. "Do you want Mel back or don't you?"

"Yes, but…" Seth massaged his temples. "Let me get this straight. *You'll* pretend to be my new girlfriend in the hope that jealousy will trigger second thoughts?"

"I'm thinking more along the lines of Mel having an epiphany, but yes."

His mouth, with its permanent tilt at the corners, tightened as though he held back a smile by sheer force of will. "Have you ever been in a serious relationship?"

"Outliers have insight. Ask Malcolm Gladwell."

He laughed out loud. "I'm sorry, but there's no way you can pretend to be dewy-eyed over a guy. It's not your style."

She sighed. "You really have no idea how good I am at this, do you?"

"No?"

"Watch and learn, grasshopper." Leaning across the counter, she dropped a manicured hand on his bare forearm and gazed into his eyes. Sunshine eyes despite their moody blue color. She'd tried to describe the exact shade in press releases and could only come up with smoky. Now she saw why—striations of brown radiated from his pupils into the faded denim-blue. Another area in which this man was recalcitrant and uncooperative.

Seth laughed, making her aware that she was frowning at him, and she softened her gaze. "You know what I love about you?" she breathed. "You're a fraud."

The corners of his eyes crinkled. "Nice start."

"Everyone thinks you're this affable, easy-going guy, but it's not true." She assessed him through half-closed lashes. "Before you broke up with Mel, I watched you wiggle away from women's attempts to seduce you. You'd flatter and charm, kiss their fingers as you went to buy them a drink that someone else always delivered. Moss and Jared were the most vocal in band meetings on tour, yet somehow Zee usually ended up adopting your suggestions."

His smile was all sweetness, but under her palm, his forearm tensed.

Dimity thought of Rage in chess terms. Zander was king, and Dimity, queen. In an ideal world everyone else would be pawns, but she begrudgingly accepted she didn't live in an ideal world. Until now, she'd wondered if Seth might be a bishop or a knight.

With a shock, she realized he was a far more dangerous rook. A rook began the game quietly in a corner, but was one of only two pieces that could checkmate the opposition alone with their king, making the piece one of the game's heavies.

Often, the player who employed her rooks most effectively would win. *Even more important to keep a close watch on Seth.*

She became aware of the warmth of his skin over muscle and unbidden, the image of him naked and pagan shimmered in her mind's eye. She curled her fingers around his forearm as all her impressions of him crystallized and found their final shape. "You're a covert rebel," she said slowly. "But I'm onto you now. I'm the only one who sees behind the Mr. Nice Guy facade and wonders what it would be like to let the beast loose."

"Is that so?"

His eyes drilled into hers, his pupils dilated, and unexpectedly, heat pooled deep in her belly. His breathing had become more deliberate, in contrast with her own, which she struggled to catch. For a charged moment they stared at each other, neither backing down, then Seth blinked. "Wow, you're really good."

"Aren't I?" Slightly giddy, she checked the label on the bottle of champagne. "This stuff works better than a master class in acting." *Definitely time to stop drinking.* "So, back to Mel. Are you really leaving something on the table here? *Really*?"

He blew out a long breath. "Fuck it, let's do this. What the hell have I got left to lose?"

"Only all hope."

He shook his head at her, rueful and weary. "It was a rhetorical question. Can you pull back on the remorseless honesty a tad?"

"Sorry." Still unsettled by their earlier frisson, she momentarily forgot her resolution and gulped more liquor. "If it doesn't work out, there's always the screamer to fall back on."

"That's the second time you've mentioned Suzanne tonight," he commented, picking up his fork again. "You must've witnessed raunchier sex, working in rock 'n' roll."

"The shock came from seeing you end your self-imposed celibacy." She found it hard not speaking her mind when sober; with champagne aerating her bloodstream she had no chance of guarding her tongue.

"After your breakup, I couldn't work out whether I admired or despised your willingness to suffer when you had so many women wanting to help you feel better."

He was silent a few seconds, then pushed his plate aside. "I'd gotten used to having sex with someone I loved. It was a tough habit to break."

His expression was so bleak that she had to look away. This was why she kept relationships transient. Love hurt.

Her discomfort must have shown on her face because he forced a grin. "Suzanne did make me feel better."

"I'm so glad," Dimity said warmly. "Even if she did over-act the hell out of it."

Lifting the shot glass to his mouth, he paused. "Excuse me?"

"The orgasm. She faked it. I mean, c'mon, no one gets that carried away, and not with—" Hearing herself, she stopped.

Very gently, he replaced the glass on the counter. "With?"

"I wouldn't want to hurt your feelings."

"Oh, we're way past that, you and I," he said and she felt a prickle of recognition at the glint in his eyes. It had to be a trick of the light. She looked up at the ceiling halogens. Except it had been full daylight the last time she'd seen that glint. It was starting to bother her how susceptible she was to it.

"Not everyone has to be a bad boy in rock," she pointed out. "I'm sure you're an awesome lover. Tender, considerate…" She struggled to think of all the positives associated with a beta male. "And probably awesome at kissing and cuddling afterward."

The outrage on his face. She got the giggles.

Seth folded his arms and waited until they subsided. "Take it back."

"Never explain, never apologize." Zee's maxim worked for her, too.

The stool scraped the hardwood floor as he shoved it back and stood up. "I'm more of a show, don't tell guy." He added pleasantly, "Last chance."

"Listen to you, being all masterful." Now she'd glimpsed the other side of his nature, it tickled her to tease the friendly lion. Payback for all the times he'd used passive resistance to frustrate her makeovers.

"Have it your way." He strolled around the counter.

"What are you going to do…*cuddle* me into an apology?"

"Nope, I have it on good authority that I'm too fucking nice." He pulled her off her stool. "Still want to get laid?"

She laughed, delighted. "You think you can win a game of chicken against *me*?"

"I know I can." Sweeping her plate aside, he caught her around the waist and lifted her onto the counter. The marble top was cold through her jeans.

"You want Mel," she reminded him.

"Yeah, I do. But as you reminded me an hour ago, she's made her bed with another man and right now they're lying in it. Tomorrow we campaign to get her back. Tonight, I'm available to fuck a friend who needs to learn why nice guys make the best lovers." Casually, he started undoing the buttons of her shirt.

"I thought you said I was too skinny," she commented, unfazed. He wouldn't go through with this, not Seth.

"You *are* too skinny," he said, pulling the shirt open. Her bra was balcony, her wares beautifully displayed. "But parts of you are perfect." He traced a finger over the upper swell of her breast and she couldn't stop a small gasp of surprise escaping. She hadn't expected him to touch. And certainly hadn't expected her responsive shiver.

He lifted his hand to brush his thumb across her mouth. "Plump and succulent," he added huskily. Leaning forward, he caught her lower lip between his teeth, teased his tongue across its fullness and released.

Astonishment held Dimity immobile. Her lip tingling, she stared into his eyes, mere inches from hers.

Seth laughed, deep in his throat. "Honey B, you can't handle a nice guy. Leave the cage door alone." He eased back.

Instinctively, she put out a hand to stop him.

Chapter 4

FOR A LONG MOMENT THEY both stared at her hand, curved around his wrist. Dimity opened her mouth to make a smart-ass rejoinder, but heard herself say, "Why are nice guys the best lovers?"

Seth's gaze lifted to meet hers, no longer teasing. Her pulse quickened.

"Three reasons," he said. "We pay attention. Every woman has a sexual fantasy. We find out what it is, and give it to her."

"What was Mel's?" she said, fascinated, and saw pain flicker. "I'm sorry, forget I asked." She really needed to learn tact. "What was the swimming pool screamer's? Other than the desire to be a siren on an ambulance?"

"She wanted to be a mermaid, taken by Poseidon," he said.

"It's impossible to have sex with a mermaid. They don't have legs."

"Suzanne had great legs." He brushed his fingers up her calves over her skin-tight jeans and curled them under her knees. "So do you." Gently, he pulled her knees apart and stepped between until only a few inches separated them. She could feel his body heat through her opened shirt. "And don't get me started on your ass."

She was turned on, and he knew it. So was he. And they were drunk and loose and one of them would stop very, very soon. Dimity cleared her throat. "What's my fantasy?"

Tilting his head, Seth considered. "It might be control, because you're a take-charge woman. Or it might be to lose control—have it taken away." Catching her hands, he clasped them behind her back.

She swallowed.

"Oh, yeah," he said huskily. "It might be that."

"What's the second reason?"

Reluctantly, he released her hands. "Nice guys like women." Carefully, he refastened the buttons on her shirt, one by one. "And you're not as tough as you make out." He must be referencing the earlier incident with Luther, which only gave her more to prove. She couldn't handle anyone thinking she was sensitive.

"You can't hurt me." She took over the re-buttoning of her shirt. "No man can. And I'm not hung up on Luther. I just liked the idea of an honorable guy crushing on me. Being good enough." She realized she was explaining herself poorly when Seth frowned. "I'm not talking about feeling worthy—obviously I don't have self-esteem issues, but I liked him seeing me as decent and full of moral fiber-iness."

"The word you're looking for is *nice*," he said.

She scowled. "Take that ba—"

He kissed her, and it was slow and tender and fiercely sweet. But she didn't want his sweetness, and had no idea what to do with tenderness. It scared her, exposed her.

She broke the kiss. "No offense, but you're home-baked cookies and I like my beefcake raw."

"Bitch," he said appreciatively, and kissed her again. It was a punishing kiss, a hard kiss, the kiss of an exasperated man, and she felt herself responding. She'd been intrigued by this side of Seth since she'd seen him with the groupie who didn't know him well enough to value the contradiction. She wanted the titan she saw on stage, the pool-side debaucher.

This time he was the first to end the kiss. "Well?" he demanded roughly.

"Meh," she croaked.

He kissed her again, a ravishment, a porn-star kiss, carnal and rude and shockingly intimate.

A man kissing a woman, no friendship in it. No kindness, no pity, no understanding, no sweetness. It was the kiss of a man driven past civilized and Dimity loved it, from him.

Sober, she'd have said her curiosity was strictly scientific. Drunk, she couldn't lie to herself. She wanted to provoke the abandon she saw when Seth performed on stage. She wanted to be the object of his singular focus. She wanted to know what that rampant power felt like, unleashed on her body.

He stepped in closer and she stifled a moan as his erection met the apex of her thighs. "I will fuck you," he said, "unless you tell me no.

It's freaky and at least one of us is going to regret this sober, but I want you. So if you're going to put the brakes on, Dimity, do it now."

It was a Herculean effort to ignore the press of his cock against the throb between her legs but she managed to instill carelessness into her next words. "Strategically, it'll be much easier to pretend we're dating if we've comfortable with each other's bod—"

She gasped as he slid her closer against his heat. "Where's your bedroom?"

"Top of the stairs, turn left, end of the corridor." She sucked in a breath. "Hurry."

"Way ahead of you." Lifting her into his arms, he strode out of the kitchen, taking the stairs two at a time. Her bottom hit his thighs on every step. His thighs were hard and strong. She wound her arms around his neck and hung on.

"For the record—" Seth wasn't even out of breath at the top of the stairs "—I'm also fucking good at cuddling afterward."

"Save it for someone who cares."

His gaze darkened as he adjusted her weight. "Woman, have you *no* sense of self-preservation?"

In response she stretched sinuously in his arms, making the re-buttoned shirt tighten across her breasts.

Muttering an oath, he stopped outside the closed door and Dimity turned the crystal door knob. She hadn't directed him to her bedroom—that would have been too intimate—but the guest room referred to as the princess suite. Praying the bed was made up, she reached inside and flicked the switch.

A massive central chandelier blazed into radiance. Seth paused on the threshold and blinked. His astonished gaze slid over the silk wallpaper, the sly nude in the Rubens print, the pastel pink taffeta curtains with tasseled ties that matched those on the drawers of the Louis XIV parquetry nightstand, then he threw back his head and laughed. "This is so you. In your face and flawless."

Dimity smiled. "Yep."

He strode across the faded Persian carpet and tossed her on the fairy-tale, four-poster bed.

She landed with a small oomph of surprise.

His sexed-up gaze full of evil intent, he said softly, "Let's mess this place up."

She dissolved into a puddle of lust. She'd barely touched him yet and she wanted to, suddenly and desperately. Rip off that plaid shirt, haul down those worn jeans, bite and lick and taste. "Come here."

Not bothering to take off his boots, he crawled on the bed toward her, tossing throw pillows left and right in his wake and giving her the strangest sense of being stalked by a jungle cat, golden and lethal. She wasn't sure whether to offer herself up or run.

Her eyes must have given away her confusion, because he laughed softly. "Too late for wisdom."

Arms braced above her shoulders, he dipped his head and kissed her.

He smelled of fresh sweat from his performance, not unpleasant on a healthy male in his prime. How long since she'd had sex with a man who wasn't perfumed by colognes and hair products?

Catching his jaw between her hands, she held him there, wanting more of his skilled tongue. Her palms rasped on his stubble as he chuckled and pulled away. "Patience, princess." Straddling her, he removed her bracelets and gold chains and dropped them over the edge of the bed. He fingered the open collar of her chiffon shirt. "Like this blouse much?"

"It's my fav—"

He ripped it in two. Buttons scattered across the quilted satin bed cover. "Oops," he said in exactly the tone she'd used before sending the text to Mel.

It dawned on Dimity that maybe, just maybe, she'd underestimated him. And the thought was so extraordinarily erotic it stifled the protest in her throat.

Unceremoniously, he divested her of clothing, not even lingering over her exquisite La Perla lingerie. Not giving her time to employ any of the usual allure and tease tricks she used to drive men crazy.

By the time she was naked, her heart hammered against her ribs with such delicious anticipation she worried whether she shouldn't be reasserting her independence.

"I think—"

"Don't." Lowering his clothed body on hers, he kissed her hard, his tongue probing and insistent. Her train of thought derailed. Clutching his biceps, she pressed her naked breasts against his chest and kissed him back, so turned on that even the soft worn flannel of his shirt felt deliciously abrasive against her sensitized nipples.

She shifted, restless as the ache of lust became relentless, and fumbled for the fastening of his jeans. Her fingertips touched skin, sleek and smooth, brushed a velvety tip, tantalizingly close, but the way they were lying stopped her exploring further.

With a murmur of frustration, she tried to pull him higher. Rolling onto his side, Seth threaded one hand through her hair, twisting the long golden strands around his fingers like a chain that bound the two of them together. "What would make you scream, I wonder." His gaze devoured her body, and everywhere it lingered—throat, breasts, her sex—responded by growing hot and tight. He hadn't really done anything yet except kiss her, and she was wet and aching for him.

"My orgasms are private. And I think women who—"

He leaned in and grazed his teeth along the tendon in her neck before gently biting the muscle where her neck joined her shoulder. Tension melted from her bones. "Don't tell me what you think," he whispered in her ear, his breath like a breeze on still water, sending a shiver through her blood. "Tell me what you want, what you crave. Tell me—and I'll give it to you."

She rolled on top of him and sat up, letting her knees fall open so the weight of his clothed body pressed against her softest flesh.

"Fuck me hard and do it now. I want to be taken and used and I want to use you."

He started shoving down his jeans before she'd finished her shaky command.

"Hell, I haven't got protection."

Scrambling off him, Dimity yanked open the drawer on the nightstand, fumbling under the box of tissues, chocolates and aspirin for the foil packets that were in all the guest rooms. Thank God she lived with a rocker.

Seth tore open the packet she thrust at him and reached under the tails of his shirt to sheath himself. While he did, she tried to rip the shirt apart as payback, but the worn cotton was stronger than it looked. *Dammit.*

Laughing, he rolled her onto her back and positioned himself between her legs.

On his first thrust, their eyes met in an agony of mutual relief. He began to move, gritting his teeth as he found a rhythm that worked for them. Her pleasure spiraled and coiled tighter and tighter. She gripped his arms. "Seth…yes, there…keep. Ohh."

The chandelier blazed behind him but it couldn't match the brilliant focus of his gaze. She knew what he wanted. Loud.

"Don't. Get. Your. Hopes. Up…"

His response was to fuck her harder.

The first tremor of her orgasm hit and she closed her eyes. Oh God, this was good, so good, she was going to co—

He froze and she opened her eyes on a hoarse scream. "Don't *stop*!" Then, seeing his triumph, she pounded his chest with her fists. "Damn you, that doesn't count."

Seth caught her hands, entwining his fingers in hers and began to move again. The laughter left his eyes. She couldn't look away.

"Scream for me," he rasped.

"I…don't…"

He found an even better angle and she stifled a moan.

"Scream for me!"

She was losing control, losing her mind… She grabbed his hair, yanked him down and smothered her cry of release in his kiss. Felt his smile before he bucked into her with his own hoarse cry.

It took them a while to get their breath back, longer to get their senses.

She was half-dozing when he kissed her forehead and rolled off her to stagger to the bathroom, and she shivered in the chill room and scrambled under the covers. The sheets weren't much better, and when he returned and spooned himself around her she didn't protest as she normally would.

"That was…" He paused.

"Yeah," she said. "And as soon as you've warmed up the sheets you have to leave. There's another guest room next door."

His chuckle gusted across her neck like a warm breeze from a southern ocean, full of alcohol and pirate glee. "Hard-ass."

"I work out."

"Yes, you do." He nudged her butt cheeks, all satisfied male limpness.

"Seth?"

"Y'huh?"

"Promise me you won't go all weird on me in the morning."

"I'll try." He was already half asleep. "Does this help or hinder our campaign to get Mel back?"

"Helps," she said firmly, because saying made it so.

♪ ♫ ♩

Seth's first coherent thought on waking in Dimity's palatial bed was, *What the hell was I thinking?*

He rolled over to apologize for jeopardizing a friendship that was one of the pillars of his new life, but the bed was empty. The sheets smelled of sex and Dimity's berry-floral perfume—a sensory combination that exacerbated both the guilt and his morning hard-on.

There was a metaphor for the current state of his life in there somewhere, but his head hurt too much to make the connection. All he knew was that whatever bender of self-pity he'd been on since Mel had announced her engagement stopped now.

Crawling out of bed, he stepped over his boots and crumpled jeans and stumbled into the shiny, white marble bathroom to relieve himself. Then, ignoring the claw-foot bath, he yanked the gold-plated faucet on the shower to cold and wrestled to remove his shirt and tank. Why was he still wearing them?

Oh yeah. They'd been in too much of hurry to take them off. With a groan, he leaned his forehead against the open shower door and tried to think.

Flirting with Dimity had been comic relief for both of them. Neither had taken it remotely seriously, so how the hell had they ended up in the sack together? He was rarely irresponsible and Dimity never…

Just how drunk was she when she'd made the decision?

His memories of last night were patchy after they'd arrived at Zander's mansion, and all to do with Dimity's eyes and Dimity's breasts. Steely and soft respectively.

No, she'd been in charge. Right up until she'd ceded it.

Jesus. He scraped a hand over his jaw, the scratch of a two-day beard only reinforcing what a state he'd let himself get into.

When she'd ditched her own plans at the bar to keep him company, he'd realized he was in a bad way. If she hadn't needed a friend herself after Luther's graceless rejection—not that Dimity would ever admit that—his pride wouldn't have let him go along with it.

Some friend he'd turned out to be.

Ignoring his sorry reflection in the mirror, he grabbed two tiny unopened bottles of Bvlgari shampoo and conditioner from the basket of toiletries on the marble vanity top and paused, frowning.

It seemed odd that she'd take him to what was clearly a guest room, but she'd often said she liked her sex impersonal. Which only made their situation going forward so much worse.

Currently, his life was shit. His dream career—the one he'd chosen over Mel, alienated his father for—was likely over; the love of his life had moved on to a dependable man; and now he'd completed the trifecta of poor choices by jumping a friend and his mentor's PA. Hell, who was he kidding? After Zander, Dimity was the most influential person in the band, deferred to by everybody from the band's manager to the grungiest roadie.

Maybe he was making too much of this—Dimity never did anything she didn't want to, and she'd wanted to do him. Grimly, he doused a small glow of male pleasure and ripped the tissue off a miniature soap. However she felt about it, he'd used her carelessly, thoughtlessly to ease his grief over another woman, and that was unacceptable to *him*. Fuck other people's standards, it was those he set for himself that mattered.

From here on in, he was fronting up to the consequences of his choices. After all, wasn't that why he was going home for a visit? To mend fences, and make amends to the people who'd once relied on him to do the right thing.

Bracing himself, he stepped into the shower, whimpering as the icy needles hit his skin. Too bad. He needed to be fully cognizant for the coming conversation.

When he'd scrubbed himself human, he cleaned his teeth, shaved, slapped on aftershave for the sharp sting of punishment, then dressed in last night's clothes.

Until the reality show that had changed his life by catapulting him into the public eye and then into one of the most famous bands in the world, he'd led a very normal life. In an industry where excess was celebrated, only wanting his share made him a novelty, a good guy. But good was relative, as Mel and his father would attest.

Really, his reputation in the rock world all came down to saying please and thank you. To waiting his turn to talk, not taking himself or anyone else too seriously, employing the manners he'd been brought up with.

He only had two real talents—he could lay down drums like no one else, and he didn't waste mental energy on rationalizations, excuses or denials. By acknowledging his flaws, he freed up the mental energy that most people used to cover themselves up.

Dimity Graham was in full camouflage, always had been. But her public persona was so entertaining, so ballsy and fun, that he couldn't stop himself tweaking her camo cap occasionally just to cause a disturbance in the force.

Last night had changed that.

What they'd done in bed was fun, nothing more. But what he'd seen in her uncomfortable little conversation with Luther was far more intimate. Vulnerability. It was the reason he'd stood up from the couch to divert the bodyguard's attention, instead of laying low and saving her further embarrassment.

She would pretend nothing had changed this morning—he knew that instinctively, having witnessed her response to Luther. But he wasn't going to let her. Their friendship deserved better than taking the coward's way out.

As he sat on the bed to pull on his boots, a memory flickered, as insistent as the headache thumping behind his eyes. Shit, he and Dimity had made some arrangement…she was going to help him make Mel jealous with some cockamamie, pretend-to-be-your-girlfriend plan. He just hoped to hell they hadn't done anything he couldn't take back.

Apart from the sex, you mean?

Ignoring the taunt from his conscience, he patted the pockets of his jeans, hunting for his cell. They'd sent texts. Saying what?

His cell wasn't in his jeans. Or the breast pocket of his shirt. Standing, he threw aside the rumpled covers—nothing—then dropped to floor level to search under the bed. Another memory loosened. They'd started fooling around in the kitchen. Walking to the door, he made a plan.

One. Find his cell.

Two. Make coffee and take a pot to Dimity's office. Likely, she was already there looking as fresh as a daisy, and with half a dozen machinations behind her. God, he hoped so. Hoped he was wrong about the damage this hook-up had done to their friendship. In a town where most people were phony as hell, he needed the few who kept things real for him. Dimity was top of that list.

Which led him to three. *Do whatever it takes to make things right.*

As he neared the kitchen, he heard Luther's deep growl. "Tell me this doesn't mean what I think it does."

Through the open door, Zander's head of security stood in profile, holding Dimity's elegant pumps aloft in the manner of a lawyer presenting exhibit A. Beyond him, the counter still held the detritus of last night's debauchery, half-empty glasses of booze and plates of leftovers pushed aside.

Seth waited for her to tell Luther to butt out. But her voice, when it came, was so quiet he barely recognized it as hers.

"I wish I could."

"Goddamn it, you were supposed to watch out for him." Luther dropped the shoes in disgust. "The guy was heartbroken as well as half-drunk when he left in *your* care."

Seth had heard enough. "If you want to do some slut-shaming, mate, shame me," he said, walking into the kitchen. "I took advantage of a friend last night, not Dimity." Ignoring Luther, he walked over to her. "Never explain, never apologize, remember?"

She lifted her chin. Her makeup was flawless, but she'd missed the beard burn on her neck. "He's right though," she said briskly, not quite meeting his eyes. "You were drunk and—"

"So were you." He turned to Luther. "This is not your business."

"Fine." The bodyguard's gaze flicked to Dimity, still full of reproach, and Seth heard her swallow. For some reason, she was ridiculously susceptible to the bodyguard's disapproval. Luther was a great guy but the former soldier couldn't see one shade of gray, let alone fifty.

Sure, he could tell the bodyguard that he and Dimity were dating now, but that wouldn't wash—Luther knew where his heart lay. And he'd seen him in pieces only yesterday, which made Seth the victim in Luther's eyes, no matter what he said.

There was really only one way to make the big man believe he could act so irrationally, incautiously, so completely out of character.

Act out of character again.

So he hit him.

CHAPTER 5

"FUCK, THAT HURT," SETH SAID, watching Dimity empty an ice tray into a crystal bowl. "I don't know how the pros do it."

"For a start, keep your thumb outside the fist, touching the second seam of the index finger." Carefully, Luther rotated Seth's thumb through a range of movement. "You're lucky this isn't broken."

The bodyguard's jaw was reddening, but that was the only sign of the assault. That, and a mix of astonishment and anger in his dark eyes. He wasn't looking at Seth as if he was Dimity's victim anymore, so mission accomplished. *Perhaps too well.*

"I can tell you really want to hit me back," Seth commented.

"You got that right."

"I'd offer, but I've discovered my pain threshold is really low."

Luther didn't smile as he released Seth's hand. "What the hell was that about?"

"I can't let you blame her," he said, gingerly stretching out his fingers, his swollen knuckles. "This was on me."

"Then maybe I *will* hit you," Luther said slowly. "Dimity?"

"I'm tempted to say yes." She whacked the ice tray on the counter to release the last few cubes. One bounced out of the tray and skittered across the floor. "But that won't teach either of you to let me fight my own battles."

The suppressed violence in her tone suggested she was the biggest menace in the room. The two men looked at each other.

"Clean up this mess before you leave," Luther said to Seth—and he wasn't referring to the kitchen. He left.

"You said you wouldn't go all weird on me." Dimity dumped the crystal bowl on the counter, grabbed his hand and shoved it into the ice.

He sucked in a breath at the icy burn. "I promise not to defend your honor again." He caught her hand with his free one until she looked at him, and tried to sound nonchalant. "Good morning, Dimity."

"Stop scanning me for love sickness. I'm immune to the power of your mighty wang."

Squeezing her hand in relief, he released it. "As long as you'll agree that it's mighty."

"I'll agree that you're a lover not a fighter," she retorted.

"I'm gonna take that as a yes," he said. "Can we also agree that our campaign to get Mel back was a stupid idea."

Her mouth set firm. A mouth that tasted as luscious as it looked. Sober, he didn't want that knowledge. Didn't know what to do with it.

"If I'd known you wouldn't respect me in the morning," she said, "I'd never have fucked you."

"From what I remember, I fucked you," he clarified, and for a joint instant they were naked in that bed together. Both looked away. "And how am I disrespecting you?"

"By discounting a brilliant idea, because you're embarrassed and not sure how to be friends anymore."

His first impulse was to deny it, which only lent truth to her allegation. He *absolutely* didn't want last night to affect their friendship. And there'd been a note in her voice that his musician's ear picked up. Sadness? Fear? Why was he suddenly attuned to the nuances of this woman?

He forced himself to consider her plan dispassionately, as though they'd never been naked together. For all their give-each-other-shit banter, he'd worked closely with Dimity for well over a year and respected her as a strategist. She had quirky, sometimes crazy ideas and they always paid off.

Like the time they'd showed up at a gig by a retirees' chorus who sang covers of iconic rock songs. Zander singing a duet of 'Summer Daze' with a ninety-two-year-old while the band harmonized with the choir had become a YouTube sensation. It was still one of Seth's favorite performances.

"So even sober, you think the idea has merit?"

"I do," she said. "But don't take my word for it. Read the texts from Mel again."

"I would if I could find my cell."

"Here." She reached behind the fruit bowl and handed it to him.

"You left it on the counter. I may have sat on it at one point, so I hope it's working."

Wiping his chilled hand dry on his shirt, he accepted it. "What the hell was I thinking?"

"I haven't got time for this," she said, tipping the dregs from the glasses and stacking them in the dishwasher. "I need to concentrate on work. Luther's not going to tell, so if we enter into a phony relationship, no one need know it's been consummated. In fact, I'd prefer it that way. Let's not compound one drunken mistake by making a big deal of this."

"I hear you." He read his text messages. Mel's added up to something, he just didn't know what. Between his hopes, his hangover and Dimity's subtext translations, he might as well be reading Sanskrit.

Grabbing the plates of leftovers, he carried them to the trash. "Be honest." The congealed chili fell into the bag with a soft plop. "Why are you helping me with this, really?" Her offer wasn't just for love…*friendship*…that was for sure. Sentiment didn't hit the top ten on her list of priorities.

She emptied the half-full bottle of flat champagne down the drain, and the glugging sound worsened his thirst. "You're the one member of the band the public universally loves," she admitted. "The nice guy, the sensible guy. Your support for Zander is vital."

"He already has it." He stacked the dishes in the dishwasher, annoyed that she'd question his commitment. "Got any Advil?"

"You're also the canary in the mine—as long as you're chirpy, no one thinks the band is doomed." She opened a drawer, retrieved the headache tablets and gave him two. "I can't have you wandering around looking like the world's coming to an end."

"Okay, *that* I don't have under control, yet." He found a glass and chased down the pills with water—sweet, cold water—then rinsed and refilled it. "Here." He offered her the glass. "Hydrate."

"And honestly?" Her blue eyes met his, full of resolve as she accepted the glass. "I can fix this for you."

Even knowing himself a fool to clutch at hope, Seth couldn't resist her absolute confidence. "Fine. I'm in."

"You won't regret it." She drank the water while he wiped the countertop, then her manner became business-like. "Until we leave for New Zealand, keep communication with Mel limited to texts. If she wants to talk, make excuses, say you're busy. She needs to feel what it's like not to have you in her life. No nice guy qualms, Seth, you hear me?"

"Yes." He needed a few days to process what had happened last night anyway, to try to make sense of it. Catching sight of the clock on the stove, he swore softly. "Listen, I've got to get going. Moss, Jared, and I have that meeting with Beau Davies and I need to change out of my slut's clothes."

"Why are you meeting Beau?"

He thought she'd know. "I have no doubt Zander can restore his reputation—I've seen his power of reinvention firsthand. But if his singing voice doesn't recover—"

"It will."

"But if it doesn't—" the specialist had put the odds of a full vocal recovery at forty percent "—we'll need to form a new band and find a new lead singer." He texted for a cab. After he changed clothes he and Moss still had to pick up Jared. It was going to be tight. "If Jared and I can't talk Moss into moving into it, Beau has a great voi—"

"You boys play among yourselves." The dishwasher tray rattled as Dimity dropped her empty glass into it. "I'm not wasting my energy on worst-case scenarios."

"C'mon," he teased, pocketing his cell. "You've gotta have a Plan B, a machinator like you."

"Rage will tour again." She slammed the dishwasher shut. "And I think it's incredibly disloyal that you're all meeting with Beau behind Zee's back."

Seth stared at her. "What are you talking about? Zander organized it."

♪ ♫ ♩

Dimity barely waited until Seth left before she phoned Zander, not giving a damn what time it was in New Zealand.

His cell was switched off.

She phoned Elizabeth's cell. "Hi," said a Kiwi accent. "You've reached the voicemail of Eliz—"

"Argh!" She cut the connection.

Diamanté padded in, looking for breakfast. "What the hell's Zee playing at?" she asked the cat, picking her up for a pat. "I thought I'd talked him out of this."

Zander had argued for a worst-case contingency plan almost from the moment he woke from surgery. *I know you don't want to hear it,* he'd written on his tablet, unable to speak through the early part of his vocal recovery, *but I'd be negligent if I didn't factor worst-case in.*

She'd backspaced until the whole namby-pamby sentence disappeared.

"Plan B is one thing. But we don't build panic rooms and we never will, so get that idea out of your head right now!" She hadn't realized she'd been yelling until he'd typed:

I've lost my voice, not my hearing.

He'd been depressed after losing Elizabeth—that's the only reason Dimity excused his heresy. "Screw the odds," she'd said passionately. "Your singing voice will recover and Rage will rise, stronger than ever." She thought he'd adopted her optimistic view, especially after Elizabeth stormed her way back into his life. Now, it seemed he'd only stopped talking about worst-case scenarios to *Dimity.*

In her arms, Diamanté began to purr. "Sure, the guys are holed up writing new songs," Dimity explained patiently. "Sure, Zee wants them at music events and in the public eye as much as possible...both those things are good for Rage. But encouraging them to talk to another singer—even informally—is taking their fears outside the family. And that's not good for anyone's morale, let alone public confidence. Am I the *only* frickin' one who sees that?"

In response, Diamanté dug her claws into Dimity's forearms, reminding her of their differing priorities. Taking the hint, she put the cat down and poured some dry food into a bowl, then grabbed her phone to try Zee again, pausing before she hit redial. This week he was seeing his specialist and the big question would be answered once and for all.

Slowly, she put down her cell. If her nerves were on edge, Zander's must be totally shot, despite his bravado. She needed to be more supportive—Samwise Gamgee carrying Frodo Baggins the last fifty feet up Mount Doom at the end of their long and perilous journey. Did Sam stop to lecture Frodo about his attitude, within sight of their goal? No, he didn't. *Quit panicking and think about something else.*

Like what...Seth? With an audible groan that caused Diamanté to glance up from her breakfast, Dimity attacked the final cleanup like a crime scene, removing all evidence, and even taking the trash bag outside so no scent of chili lingered.

It had been a long time since she'd made a strategic error, and screwing the heartbroken drummer when the band needed stability reflected an appalling lack of judgment. Her personal needs didn't override her professional goals…ever.

When she'd crept out of the bedroom following their wild night, she'd guessed Seth would be concerned about how she 'felt'. For a moment, with his compassionate gaze on her this morning, she'd wanted to admit to confusion…an impulse that still horrified her. Fortunately, it passed, and she'd been able to project the woman he'd expected—tough, controlled, strong.

It had been a huge relief when he'd recommitted to her plan. Deep down, she still felt that she'd taken advantage of him. Accounts would only be squared when she'd helped him reunite with Mel. At least that was an outcome she could influence.

She was chopping fruit for her muesli—sex had certainly given her an appetite—when Luther strolled into the kitchen. "You sort things out with Seth?"

"What…yeah." She stopped slicing banana. "Listen, when you were in New Zealand recently, did Zee talk about his specialist appointments at all?"

"No."

"And he was okay, not depressed or anything when you left?"

He shot her a glance as he opened the refrigerator and pulled out salmon and cream cheese. "If you're asking if I know his prognosis, the answer is no. Far as I'm aware, he hasn't seen the specialist. And after Elizabeth, he'd tell you first."

The reminder steadied her. Zander wasn't hiding anything from her because his voice was screwed. He was going behind her back because she'd made her disapproval clear, and because he didn't want her seeing him scared. And he was right…she didn't want to see it. It was tough enough mastering her own fear. Relieved, she scattered banana over her muesli and reached for a pineapple.

Luther cleared his throat. "Listen, can I ask you one question about Seth, and then I swear I'll mind my own business?"

She braced herself. "One."

"How?" He dropped a bagel into the toaster. "I'm missing the link between the you two who left last night and the you two I saw this morning."

He wasn't the only one. "I don't know, it wasn't planned." Alcohol played a factor, but there had been more behind it, much more. "I wish I could work it out myself...why are you smiling?"

His mouth relaxed. "I'm not."

She chopped off the pineapple's crown. "Let me ask *you* a question and then I swear I'll mind my own business. Who is she?"

Ha. That got rid of the smirk.

He returned to making his breakfast. "How about we both agree our private lives stay our own business?"

"That suggests the two of you haven't gone public yet." As she cut a couple of slices from the pineapple and removed the skin, her mind raced around their acquaintances. Zander had first suspected a crush on tour, which narrowed it down. She had to be an employee, they'd been too busy to form meaningful civilian relationships. Several of the sound techs were single women.

"Stop," Luther warned. "I can practically see the cogs moving. Leave this alone, Dimity. I only told you so you'd understand why I'm impervious to your incredible beauty."

"That is a way better explanation than you made last night."

"I know...I was nervous. We've always had a good working relationship and I didn't want to screw that up."

"You haven't." She circled a smaller knife around the central core of each golden slice. "Well, if you won't tell me, I'll have to start my own investigations."

He laughed as he slathered his bagel with cream cheese and topped it with salmon. "I've been in Special Forces. I know how to hide my tracks, and you haven't got a hope of breaking me."

She paused to admire him. "Wow, no wonder I wanted you to crush on me. You're a worthy opponent, but don't worry—" airily she waved her knife "—I've moved on."

This time he made no attempt to hide his grin. "With Seth."

"Very funny. I'm helping him get his girlfriend back." Assuming Mel deserved him. "And you still owe me one serious answer, since I gave you one. Is she an American?"

"No, Mel's a Kiwi."

"Don't play dumb."

"Hey, I wouldn't have told you anything, if you hadn't caught me off guard."

She watched him pour himself some juice. "You just said you couldn't be caught off guard."

"Where the hell were you when we needed an interrogator in Honduras?"

Neither of them had to ask the other to keep their secret. It went without saying.

A thought occurred to her. "Luther, does this woman even know?"

He paused for the briefest second, then picked up his breakfast. "I wonder if the sun's hit the back porch."

Got ya. "I'm available for consultancy services, once I've helped Seth. I mean, your rejection of me was so badly done, God knows what your skills are like when you actually care about someone."

"I also know half a dozen ways to kill someone," he called over his shoulder.

"Pffft. You military guys all say that." She felt better after their skirmish, more herself.

Her cell buzzed. Wiping one hand clean of pineapple stickiness, she answered it, activating a video link. Jared's wife, Kayla appeared on the screen.

"Oh no," Dimity said, dismayed. "I forgot we were having brunch—" she looked at her watch "—in half an hour."

"Don't panic, I'm calling to cancel anyway. Jared has a band meeting and can't watch the kids. Unless you want me to bring them?"

Dimity propped her cell against the backsplash so she could segment her pineapple slices. "Babe, we've talked about this."

She made no bones about the fact that babies scared the hell out of her.

Kayla grinned. "Just *kid*ding."

"Oh my God, that's a terrible pun." She searched her friend's face as she finished her prep. Bright smile, too bright eyes. Kayla and Jared were struggling up their own Mount Doom. The family had come along on the last tour leg because rock bands and preschoolers were such a natural fit…*not.*

Trouble ensued, mostly because Jared's ego had gotten out of control and he'd acted like a jackass, but he came to his senses when Kayla took the kids home early. Dimity had organized the repatriation, at which point she and Kayla became friends.

The couple were using Zander's recuperation time to heal their marriage, but Kayla's relentless cheerfulness suggested it wasn't going as well as they'd hoped.

"Oh, what the hell." Resolutely, Dimity ignored the flutter of panic. "Bring the brats to brunch."

Kayla started laughing in earnest. "Your face. No, we'll reschedule. I've promised Maddie we'll go swimming now. But first tell me how the hunt went." It had been Kayla who'd insisted Dimity take a night off and celebrate her mother's remarriage, though she'd chosen the manner of it herself. "Did you get laid last night?"

"No," Dimity said reflexively. Moss had seen her at the club, seen her leave with Seth. Absolutely she wasn't confessing to getting laid last night.

Kayla peered closer. "Is that *beard* burn on your neck?"

"No!" Dimity's hand flew to cover the evidence. "One of the kids must have smeared jelly on your screen."

The other woman's brown eyes narrowed. "Furtive…almost guilty. You *did* get laid last night. And you're covering the wrong side of your neck." She glanced away from the screen. "Hi, Seth, Jared's in the den. I'm teasing Dimity about the beard—"

"Zeesontheotherlinecallyoulater." Cutting the connection, Dimity sent her cell spinning across the counter, a snake about to bite her.

Sitting on the floor, cleaning her paws, Diamanté froze mid-lick.

"What? He'll make an excuse. It'll be fine. We've got this."

Diamanté resumed her grooming.

Dimity washed pineapple juice off her hands, her neck, her cell's screen, and reminded herself that rallying was her superpower.

She was pretty damn good at denial too.

CHAPTER 6

Dimity's workload meant she didn't see Seth in person again until she walked into the business class lounge at LAX five days later, by which time she'd relegated their inexplicable hook-up to the annuls of 'herstory'.

He stood at the buffet piling crackers, grapes and cheese onto a plate, dressed down as usual in a charcoal T-shirt and jeans with a fine-knit black hoodie tied around his waist. Soft scuffed tan boots matched the scruff on his jaw and his tousled dark red hair. Just Seth as she'd seen him at a dozen airport lounges on tour, her easy-going, unmanageable, flirt buddy.

So it was an unpleasant shock when her heart rate increased, it got harder to breathe, and she felt a tingle in places she thought she'd returned to dry dock. Muscle memory—it had to be.

Besides, she had far more important things to worry about. Despite her rationalizations, her sense that Zander already knew his diagnosis had grown with every phone call, but all she could get out of him was, "We'll talk when you get here." *Here* was only fifteen hours away.

Seth saw her and smiled and her pulse did another leap. *Down, girl.* "You look like a construction worker," she commented, frowning as she joined him. "All you need is a hard hat."

"Another fantasy?" He started filling a second plate.

She took a few seconds to regroup. "We're not talking about *that*." He'd told Kayla and Moss that he'd passed out on one of the mansion's many beds, ruining Dimity's plans, and they'd bought it without question. As she poured herself some coffee from the urn to his right, she registered the second plate. "What are you doing?"

"I look after my girlfriends. You need to get used to it. And before you accuse me of sexism, it works both ways." His expression was all innocence. "Cream and one sugar, thanks, Honey B."

"Sure, Red, let me just get rid of the boring ol' business stuff that's paying for all this." She dropped her briefcase and jacket at a nearby table and returned to pour a second coffee.

The guy serving himself beside them did a surreptitious double take—obviously trying to work out where he'd seen Seth. People rarely made the connection to one of the world's most famous—now infamous—rock bands. His manner was too humble, too self-effacing for a rock star. Probably, the guy was wondering if they'd been in Little League baseball together.

Seth carried their plates to the table.

Dimity passed him his coffee as she sat and he grimaced after the first sip. "You forgot the sweetener, Honey B."

"I'm concerned about your cholesterol levels, pun'kin."

"Everyone knows I only date women smart enough not to try and change me."

She tossed him the sugar sachet hidden in her palm. "You'd better fill me in on your family so I can say, 'Seth has told me so much about you.' Do you have a picture?"

"Yeah." As she piled cheese on crackers, he pulled out his cell. "This was at my aunt's sixtieth last month."

The shot had been taken informally on a beach and Dimity saw exactly what she expected: a numerous, sandy-footed family with unaffected smiles, an embarrassing number of children and three Labrador-cross dogs. "There's Mum and Dad..." Seth pointed to a smiling, gray-haired couple before indicating a younger pair. "And my little sister, Janey, her husband Tom, and baby Emily." Absently, he stroked the bald infant's face. "I was at Emmy's birth."

How could she forget? His sister and her husband had been living in London at the time and he'd made the dash from Dublin after a Rage concert, barely making it to their next in Belfast.

He flicked to another picture of himself teary-eyed and holding a squalling newborn.

"Why is she covered in white grease?"

"It's vernix. Premature babies are often born with the natural protective coat—"

"Stop!"

"Sorry, I forgot your phobia." He swiped to the earlier photo and identified every relative while she nodded and asked questions, and tried to desensitize herself to his close proximity. How did they do it in homeopathy? A gradual exposure to the substance you wanted to rid from your system. After a couple of minutes, her heart rate slowed and she could smell other things beside sandalwood soap. This was why she preferred drive-by intimacy—no consequences.

The earth hadn't moved when they'd slept together, but it had shifted an inch or two, and she itched to return everything to its rightful place. Seth knew her better now than she wanted him to, and she felt exposed in some indefinable way.

"So is the whole tribe going to be meeting you at the airport with welcome home signs and balloons?" She didn't need to see a picture of Mel. Until their breakup, her smiling face had been Seth's screensaver.

"At five-thirty in the morning? No. I told them not to bother."

There was a curious tautness to his tone. But before she could question it, he added, "Okay, your turn."

"My mom's not critical to operations."

"C'mon, I showed you mine."

There was a micro-second of mutual awareness which she covered by turning on her iPad and pulling up a photograph. "Brace yourself." Dressed in diaphanous white, she and her mother sat on white velvet and gilt chairs under a glittering chandelier. Dimity had realized young that she could either be ashamed or entertained by Helena's idealized worldview. And chosen to be entertained.

"That's your mum?" Seth blinked. "You look like—"

"Sisters. That's where a lot of my money went, on eternal youth. Hopefully, her new husband has more success in convincing her to age gracefully."

He looked as appalled as she'd felt looking at that vernix-covered baby. "You don't buy into that shit, do you?"

"To a point, sure. Unfortunately, I've nursed Mom through a couple of recoveries so I'd probably wimp out."

"Good," he said. "Dinosaur's eyes staring out of a young face…it's creepy."

"And here's my dad." It was an old photograph, taken when she was ten years old and still had hopes of keeping her parents together.

"Do you see much of him now?"

She switched off the screen. "He takes me out to lunch on my birthday or as close to it as we can schedule." She didn't like this telekinetic link she had with Seth since they'd slept together—she could sense his sympathy.

But he only said, "Another type A?"

She smiled. "I'm a chip off the old DNA."

Her cell rang. It was Zander's realtor, with a higher offer on the New York loft. Excusing herself, she moved away to take it.

Seth didn't talk much on the flight and she spent the first couple of hours working through fan mail. Weary of second-guessing Zander's prognosis, she took a sleeping pill after the dinner trays had been cleared, figuring she'd get the bed made up after she finished her peppermint tea.

Through the gap between the seats in front, an old Katharine Hepburn/Spencer Tracy movie was playing, and she watched idly as she waited for tiredness to kick in.

Seth fell asleep before the last drinks were cleared, as naturally as a cat napping, still with his headphones blasting the muted strains of heavy rock, and his hand on her armrest. It was a square hand, with a sprinkle of freckles and finely shaped nails, cut very short. She resisted the impulse to slide a fingertip over two bruised knuckles.

Idiot for defending my honor.

Reaching past him, she pulled the cord of his headphones from his armrest, then sat back and examined his profile—the sweep of dark red lashes over a lightly tanned cheekbone, the stubborn chin and wide mouth, none of which added up to gorgeous. Or explained the slightly panicky feeling she got looking at him.

For another minute she watched him sleeping, trying to work out why he was having this effect on her, but there was nothing in his face to solve the puzzle, only the unwelcome tenderness in her own heart.

Annoyed, she pulled up a note-taking app on her iPad and started brainstorming ideas for rousing Mel's territorial instincts, including making Seth's screensaver a picture of a honey badger and changing his Facebook status to "in a relationship." She only paused to watch Katharine soundlessly tell Spencer she loved him.

♪ ♫ ♩

The Maori guy processing their passports looked at Seth's name, then at him and broke into a wide grin. "Welcome home."

"Thanks." Being hailed as a friend by strangers was one of the things Seth enjoyed about becoming famous.

"You home for good now the band's broken up?"

Beside Seth, Dimity stiffened. Casually, he draped an arm over her shoulder. "Just taking a break while our lead singer recovers from vocal surgery."

"I used to be one of his biggest fans. On this, I've got no sympathy for him."

"Why is that—" Seth looked at his name tag "—Tane? We're always open to fan feedback." He repeated the band's mantra for Dimity's sake. She'd gotten overprotective of their boss since the scandal broke.

"Lip-syncing from rock's hard man just didn't sit well with me. He should have canceled that charity performance."

"The charity wouldn't have been able to find another headliner at short notice." He explained for the hundredth time. "The veterans would have suffered the financial shortfall."

"Okay, but why go on to play two more concerts? All his talk of paying small contractors, covering wages—what about short-changing loyal fans?"

Dimity's shoulders were rigid with suppressed outrage. Seth tightened his grip. "All the concerts got great reviews. It was only after the lip syncing came out that the press called foul. And Zander offered a full refund to any dissatisfied concert-goer."

"Really? Why wasn't that reported?"

"It was." Dimity broke free of his hold. "Only humans are evolutionarily predisposed toward focusing on the negative because potential harm is more of a priority than a potential benefit!"

Tane looked at Seth.

"If I tell you a saber-tooth tiger's coming and she tells you the roast dinosaur is done, which one gets your attention?"

"Got it." Tane stamped and returned Seth's passport, picked up Dimity's. "First visit to New Zealand?" he said politely.

"Second. Know how many actually took up the offer of a refund? Less than five percent."

"Is that right?" He asked his questions, stamped and returned her passport, then smiled. "I'll be sure to pass that on." He offered Seth a quick handshake. "Hope to see Rage in concert again soon."

"Thanks, mate." Seth didn't share his hope. Everything Zander had done since his surgery—setting up informal meetings with other musicians, making his home studio available for writing new songs, and encouraging them to attend key music events—suggested their lead singer was expecting the worst. Regardless of what his PA thought.

Seth hoped like hell Zander made a triumphant return, but if he didn't—couldn't—his efforts on their behalf had given Seth confidence that he, Jared, and Moss could form a successful new band. And the stress of this waiting game was nothing compared to the stress surrounding his departure from New Zealand.

He deeply regretted hurting the people he loved as he chased his dream of becoming a professional musician, but not for a second did he regret his choice of vocation. This was who he was meant to be.

"You've got to stop taking all this personally," he reminded Dimity as they waited at the baggage carousel. Her lack of a Plan B seriously worried him. It wasn't like her to rely on miracles.

"The glacial pace of getting the truth out there and accepted is just so frustrating." She dumped her laptop in the tray of the empty luggage trolley. "Thanks for saving me from a cavity search."

"You're welcome."

Her offloaded her pink suitcases from the carousel and shouldered his leather duffel bag, nervous at the thought of seeing his father.

Rage's tour schedule had been so consuming that he hadn't seen his parents since he'd returned to LA after winning a place in the live audition show. He talked to his mother and sister weekly, but he and his dad had spoken maybe a dozen words during the past fifteen months.

His father hadn't cut ties, but Frank Curran's icy disappointment was proving a higher wall to scale than anything George R.R. Martin had devised.

Whenever Seth phoned home he ended every call with, "Give Dad my love."

His mother would say softly, "I'm working on him."

His sister, Janey, would blow it off. "Don't worry, he'll get over it."

Twice his father had answered the phone only to say, after he'd identified Seth as the caller, "I'll get your mother."

The only real exchange they'd had since Seth left was when the press speculated that Rage wouldn't survive its lead singer's latest disgrace.

"So, you gave up a secure future for nothing." The triumph in his father's bitterness cut deep.

"You can have a relationship with me, or the last word, Dad," Seth said quietly. "But not both." His fingers were sweaty on the handset before his father finally answered.

"I'll get your mother."

Whatever the hell *that* meant. He was home to find out.

♪ ♫ ♩

Even at five-thirty a.m. the arrivals hall was chaos, multitudes of people hugging amid cries of welcome and tears of joy. Seth couldn't stop himself scanning the crowd for a familiar face, though he'd insisted on catching a cab to his parents' place.

He was sitting on Dimity's luggage trolley taking his cell off flight mode when someone tapped him on the shoulder.

"Surprise!"

His sister stood there beaming, an owl-eyed baby perched on her hip.

"Janey, what are you doing here?" Jumping to his feet, he caught her in a hug. "I told Ma I'd catch a taxi." One arm still around her shoulders, he reached out, awestruck, to stroke the small, downy head. "Hey, beautiful girl."

"Em wakes at dawn so I figured I might as well be at the airport as home. Mum was amping to come, too, but I told her to make your favorite breakfast instead—pancakes and homemade blueberry syrup."

"Wait…that's *your* favorite breakfast."

Her brown eyes widened. "Oh, did I mix them up?" She patted the pink suitcases he'd been sitting on. "Please tell me these aren't yours."

"They're mine." Returning from the ladies' room, Dimity looked at the baby and positioned herself safely on the other side of the trolley.

Seth chuckled. "Dimity, this is my sister—"

"Janey." Smiling, his faux girlfriend offered her hand across the trolley. "I've heard so much about you."

"And I've heard so much about *you*."

His sister's glee clued Seth in. "That poor baby didn't wake up by herself, did she? You pinched her."

Janey laughed. Confused, Dimity glanced between them.

"I think she knows we're an item," he explained for her, suddenly uncomfortable. It was one thing to plan this soap opera in La La land, where melodrama was normal, another thing to play it out here, in the real world. "How did you find out?"

"I have my sources."

Mel, then. It wasn't too late to put the brakes on this. "It's early days," he began to say.

"And even earlier nights," Dimity finished. Tucking her arm through his, she gave Seth one of her strap-in-for-a-wild-ride smiles.

Familiar from their professional interactions, it usually roused an answering "Yee-haw." Now that smile was hopelessly tangled with hot sex. For a straightforward guy, he'd gotten himself into a shitload of complicated.

"I'm *soooo* jealous." Janey shifted the baby to her other hip. "Since Em arrived, all Tom and I want to do in bed is sleep."

"Can I hold her?" Unable to wait any longer, Seth stole his niece from her mother. Last time he'd cuddled her she'd weighed seven pounds, and her new chubbiness was a tangible reminder of how much he'd missed by living overseas. "Hey, gorgeous, remember me? I'm your Uncle Seth and I saw you being born."

"Ugh," Dimity murmured. Fortunately, Janey didn't hear.

"She likes you." Janey eyed her daughter fondly.

"Yeah?" All Seth saw was the same grave watchfulness. Then Em cooed at him, little spit bubbles forming on her rosebud mouth, and he lost his heart.

Dimity shifted uncomfortably, drawing Janey's attention. "I know, adorable right? Want a turn?"

"God, no!"

"She's scared of babies," Seth explained.

"It's not personal," Dimity assured Janey. "I'm wary around any wild animal."

"*Okaaaay.*" His sister looked at him. "Look after bubs, while I get the car."

"Just to tell ya," he commented, when she'd left. "It's always personal with mothers. And if you want to make a good impression you'll need to disguise your horror when you look at Em. Won't she, sweetheart?" Em returned a toothless grin and Seth kissed her downy head, unashamedly breathing her in. "Damn, that baby smell is addictive."

"Okay, now you're just being creepy," Dimity said.

"C'mon, take a sniff," he coaxed, holding out the baby. "Her nappy's clean."

"Diaper," she corrected, tentatively leaning forward.

Em grabbed a fistful of hair making Dimity shriek. "Get it off!"

Laughing, Seth stepped in to create slack and tried to pry open the tiny fist. "This girl's got a grip like a wrestler."

"Seth," Dimity wailed, and he put his free arm around her. Now two blond heads lay against his chest.

"We'll need to offer her something in exchange. My wallet's in my jeans."

Dimity fumbled behind him, patting down his ass for the wallet.

Em brought her fist to her mouth and chewed on Dimity's hair.

"It's okay, baby girl," his voice trembled with suppressed laughter. "Just relax."

"Oh, sure, comfort the assailant."

"I was talking to you."

"Funny." Her face still buried against Seth's shirt, Dimity yanked his wallet free and thrust it behind her. He released her to make the trade.

Keeping a proprietary hold on Dimity's hair, Em made a grab for the wallet with her free hand.

He lifted it out of reach. "Nah-uh, first release the hostage."

Em gurgled and let go. He made the exchange.

"Is it safe yet?" Dimity's muffled voice said.

"Nearly."

Carefully he rubbed the sodden end of her hair dry with the sleeve of the sweater tied around his waist, dropped a kiss on the baby's head, and one on Dimity's because… Shit. Because?

Yeah, seeing the fearless one freaked out by a baby was so damned cute.

Her muffled voice said, "Did you just *kiss* my hair?"

"Awww." Janey's voice saved him from having to confess. "Aren't you three sweet? I *knew* Em would win you over."

Dimity opened her mouth to set her straight and, wishing he'd laid down more ground rules, Seth caught her eye. This was his *family*. He was home to reconcile with his father, and tighten bonds with his mother and sister. Would she understand his silent plea?

She turned to Janey with her sweetest smile. "I guess it's just a matter of meeting the right baby!"

♪ ♫ ♩

The Fiat's front passenger seat held assorted rattles and a dry crust. Seth removed the crust and climbed in while Janey buckled Em into her car seat in the back, and dumped the jumbo pack of nappies and baby bag alongside her. She'd cleared them from the boot to make room for his suitcase.

"Where exactly were you planning on putting Dimity's luggage?" he asked as his sister settled behind the wheel. His 'girlfriend' had turned down a ride to the ferry terminal, opting for a taxi. Zander and Elizabeth were living in semi-seclusion on Waiheke Island, thirty-five minutes by boat from downtown Auckland.

"Stacked where you're sitting. You two in the back, Dimity on your lap, holding nappies. Simple."

Dimity on my lap for forty-five minutes? Yeah. Real simple. But he smiled, thinking of her reaction to being stacked in the car like a Russian doll.

"Mum's going to be disappointed she's not staying." Janey fastened her seatbelt and started the engine. "Is she at least coming to your welcome home party tonight?"

Seth stopped tapping out a rhythm with two rattles. "Party? Tonight?"

"Yikes, I forgot that it's a surprise. Blame the baby brain." Checking the side mirror, Janey pulled into traffic. "Please pretend you don't know."

"Lucky I slept on the plane." He opened the window to dispel the last of his jetlag. You could almost taste the humidity that kept everything so brilliantly green—it was soft, caressing, home. So many things he'd once taken for granted had become precious through absence. The flat vowels of a Kiwi accent, driving on the left-hand side of the road, the spring birdsong. God, he'd missed it.

The life he led now was so different he might as well be living in a parallel universe. Maybe that was why he had to stop himself telling Janey she'd missed the turn-off to the apartment he'd once shared with Mel. The pain around his departure felt as sharp as if it had been yesterday. His father's disappointment, Mel's forced cheerfulness, his own guilt. Baggage he'd been carrying ever since.

He'd returned once to Auckland for an overnight concert as part of the Australasian tour leg. He'd sent VIP passes to his family, hoping that if his father saw him perform live he might understand that the things that mattered weren't always tangible—masonry and steel beams—but could be ethereal like the emotions evoked through music.

Mel had been at a swim meet in Australia. Janey and Tom had a good time. His mother had canceled an hour before Seth went on stage. "Your father's not ready," she'd said. "I want to be there, but right now Frank needs me on his side more than you do."

Seth understood that—he did—but it hurt. He'd come to rely on his mother's neutrality, her determined optimism. Instead they'd shared a brief, clandestine coffee at the airport before the band flew to Wellington and pretended everything was fine. Now, with Zander's singing future uncertain, his parents might *never* hear Rage live.

He forced his thoughts in a happier direction. "Can I take this welcome home party as a sign of a thaw?" His mother took a happy-clappy approach to problems, but his sister would be honest with him.

"Mum's told Dad he has to be on his best behavior, but he's still bitter." Her tone was apologetic. "Are you sure you wouldn't rather stay with Tom and me?"

"No. I don't want Dad thinking we're drawing sides, when I'm home to smooth things over. Besides, Ma would be hurt."

"And she's made pancakes," Janey grinned at him. "Your favorite."

"I'll get even," he promised, glancing behind to check on his niece. "Em's catching up on missed sleep."

"Speaking of being kept awake all hours, your new girlfriend seems…interesting."

"She is." For Janey's benefit, he and Dimity had exchanged a self-conscious peck on parting, one that turned into laughter when their eyes met mid-kiss. Yeah, their friendship would survive one sexual encounter. That meant a lot to him.

His sister shot him another look. "Rebound?"

"We haven't been labeling it."

"I'm here for you."

"Thanks." She waited a few seconds, then grumbled, "Well, *that* wasn't worth getting up at dawn for, was it Em?"

Seth grinned. "She's asleep…and I'm not discussing my love life with you." Which meant he had to be consistent and not pump her for information about Mel's new guy. "How's Tom? Still wanting five kids?"

That distracted her. "I've told him he'll be lucky to get a second if this one doesn't sleep through the night soon." For the rest of the ride they talked about her husband, how they were resettling in New Zealand after four years abroad, and their house renovations.

Their parents still lived in the home his father had built for them as newlyweds, but the neighborhood had gentrified in tandem with their rise in fortune.

The house itself had been renovated and extended until neither it nor the 'hood looked anything like the modest suburb of Seth's early childhood, when six-foot-high fences were only for people with dogs, and large yards hadn't been halved by the addition of extra rooms or a pool.

His parents had exercised restraint in their upgrades. His mother Gayle would never give up her fruit trees or vegetable garden for a fourth bedroom.

She came hurrying the moment she heard the front door. "Seth! And I haven't got my face on, yet."

"Looks like the same face to me," he said, holding her as tightly as he could without crushing her.

"Silly." She smelled of pancake batter. Smiling, she pulled free to look at him. Older, he thought. She got older. People did, but still he couldn't help wondering if he'd contributed to the new furrow between his mother's brows. But the affection in her eyes never changed, and the sweet scent of blueberries and sugar simmering on the stove wafted from the kitchen. *God, it's good to be home.*

"Where's this new girlfriend of yours?" Gayle glanced around him to the door. "Isn't she with you?"

"She's in New Zealand primarily to work so she's staying at Zander's. But, Ma—" he got uncomfortable again "—it's not serious." If he had to mislead his mother, he'd stick as closely as possible to the truth.

"No, you should play the field," she said. "Enjoy being single." One gentle squeeze of his arm told him how sorry she was about Mel.

"Listen to you being all rock 'n' roll." She tried so damn hard to keep everyone happy. For the first time, he wondered what she gave up to do it. Having tried—and failed—in his own balancing act, he had a new appreciation of the skills required to keep all the balls in the air. And the cost.

"Is that my granddaughter?" Gayle plucked a sleepy Em from her daughter's arms like a piece of ripe fruit and smothered her in kisses.

"Don't mind me," Janey said in a long-suffering voice.

"Oh, does little Mummy feel left out?" Seth swooped in to pepper her face with kisses while his sister, laughing, tried to beat him off. "Get him off me, Mum."

"The prodigal returns," his father's dry voice said behind them.

CHAPTER 7

The ferry to Waiheke Island was packed.

"It's a public holiday," one of the ferry staff explained as he helped Dimity stow her expensive luggage alongside beach bags, boogie boards, backpacks, and kids' trikes. "Lots of day trippers heading to the beaches and vineyards."

Just her luck. She roamed the outside decks and found a seat near the bow, which was surprisingly uncrowded, then realized why when the ferry hit the open harbor and the wind, still carrying a hint of winter chill, whipped her hair into a frenzy. Nearly everyone shuffled inside, but she tied up her hair and stayed where she was, welcoming the fresh air. She needed this opportunity to regroup.

In his natural habitat, Seth was even more attractive than he was in L.A. And that was good, she thought, watching the sun's rays bounce light off the choppy sea. It meant Mel didn't stand a chance of resisting him.

Their parting kiss had been self-conscious, but thankfully, Janey put it down to her presence, and they'd all laughed about it. Did Seth know how few people could so effortlessly make her laugh?

She'd had to resist the urge to linger, but it was exhausting pretending their futures weren't hanging in the balance—everyone thought Zee's prognosis was still a couple of weeks away.

"See you at Waiheke. I'm sure we'll meet again soon, Janey."

Seth's sister had been nice; his niece terrifying. Something about babies' dependency, combined with their expectation of being loved, left her feeling completely helpless.

She hated being scared.

Standing, she walked to the bow where the wind was fiercest and imagined it blowing through her, collecting and flinging every anxiety, every doubt into the boat's churning wake. But her greatest fear still circled like a shark.

What will we do if he has no voice?

She hadn't considered a Plan B because it felt disloyal, and because she didn't want to tempt fate—two insanely illogical reasons. Her mentor had proved time and again that willpower could move mountains. And crazy as it was, she felt very deeply that her faith, added to his will, was necessary to push them over the greatest hurdle they'd faced together. And that was enough woo-woo bullshit for one morning.

Retreating to shelter, she reviewed Plan A. Once Zee had the all clear, her first priority was relocating the lovebirds to LA so he could launch a charm offensive. Grabbing her iPad, she made a note to contact the specialist freight company who'd shipped his guitars to New Zealand. Elizabeth had already said she could write anywhere until her university lecturer job kicked in March first next year, by which time Dimity would have talked her out of returning. To her note she added: *Get freight quote for Elizabeth's furniture.*

Zee's manager Robbie had asked Dimity once if she was jealous of Elizabeth's influence. But Elizabeth wouldn't dream of interfering in Zander's career any more than he would dream of interfering in hers. His respect for her work had given him the idea of asking her to write his memoir in the first place. He was also canny enough to recognize that a Pulitzer Prize-winning biographer of long-dead icons writing the memoir of a polarizing and very much alive rock idol would generate killer publicity.

The publisher, Max, had canceled Zee's book contract after his fall from grace, no longer believing sales would justify his million-dollar advance. Unbeknownst to Zander, Elizabeth had pitched another book—*In Bed With A Rock God*, her account of touring with Rage on its last scandal-ridden tour and falling in love with its disgraced lead singer.

Her goal was to soften the public's perception of him—in Dimity's view a brilliant idea; in Zee's an enterprise fraught with peril. They were both right.

Either way, Elizabeth's book would be a bestseller. Once they'd won their case against the insurers, they'd reschedule the remainder of Rage's tour with extended dates thanks to the buzz generated by Elizabeth's memoir. Everyone a financial winner. Dimity switched off her device with a smile. Now *that* was a happy-ever-after she could buy into.

The speck that was Waiheke Island grew in size until its low sweep of fields and trees filled the horizon. The vessel dropped speed, and a siren blast warned small craft of her impending arrival into Matiatia Bay.

Dimity found the bathroom, combed her hair, reapplied her makeup, and prepared for victory. It didn't take long to find two recruits to help with her luggage—a hippy and a local vintner—and she sailed down the gangplank confident that she looked every inch the glamazon PA to a famous rock star. Her cell pinged a text.

Walk to end of pier, turn right. We're waiting under the pohutukawa trees.

Elizabeth's bright orange hair was easy to spot. She'd twisted and clamped her unruly curls into a bulldog clip, but the sea breeze had teased strands free and they danced around her head like a welcoming flag. She was striking, too, for her air of indefinable elegance, making even an off-the-rack green dress and coral cardigan look like designer labels.

It took Dimity longer to identify the man standing beside her.

Zee normally wore clothes as flamboyant as his personality. Today, he was almost nondescript in jeans so worn and faded as to be nearly white, and a loose-fitting T-shirt that covered his stellar physique. He'd replaced his trademark Stetson with a cheap navy cap emblazoned with *I'd rather be fishing* and wraparound sunglasses hid his distinctive pale blue eyes.

With the wharf crawling with day trippers, a disguise made sense, yet she was shocked by how easily he slotted into this environment.

"I see you've changed your mind about staying longer than a week," he called, nodding hello to her porters. "Unless those suitcases are full of new subpoenas."

Hugging wasn't something they did, so she was caught off guard when he pulled her into one. "Save the touchy-feelies for Elizabeth," she said fending him off. "That goes for you, too," she warned his fiancée, who ignored her.

Dimity suffered the hug. "I remember why I never liked you," she complained. "You keep trying to be my friend."

Smiling, Elizabeth released her. "It's because you're so bloody sweet."

"It's a curse." Dimity turned and thanked her helpers. "Zee, do you have New Zealand dollars?"

He shook their hands instead. "She's new to community," he explained, and they stopped looking offended. She'd forgotten that Kiwis didn't tip.

When they'd left, Dimity looked around. "Where are your local bodyguards?"

"It's been two months since the scandal broke. Maybe in LA the paparazzi would still be lurking. Here on Waiheke, I stopped being of local interest after a week."

"He was supplanted by concerns over wastewater management."

"Septic tanks," said Zander.

Dimity gave them both a withering look. "You two know it's all those raging sex hormones that are making you idiots, right? It's called *dope*-a-mine for a reason."

"We're parked a short walk away." Zander picked up the two largest suitcases and looked at Dimity's shoes. "Only you would wear heels that high to an island."

"Think of me as an envoy from the real world. Clearly, I've got here in the nick of time." She shook her head at Elizabeth. "If you still find him attractive dressed like Gilligan, it must be love."

"It is." Elizabeth looked at Zee, who dropped Dimity's suitcases on the path and pulled her into his arms to kiss her.

Dimity rolled her eyes. It was going to be a long two weeks. "I hope my bedroom is soundproof."

"Yeah, we've thought about that." Zander picked up the suitcases again. "Your bedroom is in a separate building. Doc likes to make a lot of noi—"

His lover clamped her hand over his mouth.

"Some things stay private?" he mumbled through her fingers.

"Some things stay private." Removing her hand, she straightened his cap.

Dimity shuddered. "For the love of God, keep this mushy stuff private, too. It's turning my stomach."

"And to think I really did miss you." Zander led the way to the car, dropping Dimity's suitcases beside a mud-covered Land Rover Defender. "This is ours." In LA he drove a Dodge Viper.

"Very funny." She kept walking, only turning when she heard the beep of an electronic key. "*Seriously?*"

"The dirt road to our rental property is only accessible via four-wheel drive, and the recent storm has turned every pothole into a muddy wallow." He gestured to the mud coating halfway up the doors. "If you're worried about my security, consider it camouflage." Swinging open the rear door, he sidestepped the tire attached to it and picked up one of her bags. "You must be wiped out after your flight."

"They were in business class, not the Gulag," Elizabeth pointed out.

Dimity and Zee exchanged a look as he hoisted her bag into the trunk. She missed the private jet as much as he did. "Socialists have no appreciation of the needs of rock royalty," he commented.

"Yeah, I saw some of Your Highnesses' behavior on tour," Elizabeth said dryly. "You know what happened to the royals in the French Revolution, right?"

"Everyone got to eat cake?" Dimity said. She had a broad education and enjoyed Elizabeth's intellect.

Laughing, Elizabeth pushed aside groceries to make room for the second suitcase. "How's Seth? I hope you've been kind to him since his ex got engaged."

Unexpectedly, Dimity's face went hot. "So kind I'm going to help him get Mel back. We're pretending to date," she added casually. "So, if you see pictures of us together you'll know why." *Please think this is sunburn.* Elizabeth started lifting the second suitcase and Zander moved to help her, but he was staring at Dimity. She couldn't see his eyes behind his shades, but his brow was creased in a slight frown. Her guilty blush deepened.

"I don't know if it's wise to start tinkering in other people's relationships," Elizabeth said.

Desperate times. "You and Zee wouldn't be together if I'd let you rush to his side after the—"

"You're right, I'll stay out of it."

Zander took the bait. His attention shifting to his lover. "What's this about you and me?"

Dimity had stopped Elizabeth rushing to Zander's side after the scandal broke because he would have read it as pity, not love, and rejected her. Instead, Elizabeth had effected a reunion by playing smart. By unspoken agreement, neither woman had ever told him of Dimity's intervention. Not even a man in love liked to think he'd been managed.

"Enough small talk." Dimity seized control of the conversation.

"Your speaking voice sounds stronger. When will you hear about your singing voice?"

Zander swung the rear door closed on the suitcases and unhooked her laptop from her shoulder. "Let's get you settled in, first."

His hesitation told her everything.

She grabbed his arm as he opened the passenger door. "The specialist has given you a prognosis, hasn't he?"

Zander dumped her laptop in the back seat. "I've got some lamb steaks marinating and a bottle of local wine in the fridge."

She tightened her grip on his arm. "Zee, don't torture me."

He glanced at Elizabeth, as if for reassurance, and dread pooled in Dimity's stomach. *Oh God. It's over.*

"I'll make a full recovery."

She burst into tears, surprising the hell out of all of them. "Ignore me," she managed between sobs. "It's stress leaving the body, that's all. I'm just so h—h—happy." She dabbed at her wet face with her sleeve but the tears kept coming, trickling into her wide smile and salting her tongue. She should feel embarrassed—Zee had never seen her cry.

If she needed to weep, she found a hidey-hole somewhere. Tears were simply a build-up of tension. You turned on the tap, flushed pesky emotions from the body and returned, refreshed, to business.

But oh, these felt like a blessing, washing away the toxic sludge of doubt, fear and frustration that had held her hostage for nearly eight long weeks. Waiting on a medical prognosis had been wearying, but ignoring her fears? Exhausting. Outcomes beyond her control were her worst nightmare. She thought she'd left powerlessness behind with her childhood.

Zander laid a hand on her shoulder. "There's more—"

"Recovering your full vocal range will take another few months." Gratefully, she accepted a handkerchief from Elizabeth. "I did research." When she couldn't sleep she'd obsessively trawled through every obscure medical paper related to vocal health.

"My singing voice isn't the only consideration—"

"Way ahead of you." Nothing like business to snap a girl out of sentimentality. Briskly, she wiped away her tears. "We have to win our case against the insurance company before we can afford touring again." For weeks her forward planning genius had been shackled to the outcome of Zander's medical verdict. Now it broke free and ran.

"I wonder if it's worth trying to settle out of court to expedite the process… Maybe we should get the lawyers to run some figures."

"Can you listen without interrupting for a minute. Please?"

She nodded, but the opportunities fired along her synapses were as distracting as fourth of July fireworks. *How do we break the news to best effect?* Ellen *will give us a slot.*

As a silent Elizabeth offered her a half-empty disposable cup, she watched Zander's mouth move.

Or should we go for print? There might be more gravitas releasing to the New York Times.

"Difficult for you to understand…"

I could also see Zander on the cover of Rolling Stone. *Rock's Lazarus rises again.*

"…You're my general…"

"Brilliant!" She beamed at him. Lip-syncing at a military fundraiser had got him into this mess. His first public performance *had* to be for the war vets.

Zander folded his arms. "This whole experience has forced me to reassess what kind of man I want to be—"

"I'm glad you brought that up, Zee, because we need to fast-track rebuilding your reputation." Dimity paced beside the dirty vehicle. "It's time to come clean about all the charities you've been supporting… No. Hear *me* out."

She took a swig from the cup she was suddenly holding—tepid coffee. "We have to make more of the war vets' support. If *they* believe your heart was in the right place when you lip-synced the national anthem, then anyone calling you unpatriotic hasn't got a case. That's why your first public performance has to be at another military fundraiser."

Absently, she shook the contents of the cup, hoping to stir up sugar. "You have to return to home soil immediately." Her spirits soared. "Maybe you and Elizabeth should get engaged or something. Have you written her a song yet? Let's spin all this lurve sludge into gold."

She took a breath and another swig of coffee. *Yes, sugar!* "The only thing I don't understand is why you've been encouraging the other band members into side projects…but I don't pretend to your marketing genius." Zander tried to interrupt and she laughed. "I'm raving, but I hadn't realized how much this was weighing on me. It sure explains a couple of the crazy things I've done lately." It was such a relief to categorize her hook-up with Seth. Her subconscious had been creating busy work to distract her from all this.

Her boss was watching her with the strangest expression. Glancing at Elizabeth, Dimity saw it reflected and was able to identify compassion, more familiar on Elizabeth's face than Zee's. A chill pierced her euphoria. "What?"

"I'll get you a fresh coffee," Elizabeth said. "Skinny milk, one sugar." She touched Zander's arm in passing, almost in reassurance.

"What?" Dimity demanded again.

"I'm not telling anyone else my singing voice is recovering—only you and Doc. Our press release will simply say my future in music remains uncertain and that my immediate priority is creating other opportunities for everyone involved with the band."

She stared at him, her brain still transitioning from warp speed. "But Rage?"

"Has had its last encore."

"I don't understand. If your singing voice is recovering?"

"I'm glad I resurrected the band when the original members left." He pulled off his cap and raked a hand through his white gold hair. It had grown since he'd cut it to raise money for the vets, a day before his doomed appearance for them.

The extra length made him look his old self again. Which made it even harder to process what he was saying. "I did it for the wrong reasons—because I'm a fucking egotist and need center stage—but my God, what a war we waged, Dimity. We revitalized one of the world's greatest rock bands."

"And we will again," she said, bewildered. "You know all the haters will run out of steam. The lawyers will win the claim against the insurance company. You'll have money to finish the tour."

He replaced the ugly cap on his head. "Remember the *Star Trek* motto? To boldly go where no man has gone before. I've got nothing left to prove and everything to lose."

"What the hell are you talking about?"

"It's time for me to focus on my relationships and prioritize family."

"You've just spent the last seven weeks bonding with family, they'll probably be glad to see the back of you. Zee, this isn't you talking." Was he on drugs for his vocal recovery? Anywhere in the world, if people had to name iconic bands, Rage would be among them.

To pull that off, twice, and then walk away? Music—the power, the politics, the game—*fame* was his life. She'd seen him living for it, had adopted his creed as her own.

Who needed a personal life when your professional life was so absorbing? And he was saying it didn't matter? That he wanted to exchange that edgy, thrilling chaos for the touchy-feely, cloying, mystifying complexity of personal relationships? Domesticity was for lesser mortals, not gods of rock. Not *the* god of rock.

"You'll never be happy away from the world's stages. Whatever kind of magical lovefest you're on with Elizabeth, it's going to wear off, get boring, get too real."

He was watching Elizabeth approach with Dimity's coffee and she followed his gaze, trying to see what he did. Yes, his former biographer was a wonderful woman—Dimity was secretly fond of her, herself— but there was nothing in her pleasant features and lanky grace to inspire the razing of empires. "The high won't last. *It can't.* You don't rely on love." He'd been abducted by aliens. It was the only explanation that made sense.

Zander was still watching Elizabeth. "How long have you worked for me?"

"Nearly three years."

"And until Doc came along I knew nothing about you unless it related directly to me. I didn't know you were financially supporting your mother or that you were crying in stadium utility closets because you were exhausted through overwork. As long as I could anesthetize my conscience with alcohol, I believed my vocal gift justified selfishness in every other area of my life. When I had to sober up to conserve my voice I also woke up to what I'd become." He added quietly, "The high we're feeling now will come and go through our lives. But my love for her will never change."

"Spare me your Hallmark moment." Dimity glared at Elizabeth as she accepted fresh coffee. "As for you, I thought you only used your powers for good?"

"I made this decision alone," Zander answered. "Doc's supportive of whatever I want to do."

"Because she has no *clue* what a disastrous mistake you're making." Dimity swung her glare to Zander. "This decision isn't reversible, Zee. The longer you stay out of the music industry the harder it will be to return to it. People forget."

"Exactly," he said. "To sustain the level of fame I've been used to I have to give everything. I'm not willing to give everything anymore."

"But to leave when your reputation is tarnished. What will that mean for Rage's legacy?"

"Twenty years from now Rage's music will matter or it won't, regardless of whether I go out on a high or a low. I lost sight of that."

"You have one of the greatest voices in rock *ever,* according to everyone who counts these things and you're what…bowing out? Singing isn't what you do, it's who you are."

"I'm more than my voice," he said. "It's defined me for twenty years, hell, it's been the only worthwhile thing about me since I was fifteen. I'm not expecting the transition to be easy. But change will be impossible if I mainline into the adulation that encourages me to stay exactly the way I am."

She felt as if she'd woken in a lifeboat with no memory of the Titanic going down. "What about your fans?" She was desperate now, clutching at straws. "You've always said Rage's fans come first."

His jaw tightened. "I'm not saying this is painless, only that it's necessary."

She was running out of arguments. While she cast about for a roadblock to stop this madness, he said gently, "It'll be okay. You still have a job."

"Doing what? Sending out your fucking Christmas cards? And what about the other band members?" Moss, Jared…*Seth.*

"They're more than talented enough to succeed in their own band. I'll help them as much as I can."

She tried to read his eyes behind his sunglasses, but the lenses reflected only an anguished woman. Automatically she began smoothing down her windswept hair and stopped. Everything seemed pointless, confusing, jarring. The sun too bright, the oily miasma of diesel and brine with its hint of moldering seaweed, the coffee she held.

She hurled the paper cup at the beach. The white plastic lid flew off, skimming through the air like a Frisbee. A spray of muddy liquid splattered across the grass. The breeze caught the cup and rolled it toward the sea.

"I'll get it," said Elizabeth, and this time it was Dimity's arm she touched in passing. Dimity shook her off. *Judas.*

"I wish I'd never helped you sort out your problems with Zander," she told Elizabeth when she returned. "Not if this is the result."

Elizabeth dropped the cup into a public trash can. "I had nothing to do with his decision."

"Of course you did. If he wasn't so damn happy, he wouldn't be doing this existential bullshit."

"Dimity," Zander warned.

She ignored him. "You've killed the career of one of the greatest bands in rock 'n' roll. Yoko has nothing on you. And you're too naïve to realize it."

"That's enough," Zander said sharply.

"Let her speak, she's upset." Elizabeth's gaze remained steady on hers. And Dimity hated her in that moment, hated her for understanding.

Itching for a fight, she rounded on Zander. "So that's it? You're abandoning us? Your Rage family, the people who have worked for and believed in you."

"I'll do everything in my power to make sure no one suffers by my action. Though frankly, given my pariah status, you probably all have better prospects without me." He took off his sunglasses and she was hit by bolts of crystalline blue sincerity. "But I'll always be there for you."

Beyond him, city-bound passengers lined up to board the return ferry, a brightly colored snake-chain waiting for the gate to reopen.

"Is this where Shep comes up with his tail wagging and you tell me you'll make me godmother of your first child and we smile tearfully and everyone's happy?"

"I'd like that to happen, but I'm sensing some resistance." Zander hit her with his killer smile, the one that always got him what he wanted. "What if I named that first child after you?"

"Don't," she said, almost too bitter to speak. "Don't you *dare* make a joke of this. The terrible waste of your talent, the end of one of rock's greatest comebacks. The pain you're causing me, the band, your fans…everyone who's believed in you and followed you."

"You're right, I'm sorry." He dropped the smile. "I need practice with this stuff. I will do whatever I can to help you all in your careers. But I have to live my best life. And Rage won't get me there." He held out his hand. "Please understand."

Dimity slapped it away. "No. I can't pretend you're not making the worst mistake of your life. I can't play along with your stupid fantasy that you're capable of being an ordinary Joe, satisfied with life in the 'burbs. You have a talent that makes you extraordinary and you're giving it all up for love? You should be committed, not congratulated." She wrestled with the door to the Land Rover's trunk but couldn't find the catch.

Joining her, Elizabeth said softly, "What are you doing?"

"Leaving." She couldn't stand to look at either of them. The ferry's engines started, a deep-throated throb. Giving up on her luggage, she tightened her grip on her shoulder bag and grabbed her laptop from the back seat.

"Go ahead and abandon us," she told Zander. "But know it for abandonment."

Without waiting for his reply, she hurried toward the pier, where the last passenger was disappearing across the gangplank.

"Dimity!" His voice was huskier post-surgery, more so when filled with anguish.

One of the ferry staff started untying the dock lines and she broke into a jog. When one foot slipped out of its stiletto, Dimity kicked off the other, leaving both behind and sprinting in bare feet. She had to get out of here.

A guy closing the railed gate at the bottom of the gangway shook his head when she pulled up, panting. "Sorry, you'll have to wait for the next one."

"Please," she gasped. "Please."

He looked up at the ferry to check its status and she took the opportunity to slip past him. "Hey!"

At the top of the ramp another guy was sliding the gangplank away from the dock. "Emergency," she yelled. "I have to get on." Her face must have given her credibility because he reached out a hand and jumped her over the small gap and onto the vessel. "Ticket?"

She looked at him blankly.

"Go on," he nodded her away. "Don't tell anyone and don't do it again."

Stammering thanks, she ducked inside and found somewhere she could wedge herself away from people. Her cell buzzed Zander's call signal—Queen's 'We Are the Champions'. Hunching further into her corner, she ignored it, watching the island recede into the distance.

As far as she was concerned, she'd just quit.

CHAPTER 8

"DAD." ASTONISHED, SETH FACED THE man who'd farewelled him with the words, *You're breaking my heart.* "I thought you'd be at work." Rain, hail or flu, his father always left the house at six a.m. returning twelve hours later. "Did you stay home for me?" This was better than he could have hoped for.

Arms open, he was halfway across the hall when his father answered.

"Isn't *that* a rock-star attitude? That it's always about you."

His steps slowed. Behind him, his mother said sharply, "Frank."

His father thrust out a hand, as effective as a stop sign, and Seth stared at it. His grandfather—Frank's father—had been a cold man, uncomfortable with physical affection, and his handshake had become a private family joke. The message couldn't be plainer.

Fuck that. Seth wasn't playing this game anymore. Side-stepping the outstretched hand, Seth enveloped his father in a hug and became conscious of frailty in the big man's frame. He'd lost weight. Frank stood stiffly, neither returning the embrace nor pushing him away. Seth read that as a positive sign.

Releasing him, he stepped away. "It's good to see you, Dad—regardless of why you're still here."

His father looked through him. "I've got a nine a.m. meeting nearby, so your mother decided we should all have breakfast together."

And good to see you, too, son. "Great, I'm starving." Seth had expected mending fences to be hard work. No point being hurt by it. Letting everyone off the awkwardness hook, he smiled at the others. "Let's eat!"

Halfway through the meal, which they ate under the wisteria-covered deck overlooking his mother's flower beds, Seth was grateful

Janey had chosen her favorite breakfast and not his. The atmosphere was too tense to enjoy it.

Frank sat opposite, the leaden weight of his disappointment evident in the new stoop to his shoulders and the downward drag to his mouth. *Did I do that?*

For the hundredth time, Seth reminded himself that he couldn't live his father's dream, only his own. For the hundredth time, it made no difference to the guilt.

Once they'd talked a lot, mostly about work. But the business had become a no-go zone. Which left small talk about relatives, punctuated by little pools of stagnant silence.

"I don't know why we have to give a blow-by-blow of everyone's lives." Frank pushed his empty plate away. He'd ignored the pancakes in favor of All-Bran, but his expression remained constipated. "Seth will see most of them at the party tonight."

"Oh, honey," his wife wailed. "That was a surprise."

"Honestly, Dad, you're hopeless." Janey winked at Seth.

"How was I supposed to know? I only found out we were having a party last night."

"Because you would have stop—" Gayle picked up the coffeepot. "Darling, more coffee?"

Seth held out his mug. *So much for the thaw.* "Thanks."

"So I guess you'll be going on tour again once your lead singer's voice recovers," Gayle said encouragingly.

"That's the plan." Only Zander's closest circle knew his singing voice was at risk. "We're waiting on the outcome of the insurance claim."

"How long will that take?"

"Could be anything up to a year."

Frank evinced faint interest. "What's this?"

Wow, he really hadn't been paying attention to anything Seth did. Either Janey and Mum hadn't been passing news on—doubtful—or his father refused to listen. Damn, but the old man could be a stubborn son of a bitch when he wanted to be. And who did he think he was punishing by not eating Gayle's pancakes? For his mother's sake, Seth forced himself to take another from the stack. "The insurers are refusing to pay out the tour cancellation insurance, claiming Zander's voice problem was pre-existing. He's countersued saying it wasn't, and now it's up to the courts."

"Assuming no settlement is reached in the meantime."

"Assuming that."

They discussed the ramifications. Seth's grandfather had worked in insurance all his career and his father's first job had been in insurance. Policy minutiae bored Seth senseless—Dimity would love the conversation—but anything that broke down barriers with his father had to be good.

"Your grandfather didn't want me to start my own business, always thought it was too risky," Frank said. "He saw a lot of start-ups fail."

"So Seth's following the family tradition by striking out on his own." Janey swallowed her last bite of pancake and smiled at her baby, who sat at their feet on a blanket, ignoring Nana's box of toys in favor of playing with the laces on Seth's outstretched boots.

"Running away to join a rock band isn't comparable to starting an engineering company," Frank said dryly.

Gayle pursed her lips, a referee poised to whistle a foul, but Seth controlled his temper. "I wasn't running away, Dad." *Be patient, play nice, he'll come around.* "I was accepting a once-in-a-lifetime opportunity."

His father shrugged. "I notice the press still have knives out for him."

"Zander did what he thought was right." There was a fine line between playing nice and rolling over. "The *press* need to get over it."

"I was really proud of you for standing by him." His mother smiled at him. "It showed character."

"Yes, *loyalty's* a wonderful thing," Frank said.

Refilling his coffee mug, Seth counted to five. *One stubborn asshole, two stubborn assholes, three—*

"We should ask Zander and his girlfriend to the party," Janey suggested. Under the table, she nudged his knee in sympathy.

"And I can't wait to meet yours, Seth." Gayle turned to her husband. "Honey, remember I told you? Our son has a new girlfriend."

"Model or actress?" Frank asked, but his tone implied *whore of Babylon or airhead?*

"Neither." Seth rarely drank sugar with his coffee but he added a teaspoonful now, to take away the taste of his father's bitterness. "Dimity is Zander's PA." *And she would have* you *for breakfast if she heard your tone.* A tug on his boots made him look down. His niece was hauling on his untied laces like reins.

"A secretary, well that's normal at least. Wacky name, though."

Her mum's wacky. "Her mother named her after a character in *Gone with the Wind*. And Dimity's responsibilities are more like chief of operations."

"Like your job used to be," his father said.

At Seth's feet, Em beamed up at him, a timely reminder that he wasn't home to escalate a cold war, but to make peace. For all their sakes. Returning the baby's smile, he responded to his mother's earlier question. "Dimity's probably too jetlagged to come tonight." He had no doubt she'd handle herself, but he definitely needed a good night's sleep to carry off that particular fiction.

"And Zander and Elizabeth are still bugged by paparazzi off the island so they'd need more notice to organize security." If Frank thought Seth had crossed to the dark side, what the hell would he make of Zander Freedman? Even reformed, his mentor was larger than life.

"Ridiculous," said his father. "Anyone would think they were important."

"Nice idea though." Doggedly, Seth ignored the comment. "Maybe another time."

"I can't wait to see what you think of Dimity, Mum." Janey bent to retie Seth's shoelace so Em could continue her game. "She's so different from…" She faltered.

Any more elephants in the room and we could form a circus act.

"Mel," Seth supplied. His mother was looking at him anxiously. To reassure her, he added, "I might have underplayed my relationship with Dimity. I'm pretty smitten."

Gayle's expression relaxed. "That's a relief. I have a confession to make. I ran into Mel yesterday and we got talking about the party and I hope you don't mind, but—"

"Hi, there. Hope I'm not interrupting anything?"

A tall, smiling man had come around the side of the house. "I knocked, but no one answered the front door."

It took a moment for Seth to recognize him. Jeff, his replacement at Curran Engineering.

"No, I'm ready to go." Dropping his napkin on the table, Frank stood with such an expression of relief you'd think he'd just been given parole. "Jeff's my ride to work," he explained to Seth. "No need to get up…I'll see you tonight."

"It would be rude not to say hello to Jeff." *One of us has to remember our manners*. Following his father across the lawn, he shook Jeff's hand. "Nice to see you again." He hadn't been involved in his hiring—a pointed omission—but had worked alongside Jeff for two weeks before leaving for LA. He'd also made himself available anytime for follow-up queries. In one bizarre instance, he'd placated a difficult client while waiting to go onstage to hear whether he'd made the final of the reality show.

Jeff pumped his hand. "I hope you're not home for your old job," he joked.

"Relax, mate, I still have one." He was getting really tired of everyone assuming the band was history. Even mentally preparing himself for the worst, he was still hoping for the best.

"And I wouldn't offer him his old job, anyway," Frank said, smiling. "You're better at it and when he left, Seth made it *very* clear he was relinquishing all rights in perpetuity, didn't you?"

"I did, Dad," he said evenly.

"So he's got no one to blame but himself." His father was still smiling at Jeff. "Shall we go, son?"

Son?

"Um, yeah, sure." Jeff looked embarrassed. "For what it's worth, I think your lead singer is getting a bum rap. I hope it all works out for you."

"I'm sure it will...Dad, a word?" Seth had reached his limit of playing target for cheap shots. He waited until Jeff had walked out of earshot. "I was hoping this visit we could get past how much I've disappointed you."

"Do you want me to pretend that your leaving had no repercussions on the business?"

"It's been over fifteen months." *For God's sake. Get over it.* He forced himself to be conciliatory. "Can't we move on?

"You're staying here, aren't you?" Frank said equally pleasantly. "Your mother's throwing a party, which I'm paying for. And what is this, if not a conversation? And now if you'll excuse me, some of us have real jobs."

He left before Seth could formulate a response that didn't start with, "You stubborn old goat." He stayed a minute—tempted to kick his mother's prize azaleas—to talk himself down.

Why the hell am I even trying, if he's just going to keep rubbing my face in the dirt?

You stomped on his dynasty dreams, left him in the lurch—did you really expect the fatted calf?

No, but there's a difference between sadness and sulking. Surely disappointment has a fucking use-by date.

It was another minute before he could bring his frustrations under control and return to the table.

He must have done a lousy job because his mother took one look at his face and sighed. "He *has* missed you, honey."

Leaning over the table, he kissed her cheek. "We'll work it out." *If I don't tell him to take a flying leap, first.* Janey's expression was also anxious. "Hey, I have presents in my bag, let me get them."

His mood did improve watching his mother and sister exclaim over their gifts—a necklace for Gayle, earrings for Janey, and baby cowgirl boots for Em. She was chewing on them when his cell chimed with a call from Zander.

"Let me guess. Dimity's driving you crazy already."

"Something like that. I need your help."

♪ ♫ ♩

By the time the ferry moored in the city, only flashes of anger pierced the despair settling over Dimity like a heavy gray shroud.

After buying a pair of cheap flip-flops from a tourist kiosk on the waterfront, she found a bar with a mezzanine deck that would lift her above the crowds strolling around the inner harbor precinct.

Choosing a table in full sun, she fanned her chilled hands on the warm wood and tried to think what to do next. Her mind was still a blank when the waitress approached ten minutes later, with an apology for slow service.

"Public holidays are always busy," she explained, taking her order pad from a front pocket in her apron.

"What exactly are you celebrating?"

"Labor Day…something to do with the anniversary of the forty-hour work week." The waitress rolled her eyes. "First I've heard."

"I can't remember working one of those, either." *I no longer have a job.* For the first time in her adult life, she was unemployed. How the hell was she going to fill her day? Scratch that, how was she going to fill the next hour?

"You okay? Your hands are shaking."

"Low blood sugar…I'll be fine when I eat." On autopilot, Dimity scanned the menu, ordered a pear and brie salad and a low-carb beer. A

Scotch on the rocks had more appeal, but it was only eleven-thirty in the morning.

The earliest she ever got to bed was ten-thirty. That left eleven hours—normally jammed with machinating, organizing, meeting, greeting, and making things happen—to focus entirely on herself, and her next step.

The shaking worsened and she wrapped her arms around herself. Maybe her next step was to breathe deeply of the sea air. Wasn't it supposed to be good for you, full of negatively-charged ions—or was that positively-charged ions? It did raise serotonin levels, the feel-good chemical that reduced stress. Not that she had any stress, as of—she checked her watch to work out her quitting time, holding her wrist steady. *Did I change it to New Zealand time yet?* She couldn't remember.

The waitress delivered her order and Dimity was overcome with relief when the other woman confirmed she *had* set local time. *See,* she told herself, *you're okay.* The beer was fizzy and cold and quenched her thirst. She drank it slowly and her shivers subsided, enough to turn on her phone and scroll through messages. Two missed calls from Elizabeth, three from Zander. She blocked their numbers and began answering the email queries that had accumulated while she'd been traveling, then remembered...*I quit.*

Dropping her cell on the table, she picked up her fork. Without appetite, she stared across her salad to the yachts bobbing in the marina. How could Zander make such an important decision without consulting her? The betrayal was a knife in her back. They were supposed to be a team. She'd even given up attending her mother's wedding to keep things running for him. Admittedly, she'd also been terrified Helena would take one look at her daughter, remember how good she'd had it, and get cold feet.

Dimity brooded while the sun wilted the lettuce and browned the pear.

"Something wrong with your meal?" said the waitress.

Dimity put down her fork. "I guess I wasn't hungry." Draining her glass, she ordered a second beer. A kid at the next table clattered down the deck's steps to the edge of the jetty and threw his bread roll into the water. Seagulls swooped, raucously squabbling over ownership. There was a mournful sharpness in their cries that suited her mood. The kid returned to his table and whined when his parents declined to donate their half-eaten meals.

"You're getting sunburned." The waitress arrived with the second beer and repositioned the umbrella to shade Dimity's face.

"Thank you." She ordered three rolls to be delivered to the kid's table.

His parents sent him over to thank her, which made both the boy and Dimity uncomfortable.

"Mum said you need sunblock," he said, thrusting out some sunscreen.

"That's kind." To her horror, tears rolled down her cheeks. Frantically she rubbed them in with sunscreen. "Go feed the seagulls," she said hoarsely. "And…be nicer to your parents, because they care about you." She heard the lameness, even before she saw it confirmed by his scowl.

After he ran off, she made a phone call.

"Mom, it's me."

"What a coincidence, Floyd and I were just talking about you."

Her spirits lifted. "You were?" Maybe her mom was missing her. Which was sweet when Helene had no ulterior financial motive anymore.

"We're at a cocktail party with some lovely people. Their son's a huge Rage fan and I told them you'd be able to get the band to sign a picture and send it to him. His name's Ryan. That's spelled R-Y—"

"A-N," Dimity finished wearily. *Still wanting something, then.* "Listen, I have some unexpected downtime." If her mother wasn't capable of providing a refuge, her daughter would settle for a bolt-hole. "I could fly over, spend a couple of weeks with you guys."

"You couldn't make our wedding, but you'll gate-crash our honeymoon?"

She thought she'd placated Helena with an expensive present, but the playful hostility in her tone suggested not. "What was I thinking," she said cheerfully. "I can't cramp the lovebirds' style! Listen, I have to go, Mom." *I can't be the grown-up right now. And clearly, I've got to stop hoping you'll ever take up the role.* "We'll talk soon, and love you lots."

"But, honey—"

"Ryan with a Y. Got it."

She ordered a third beer. She'd been in the same clothes over twenty-four hours and she could smell herself, sweat and sunscreen. There had to be a hotel nearby. After this drink she'd check in, shower and call the airline for flights out. Zander would forward her luggage.

You don't want to talk to him.

So, I'll get the concierge to make the call.

If he finds out where you're staying, he'll come see you.

Dimity dropped her head in her hands. Every small problem seemed suddenly insurmountable.

"Can I take this, or are you expecting someone?" said a female voice. Exhausted, Dimity looked up. The woman already had her hand on the back of the spare chair.

"Go ahead."

How had she come to this? Sitting alone and friendless in a bar at the bottom of the world. Two months ago, Rage had been filling stadiums, and she'd been touring in Zee's private jet and *winning*. He'd assured her that her job was safe, which meant he still didn't know her at all. It had never been about the job, never even been about the money. It was about being important to someone. Being respected.

She ordered another beer. As long as she was in a public space, pride would hold her tears at bay, but once she was alone… *I won't cry. I'm never crying again.* Her cell rang. Irritated, she reached to switch it off and glimpsed caller ID. She *did* have one friend here. Relief swamped her. She picked up. "Seth."

"Are you okay?"

It took her a second to join the dots. "Zander called you." Cautiously, she added, "What did he tell you?"

"That something he said upset you. That you won't answer his calls or Elizabeth's. That you have no luggage and no shoes. Where are you?"

She propped her chin on one hand. "Lost."

"I'm at the ferry building," he said. "Are you still at the Viaduct?"

In the marina, a launch cruised by like a sleek white shark, its sound system blaring Cold Play and a bikini-clad woman on the deck. "I'm not sure I want to be found."

"I accept the challenge." She saw him round the end of the promenade, cell held to his ear. He wore sunglasses and had changed into casual shorts and a navy T-shirt, but his dark red hair made him easy to identify, even at five hundred yards.

Dimity straightened. Seeing him when she was weak? Not a good idea. "It wasn't a challenge."

"Then you really are upset." He scanned the outside tables of the first restaurant then disappeared inside, presumably to check the interior. "Where are you, Honey B?"

The silly nickname made her lower lip tremble. She bit it. "Go be with your family," she ordered. "I'm a big girl who can deal with this alone." If she sat quietly on the top floor deck of this veranda bar, the odds of him spotting her were remote. No one ever looked up. "I already bought flip-flops."

"The local vernacular is jandals." He reappeared and moved on to the next eatery, continuing his methodical scan. "Can you be more specific about the *this* you're dealing with?"

She shifted her chair farther under the umbrella. "You'll have to ask Zee."

"I'm not telling anyone else my singing voice is recovering, only you and Elizabeth." After all the times she'd berated him for not trusting her enough to share his voice issues, the SOB had effectively tied her hands.

"Okay, let me rephrase the question." He rejoined the walkers on the promenade, his gaze sweeping the crowds. "Are you considering a Plan B?"

She tried to deny it, but the lump in her throat was too big. Picking up her beer, she took a big gulp. Seth's voice said quietly through her cell, "It doesn't have to be the end of the world. We'll get through this."

He thinks Zee's voice won't recover. How could he take it so calmly? Except when she looked down, he was standing with his head bowed and the slow tide of pedestrians diverting around him. Beat up and broken-hearted, just like her. Defeated. Just trying to comfort her.

Seth didn't deserve this. None of them did. "It's not conclusive," she blurted. "Not yet."

He raised his head. "More tests?"

"Yes." *For me.*

"There's still hope." After Elizabeth, *she* had the most influence on Zander. Unlike Elizabeth, Dimity had no scruples about using it. She couldn't—wouldn't—let her boss make such a tragic mistake.

Seth started walking. "Where are you, Dimity? I need a friend after news like that."

Nice try. But she had a nose for sympathy, even at two hundred yards. "You really think I'm going to let you see me all windblown and sunburned in yesterday's clothes?" She pushed her beer away and reached for the water glass.

He bypassed the next restaurant without going inside to search and she felt a pang of disappointment that he'd given up, before the penny dropped. "Dammit, I just told you I was sitting outside, didn't I?"

Seth grinned. "If you can see me, I must be getting close."

Doh. "I'm leaving now." She stayed where she was. Any movement would only draw his gaze. "Here are my footsteps, clickety-click."

"It's slap-slap if you're in flip-flops. An idle question. Have you been drinking?" He was at the café next door now, close enough that she could see the pattern on his Vans sneakers—plaid.

Very, very slowly, she inched to her right so the large planter box on the corner of the deck screened her from view. "I might have had a couple of beers."

"Then I definitely can't leave you to your own devices. God knows who you'll hit on."

She hadn't thought she had a smile in her. "I'm not exactly irresistible. Tangled ponytail, sweaty clothes, red eyes from cr— squinting in the sun." She looked at her bare feet in their cheap flip-flops and gingerly wriggled her toes. "My feet are so red they match the nail polish."

A shadow fell over the table. "So they do," he said.

Now he'd found her, Dimity could admit she'd wanted him to, but she still needed a few seconds to gather her reserves before lifting her head. She'd already exposed too much of herself to this man. But when she looked into his kind eyes, her poker face wobbled.

Seth pulled her up into a hug and she let him, needing his comfort more than she needed to be seen as strong. Just for a minute. And he wasn't a guy to hug and tell or view her weakness as anything other than temporary. Even so, she repeated his words from The Comfort Zone. "If you start feeling sorry for me, I'll have to ditch you."

"Feel sorry for the honey badger, are you kidding me?" His arms were strong around her. "I'm protecting my throat."

Her arms tightened around his waist. "What if everything we've worked for falls apart?"

"Then we'll build something new on the foundations." He pulled away to scan her face. "But it hasn't fallen yet...has it?"

She straightened her shoulders. "Not yet." She had no right to quit without doing everything she could to change Zander's mind. Too many futures depended on it. "You ready to return to Waiheke?"

She shook her head. "I don't want to see Zee until I can be more positive." *Positive I won't strangle him.* Her boss could suffer the fallout for another day or two. Anxiety might help her cause. "I'll find a hotel."

"Forget that, you're coming home with me." He picked up her laptop.

"Because you think I'm all sad and pathetic?" she challenged.

"No. I need a human shield."

That was intriguing. "The reunion isn't going well?"

He snorted. "Dad's still bitter that I ditched the family firm to join Rage and Mum's so determined for everyone to along that she's invited Mel and her new fiancé to my surprise party."

"Wow, even I can see that's insensitive."

"She thinks because I've got a new girlfriend, I must be over Mel." He gave her a look.

"Oh," she said.

"As in I *owe* you, Seth, for suggesting this dumb-ass idea?"

She hesitated.

"C'mon," he said. "I need you."

It was bullshit. Probably. Still, being useful would give her something to do while she let Zander stew. "Dysfunctional families I can relate to." She collected her belongings. "Let's go."

"We need to tell Zee and Elizabeth you're okay."

"I'll do it." She unblocked their numbers and sent a text to Elizabeth.

Sorry for earlier. Tell Zee I'll phone in a day or two when I've got my head around it.

Her boss was a rock once he'd made up his mind about something. After years of bloodying her forehead against his stubbornness, she should have remembered not to go head-to-head with him. If she hadn't overreacted, she might have been able to interpret his motives. Her next move was to listen more carefully.

Zee's underlying fears would lead her to the crack in that rock and show her where to apply the chisel.

Chapter 9

SETH HAD BORROWED HIS MOTHER'S car, a tiny Honda with surprising zippiness around corners. In the passenger seat beside him, Dimity sorted through her online mail.

"I guess it's not worth pointing out local landmarks," he teased, and she raised her head, her blue eyes curious.

"You have some?"

"Hell, yeah. That brick house on the corner? That's Brian's. He was my best buddy in Scouts. I stole oranges from Mrs. White's tree there…" Taking one hand off the wheel, he pointed. "And coming up on your left is my old primary school…better known to you as elementary. See that red roof over the trees? My first band used to practice in that house. Our keyboardist was my music teacher's son."

She was watching him. "Sounds like you spent most of your life living in one square mile."

"Ten square miles," he corrected. "What about you?"

"My father's a diplomat and there are two hundred and sixty-five American embassies around the world." She turned off her screen.

"And you traveled with them?"

She nodded. "Until I was ten, I went to international schools, mostly in Asia and Europe. At eleven, my parents sent me home to boarding school. That's when their marriage fell apart—I wasn't around to supervise."

He started to laugh, saw she wasn't joking, and sobered. "That's…probably true."

"Uh-huh." Dimity yawned widely. She looked pretty terrible by her standards, makeup streaked, face sunburned, hair flying in the breeze from her open window. To Seth, she looked endearingly normal. Her bloodshot eyes could be from jet lag, but he suspected not. Whatever news she'd gotten was bad—for a few seconds he'd thought Rage was done, and everything he'd worked so hard for, lost.

"Tell me the truth," he said. "Do we still have a job?"

"It's going to work out, Seth," she assured him. "There's been a hitch affecting how soon Zee can return, and I let it get on top of me—" she gestured to her appearance "—obviously. I'm sorry if I made you think things were hopeless. Truly they're not." She might look tired and tear-stained, but there was no doubting the sincerity in her voice.

"You can have a weak moment like the rest of us," he said.

She didn't look convinced. "The last weak moment I had, we ended up in bed together."

It was easier when he was the one trying to be flippant about it. But their hook-up did appear smaller, more manageable, when it was brought into the open and made light of. He didn't want embarrassment lurking like the bogey man behind their every interaction.

"Yeah. Let's not coincide our weak moments," he said, wishing he could remember what triggered their hook-up. All he could muster was an image of her blue eyes challenging him, and the wild thrill of accepting it.

He changed the subject. "And you're not talking to Zander because…?"

"He annoyed me today. Sometimes he needs a reminder that he's not the boss of me."

Seth laughed, enjoying her. "Tell me more about the places you grew up in, while we stop to buy you sunscreen. You'll need it while you're here."

The time passed quickly with her quirky stories. She sang him a song in Mandarin, one she'd learned in her Hong Kong crèche, and he glimpsed a shy and studious little girl in her neatly-folded hands and downcast eyes. She was laughing at him trying to learn it as they pulled into his parents' driveway, but sobered as they entered the house.

He watched as she touched the duck-head umbrella in the hallstand, stared at his mother's floral gardening gloves on the hall table, and stopped at every family photo, her hands clasped behind her back and her expression oddly reverent. As a child, whenever Seth had stayed with his late nana, she'd haul his reluctant ass to Sunday Mass. "Respectful fear is all I ask," Annie would mutter as she herded him into a pew. He saw that expression on Dimity's face now.

"It's just an ordinary house," he said, puzzled.

"Exactly." She closed her eyes and sucked in a lungful of the berry sweetness still lingering in the air from breakfast.

He recalled her nomadic childhood. *Growing up, had she craved my life?*

"I'm in here," his mother called from the kitchen, and Dimity took another, deeper, breath.

"She doesn't bite," Seth reassured her. "And I texted to tell her you were coming."

They found Gayle counting out silverware at the kitchen counter, surrounded by trays of hired glasses and plates. "I don't know why I thought this party could be a surprise," she commented, frazzled. "And we don't have near enough knives and forks. I'll have to make another run to the hire store." She smiled at Dimity, leaving her task to hug her. "Welcome to the madhouse."

"Um…thank you." Dimity was clearly flustered and Seth wondered if she'd grown up with much physical affection. "I'm sorry to land myself on—"

"Don't say a word, you're very welcome. Would you like a coffee? I also have some blueberry muffins if you're hungry."

"Thank you, but I've eaten. I would appreciate a glass of water."

"I'll get it." He picked up one of the hire glasses and his mother confiscated it.

"No, honey, use one of ours, we need to keep these separate. I wish to hell I'd gotten plastic goblets."

"Why didn't you?" Seth filled the glass from the faucet.

"The environment," she said glumly. "Don't you love how protecting it makes work for women?" she said to Dimity. Before she could answer, Gayle eyed her more closely. "You look sunburned—have you been sitting outside? Seth, why didn't you tell her about the ozone layer?"

"It's thinner down here." He handed Dimity the water glass. "You burn more easily."

"Oh." She stood as if not quite sure where to put herself, and he felt a stab of tenderness. In a nightclub, a boardroom, and backstage at a stadium this woman was mistress of all she surveyed, and yet she was clearly intimidated by his voluble mother's friendliness. He pulled out a chair for her. "I bought her some sunblock, Ma."

"That won't do her any good now, but don't worry. I have some aloe vera in the garden."

Dimity glanced at him, clearly needing a translation. "It's a natural balm for sunburn. But you probably want to take a shower before you apply it."

"Of course," Gayle exclaimed. "You'll want to clean up. And you must be exhausted. I hear your bags have been held up, what an absolute pain for you. I've already put extra towels on your bed, Seth."

Shit. He met Dimity's eyes. Neither of them had considered this. "I thought you'd put her in the spare bedroom."

His mother laughed. "Honey, I've reconciled myself to my kids having sex."

"It's not that. I…snore." Lame, but the best he could come up with, at short notice. Really *should have thought this through.*

"It's hereditary," Gayle confided to Dimity. "My side, unfortunately. But I've got this fantastic homeopathic remedy, Frank tells me it works a charm." She registered his disquiet. "Is your snoring really that disruptive, honey? I've made up the spare room for Janey and Tom so they don't have to wake the baby after the party."

"The homeopathic remedy sounds great," Dimity answered, shooting him a cryptic look. "And honestly, I could sleep through an earthquake right now."

"Take a nap…both of you," Gayle suggested.

Was his mother determined to pimp him out? "I slept plenty on the plane," Seth said hastily. Not that Dimity had evinced the slightest interest in a repeat performance. Neither of them were. Evincing. Anything. For the sake of their friendship, they'd put that night behind them. He had a sudden, visceral recollection of how her luscious behind felt under his palms. Apple-round. He couldn't look at her. "I'll help you with the party stuff, Ma."

"I do need a table shifting outside. That reminds me, the aloe vera." She headed toward the door. "Settle our guest in, honey, and I'll bring it up."

"Thank you," Dimity said formally. "I appreciate your hospitality."

"I look forward to getting to know you," his mother said.

"Great." Dimity actually looked scared. The strangest idea occurred to him—that she was afraid of being found wanting.

"I'm sorry," he said, when Gayle was out of earshot. "It didn't even cross my mind that Mum would put us in the same bed."

"Mine either. Guess we're both jet-lagged." She stretched out her back, yawned. "What's more shocking is that the house only has three bedrooms."

"I'll sneak the air mattress up later," he promised.

"Seth, I think I can keep my hands off you if we share a bed."

"It's not that." *I can't want you now I'm set on reconciling with Mel. And why the hell is this suddenly a problem when I've had no problem resisting other women?* "But thanks for the ego check." The reminder that he was only a hook-up for her steadied him. "I feel I've brought you here under false pretenses."

"Yeah, you really lured me in with 'My family's dysfunctional.' Though I guess you did mislead me. At worst, your mom's eccentric."

"I wanted to give you a sanctuary." He was still annoyed at himself for not anticipating sleeping arrangements. "Instead you get to top and tail on a lumpy double mattress."

She batted her eyelashes at him. "You're so sweet when you take full responsibility."

"Don't, for the love of God, start that again," he warned, but found himself returning her smile. She was right. He was making too much of this. "C'mon, I'll show you our room."

"So, top and tail," she mused as they walked upstairs, pausing to check out the family portrait at the top. "Is that like a sixty-niner?"

Like he needed that mental picture. "You won't be laughing when my cold hairy feet are on the pillow next to yours." He opened the door to his room and she hesitated. "And can you stop tiptoeing around as if you're on hallowed ground...although I guess my female fans would consider this room a shrine." However uncomfortable he might be having to share a bed, he wanted her to feel at home.

"Idiot." That got her over the threshold. "Was this your room when you were a kid?"

"Yeah, but it's been redecorated since then, and the bathroom's new." He opened the door to the ensuite. Most of his stuff was in storage, and it was a guest room now. "And what kid is lucky enough to sleep in a king-size bed?"

"This kid," Dimity said idly, going to the window. "Which house is your childhood sweetheart's?"

"Across the street." He pointed out the clapboard across the road. "Mel's parents still live there."

"Did you ever sneak her into this room?"

"Contrary to what Ma implied, she and Dad have *never* encouraged our sex lives. Mel and I consummated in my car like normal teenagers. Even when we lived together, if we came home, she stayed at her folks and I stayed at mine. You're in virgin territory." He grinned at her. "How about you, ever sneak guys into your room?"

"Security was too tight at boarding school, not that I ever wanted to have sex in a dorm."

There was a tap on the door, and his mother poked her head in. "Here's the aloe vera, and the snoring remedy for Seth."

"Thank you," Dimity said. "Incidentally, the second tray of glasses was missing two. Make sure the rental people don't charge you for them."

"Well, okay," his mother said, startled.

He grinned. "We'll leave you to nap, Honey B."

"Oh, Seth?" Dimity waited until his mother was halfway down the stairs. "Thanks for the moral support today. I won't let you down tonight…with Mel, I mean."

"That's not why I did it."

"I know." She smiled at him. "So if I open your wardrobe will I find a dozen faded plaid shirts?"

"Feel free to borrow one until your suitcases arrive." He closed the door on her dismayed face, enjoying the rare satisfaction of having the last word.

♪ ♫ ♩

When Mel arrived forty minutes into his 'surprise' party, Seth was grateful that being famous had taught him how to appear relaxed in the public gaze.

His ex hadn't perfected the same skill. She blushed red, then crimson when she spotted him, her sunny smile becoming a self-conscious grimace. Nervously, she smoothed her palms over her trousers, even stumbling as she approached, and Mel never stumbled. The man walking alongside caught her arm to steady her. *Her fiancé.*

"Let me introduce you to the guest of honor," she said, so loudly that Seth could hear her across the room.

The bastard who'd stolen his girl didn't even blink before following her. First impressions? Solid, dark-haired, average height. Nothing obvious to explain why Mel preferred him.

A hand slipped into his. Beside him, Dimity murmured, "Breathe."

He breathed. Found a smile, released her hand, and stepped forward to embrace Mel. *A quick hug, not too long, not too short. Nothing to draw attention or make her uncomfortable.* She held him tight, claiming their history, neither playing games, nor hiding her affection.

Grief hit like a punch to the gut. Her hair smelled of chlorine—she must have come directly from swim training. He was lost, completely devastated.

Mel released him. "It's so good to see you." She turned to the guy at her elbow and everything about her softened—her angular features, her hazel eyes, even her voice—when she said, "This is Kevin."

In the middle of his first epiphany—*she really loves him*—Seth took a moment to respond. "Good to meet you, Kevin."

Draping an arm around Mel's shoulders, Kevin leaned forward to shake his hand. "Big fan of what the new band members have been bringing to Rage," he said. "Hope it works out for you all."

"Thanks." Seth hadn't prepared for nice. He'd prepared for a villain, someone easy to hate.

Mel looked beyond him to Dimity, smiling, a little dazzled. Now her suitcases had arrived, his fake girlfriend was unrecognizable from the disheveled woman he'd brought home eight hours earlier, radiant in a glittering sheath dress chosen specifically to give Seth camouflage. She hadn't told him that, of course. Her exact words were: "You can take the girl out of Hollywood, but you can't take Hollywood out of the girl." But when you understood that Dimity was kind, she was remarkably easy to read.

"Hi," Mel said politely. "You must be—"

"The honey badger," said Dimity, implying an intimacy that Seth was suddenly deeply thankful for. He had back-up.

Mel's eyes widened. "He *told* you?"

"We have no secrets."

"Most women would find it a little—" Mel shrugged, and Kevin's arm slipped off her shoulder "—uncomplimentary?"

"I'm not most women." Reaching a hand past Mel's shoulder to Mel's guy, Dimity unleashed her smile. "Hi, Kevin, I'm Dimity, Seth's girlfriend."

Blinking, he took her hand, his other reclaiming Mel's shoulder, possibly for support. "And I'm Mel's fiancé."

Seth swallowed. *Checkmate.* Why the hell hadn't Dimity warned him how much epiphanies fucking *hurt?*

"Well, I owe you a big thanks, Kevin." Dimity's smile widened. "If you hadn't broken up the dynamic duo, Seth wouldn't have become available."

Janey was passing with a tray of canapés. Smoothly his sister changed course and offered them to their group, but Mel and Kevin had frozen. Seth, on the other hand, had begun to thaw now the first shock of reunion had passed. And there was an ocean of conflicted feelings straining to break through the ice.

Careful not to meet his eyes, Kevin cleared his throat. "Actually, Dimity, they'd already called it a day before Mel and I started dating."

"We're all adults here, so no need for euphemisms." Dimity's manicured fingers hovered over the hors d'oeuvres. "You mean before you and Mel had sex. What are we looking at…shrimp?" she asked an open-mouthed Janey. His 'girlfriend's' nap had lasted until shortly before the party started, and none of his family had seen her in full flight. Until now.

"Shelled prawns," Janey managed to say.

Mel and Kevin were staring at Dimity with a mix of awe and horror.

Spearing a denuded crustacean with a toothpick, Dimity dipped it in mayonnaise and bit into it delicately. "Delicious."

Seth's reaction bounced between pissed and grateful. He'd wanted to know…and not been able to ask.

"Honey B…" Picking up a napkin, he covered her big, beautiful mouth with it. "You have some sauce right *here*." Much as he appreciated her support, this topic was nobody's business but his and Mel's. And he had no desire to embarrass his ex. "Shouldn't you be passing the food around?" he prompted Janey, removing the gag.

"What…oh yeah." His sister dragged her fascinated gaze from Dimity.

"Enough about us." Mel used Janey's departure as an opportunity to redirect the conversation. "How serious are *you* two?" A pointed question when they all knew Seth hadn't wanted the breakup. Mel seemed to realize she was sacrificing him to put Dimity in her place and threw him a stricken look.

He wasn't impressed. *So, I'm trying to spare your feelings, and you won't spare mine?*

"Who knows? We're still at the fun stage." Dimity handed her toothpick to a surprised passing guest. "For all we know, this is rebound."

Her chuckle was a husky, sexy masterpiece as she slid an arm around Seth's waist. "I wonder if it's called rebound because of the workout the bedsprings get?" Only he could see her anger as she looked up at him. Anger on his behalf. He was touched by her protectiveness. But it wouldn't do.

"You two haven't gotten a drink yet," he said to the others. "What will you have?" He needed a quiet word with his 'girlfriend' before she went to war for him, so he kept his arm firmly around Dimity's waist after he'd taken drink orders and steered her toward the makeshift bar set up next to the barbecue.

"Want to fill me in on your plan?" he said, as he handed her a champagne, and poured two glasses of red wine. Because she always had one.

"You'll have more luck sparking Mel's territorial instincts if I'm myself," she said. "What woman in her right mind would want me taking over?" She sipped her champagne, grimaced, and carefully put it down, confirming that his father had bought cheap.

But to Frank, this probably isn't a celebration.

"If you want some time alone with Mel, I can separate Kev from the herd."

"I do, but not for the reasons you think." He took a deep breath. "This isn't going to work." He couldn't remember the last time Mel had looked at him the way she looked at Kevin—maybe in their teens?

"Fine," Dimity sighed. "I'll play nice."

"That's not what I—" He broke off as his father arrived with a platter of raw steaks. "Dad, you want a hand cooking those?"

"I've managed for the past fifteen months," Frank answered, smiling at Dimity. "Seth introduced you to everyone? I hope our accents aren't too difficult to understand."

"Oh, I'm picking up the nuances just fine."

"He should have told you dress was casual." The steaks hit the grill with a slap and a sizzle. "I hope you haven't been feeling uncomfortable."

"I don't really do casual," Dimity said. "Or feeling uncomfortable." She was watching his father with the puzzlement of a predator, trying to work out if this was prey or not.

"We should get these drinks to Mel and Kevin." Not sure which one he was protecting, Seth stepped between them. "Yell if you need a hand, Dad."

"You could send Jeff out. He's terrific on a barbecue."

"Jeff's here?"

Cheerfully, Frank prodded the meat with tongs. "He and his wife have become part of the family."

"What did I miss?" Dimity said as they walked inside. "Who's Jeff and why are you looking so pissed?"

"Jeff took over my job, and Dad is somebody I need to handle alone." Seth stopped to eyeball her. "No meddling. I mean it." He didn't want or need an intermediary between himself and his father. This campaign was his to win or lose.

"What do I know about fathers? I can hang out with your mom though, right?"

There was an undertone of wistfulness in her voice. Seth thought of that awful mother/daughter portrait she carried on her iPad. "As long as it's for fun."

"Fun only. Got it." She smiled at someone behind him. "Kevin, I have your drink. I hate to admit my ignorance, but I have no idea what a sports scientist does. Will you fill me in?"

"Sure, but first I was hoping to have a word—privately—with your boyfriend."

Seth hadn't expected that. "Want to take this to Mel?" He handed Dimity one of the glasses, and gave the other to Kevin.

"Of course." She left them to it.

"It's about Mel," Kevin began.

"We haven't had a chance to catch up yet, Seth." His cousin, Liam, slapped his tensed shoulder. "And I want an introduction to your hot new girlfriend." Then he noticed who Seth was talking to, and added awkwardly, "Not that your old girlfriend isn't hot. Hey, Kev, how's it going?"

"Give us a few minutes, mate?" Seth asked.

"Sure thing. See ya, Kev." Liam escaped.

Seth gestured the other man into the study and Kevin looked relieved when he left the door open behind them. *Guess my friendly smile isn't so friendly.*

"Look, this is...I wanted to reiterate...Mel and I didn't move beyond friendship until she broke up with you. She's better than that."

"I know she is." *It's you I don't trust.*

"Which is why she feels so guilty for not telling you about us earlier."

"Guilty," Seth repeated. Not *conflicted*, not *uncertain* but the dreary, soul-sapping emotion he'd lived with since he left New Zealand.

"Because of the difficulties you're having with your dad."

As though Seth needed a stranger explaining Mel or his family to him. *I don't remember inviting you into my trust circle, asshole.* He swallowed the sharp retort with a gulp of beer. Of course Kevin was Mel's confidante now—she was marrying him. "I'm home to work it out with my father."

"That's a relief." Kevin managed a weak grin. "I was worried you might try to change her mind."

Seth liked him better for the note of insecurity. But while Kevin might worry that Mel had doubts, Seth had taken one look at her face and seen none. That was the beauty of knowing someone most of your life. Ironic that the only other person he could read so easily was his pretend girlfriend, a woman who prided herself on being inscrutable.

Kevin was still waiting nervously for a reply. It would be so easy to mess with him a little. But he thrust out a hand. "You're the one she wants," he said. "I hope you'll both be very happy." Sometimes it sucked being a nice guy.

"Thanks…thanks a lot." Kevin pumped his hand. "I hope it works out for you and Dimity."

"Sure." Seth started to leave, but Kev wasn't through being grateful. "Her grandmother still prefers you," he offered, almost as a consolation prize.

"Yeah?" Seth hid a smile. Nana June was a mind-fucker, was what she was.

"Never shuts up about you. *Seth helped me order the timber for the gazebo. Seth was always offering to do work around the house. Seth could never do enough for me.*"

That last part was certainly true. No one could do enough for Nana June. He should tell Kevin that and save the poor bastard hours of manual labor.

"Well, you know what they say," he said cheerfully. "You can't choose your relatives." So, he wasn't *all* nice guy.

He went in search of Mel to grant absolution with more sincerity, after which he fully intended to drown his sorrows…except he was sharing a bed with Dimity tonight. *Just when I thought the night couldn't get any worse.* Given their history, he had to stay stone-cold sobe*r.*

♪ ♫ ♩

"She's…different," Mel said diplomatically. They'd settled on the couch in the living room. She avoided standing for hours on her prosthesis. "Not your type."

Seth wasn't sure he wanted to discuss Dimity. "She's ambitious, confident, smart…I'd say I'm staying true to type."

"Thank you, but you know what I mean. She's very blunt."

"You have no idea," Seth said. "She's on her best behavior tonight." If there was any humor in this situation, it was watching Dimity being her version of nice. Like a lion trying to befriend gazelles, every now and then she couldn't help but nip.

She was on the other side of the room, talking to his mother, their heads close together like a couple of conspirators. Seth wondered if he should worry about that. "I love her honesty," he added. "You always know where you stand with Dimity."

"Is that a dig at me?"

Was it? The old Seth would have been conciliatory. Turning his head, he pinned her gaze. "Why didn't you prepare me for Kevin, Mel? We went straight from, 'We're done, feel free to date,' to 'I'm marrying another guy.'" *Why the fuck didn't you give me a chance to change your mind before it was too late?* But a new thought followed. He'd always thought his decision to leave had been responsible for the growing distance between them. Carried the guilt and regret for that. Was that it? Or were they already starting to outgrow each other before he'd left?

She started playing with the tassel on the cushion. "When I broke it off you took it hard. It seemed cruel to tell you I wanted to date someone else and I wasn't expecting Kevin and I to get serious so quickly. When he proposed, I had to stop being a coward and tell you before anyone else did." She touched his hand. "I'm truly sorry, Seth, for making this worse than it had to be."

He set aside bitterness. "I don't suppose there *is* a painless way to break up with someone who doesn't want to break up with you."

"In some ways our breakup was more passionate than our relationship," Mel said. "Maybe you should ask yourself why you were so affected."

"What do you mean?"

"How would you describe our years together, Seth? Loving?"

"Absolutely."

"Supportive?"

He nodded, then thought, *Well, I supported you.* Yeah, he'd been the one to leave, but if she'd given his dreams the same backing he'd given hers, they *could* have made their relationship work. Or was that sour grapes talking?

"Comfortable?"

He looked at her, trying to get an inkling of where she was going with this.

"*Too* comfortable?"

"Sorry, I'm clear out of epiphanies." He was going to kill Dimity for giving him that word.

Mel leaned forward and kissed his cheek. "Think about it."

Chapter 10

Dimity's cell vibrated on the nightstand.

A chill prickled along Seth's body as she pushed free of the blankets and scrambled for it in the dark. "Mom," she whispered, "it's two a.m. here and everyone's asleep…can I phone you tomorrow?"

He turned his head on the pillow. On the other side of the bed, her shadowy form sat hunched over her cell. "I don't want to wake the guy I'm with."

"It's okay." He hadn't fallen asleep yet, though he was weary to the bone. Too many thoughts chasing their tails around his brain.

In the dark, Dimity swung her legs out of bed and stood. "No, I'm not making it up to avoid you…hang on." She turned, and her hair brushed his bare shoulder as she bent to give him her phone. "Say hello to my mother."

"Hello, Dimity's mother."

Her daughter repossessed the phone before he got a response. "Uh-huh…oh that's too bad you had a fight. Tell Floyd I figured you were joking. Of course, I know I'm welcome to come stay." She hastened to the bathroom and closed the door. Light spilled around its edges. So did sound. "Yes, you know your own daughter best." Seth heard battle fatigue threaded through the positivity. Concerned, he propped himself up on one elbow.

"Give Floyd my love and don't wear him out. Remember he's got high blood pressure… The autographed poster… Yes, I'll remember. Love you, too, Mom."

Silence.

Through the wall, he heard the creak of his parents bed, the murmur of voices, his father's questioning growl and his mother's soothing tone. Typical of an old house, the sound-proofing was lousy. The household resettled, but the thin strip of light remained under the door and Dimity didn't return. No taps, no flushing, complete silence.

He suspected she wanted privacy because she was struggling in some way with her mother's remarriage. You didn't need to be a psychologist to work out Helena was a narcissist. But he had to respect her daughter's strong need for privacy. He rolled off his elbow onto his back and resettled. Particularly when he was desperate for it himself.

He'd deliberately come to bed an hour after she had, and not solely to avoid the awkwardness of sharing sheets with a friend he'd had crazy monkey sex with. He wasn't ready to perform an autopsy of the evening, not until he'd had a chance to sit by the corpse and pay his respects. Grieve.

The bathroom door opened. In the brief moment before she switched off the light, it gleamed over the ivory shift she wore, highlighting how the satin clung to her breasts, her legs and the V in between.

Seth closed his eyes. It figured what she wore to protect her modesty would be sexier than nakedness. He'd thought, given his heartache, he'd be immune. He'd thought wrong. One glance and he could conjure the texture of her skin, smooth, so soft under his fingers, recall exactly how it felt to thrust between those shapely legs. God. He rolled onto his side facing the wall, and adjusted the silk boxers he'd worn to protect *his* modesty.

The mattress sank as she climbed in beside him. Funny how something as simple as the weight of a woman slipping into bed beside him could feel so familiar, so comfortable. And heighten his sense of loss. He and Mel had lived together for two years.

Dimity resettled. He waited for her breathing to even out and deepen, waited for his awareness of her to dissolve. Shifting closer to the edge of the bed, he let grief wash through him, grief over losing a life that he hadn't truly appreciated he was giving up.

He'd loved Mel a long time, and she'd loved him. And they wouldn't have the five kids they'd joked about, they wouldn't live in the same neighborhood they'd grown up in, and he wouldn't be in the stands when she finally won gold at the Paralympics—because she would.

Beside him, Dimity shifted. "You're sad and it's keeping me awake. You've been sad ever since you talked to Mel's fiancé."

"She's happier with Kevin. I'm letting her go."

He expected her to argue, but she said nothing.

"You saw it," he guessed, rolling onto his back. "The way she looks at him."

"I don't understand how she could prefer him," Dimity said in the dark. "I guess he could have hidden talents."

"If you say, like being great in bed, I'm kicking you out of it."

"I wasn't going to say that," she assured him. "What are the odds you have the same hidden talents?" He laughed. It helped.

"Mel said I should ask myself why I took our breakup so hard." He needed a woman's perspective. No, he needed *this* woman's perspective, astringent and insightful.

"That's interesting, so did your mother."

He was startled. "You talked to Ma about it?"

"No, she talked to me. She's been worried about you and was telling me how glad she is you've got a new girlfriend."

"What did you say?"

"That I'm toying with you."

He twisted toward her.

"Just kidding. That we're having a lot of fun."

"You're certainly the only bright spark in my life right now," he conceded. "In a 'light fuse, dive for cover' kind of way."

"Is there any other kind?"

He snorted. "So I'm lying awake trying to work out what Mel meant."

"Really?" Dimity sounded surprised. "I think it's pretty simple."

"Yeah, Dr. Love, what's your theory?"

"You gave up a lot to join the band. Mel was the last link to your old life."

Seth knew it was the truth because her words sank into him without resistance.

How much of his devastation at losing Mel had been because she represented a way home if he needed it? Too much, he suspected. "That makes my noble sacrifice in giving her up a lot less impressive."

"Exactly why I avoid self-awareness," she said. "It leads to humility."

"I changed my life and everyone changed theirs."

"They don't call it the brave new world for nothing."

"No." He rolled onto his side. "Goodnight, Dimity." She'd given him something to think about. He'd needed to break free, chase a music career, and there were consequences to that. He'd hurt people. Mel had moved on. So had his father. And that was Seth's problem to deal with, not theirs.

Dimity said quietly, "Is there anything I can say to make it better?"

"No." She didn't need to sugar-coat things. It was a relief to be able to be honest. A few seconds later, Seth felt her tuck the sheet between them and then carefully place an arm across his chest to clasp his shoulder. "This is a hug," she said. "Tell anyone I've gone soft and you're dead."

"Thank you," he said gravely. She stayed a minute then got twitchy and moved away, leaving him smiling. The honey badger was scared of hugs. Just as well. Her warmth had permeated the sheet, he could still feel the imprint of her soft breasts rising and falling against his shoulder blades. W*hat's* wrong *with you? She's trying to comfort you.* Whether it was her hug or the relief of accepting the truth, his mind was easier.

"Was the phone call okay…with your mother?" Seth risked getting his head bitten off.

"Little pitchers have big ears." Not a bite, but a definite snap in his direction.

"They're in proportion to the rest of me." He willed his hard-on to go down. "I wasn't trying to listen, but this house has no soundproofing." He waited.

"Floyd, her new husband, heard her say it wasn't convenient for me to visit, and thought she might have hurt my feelings. Helena and I laughed about it." Her self-mocking tone invited him to laugh, too, but he was recalling the flat note in her voice when she'd said, "Of *course* I know I'm welcome."

"And did she hurt your feelings?"

"God no, not for years," There was genuine amusement in her voice now. "Do I come across as vulnerable to you?"

Their friendship had survived sex, but it wouldn't survive any hint of pity. "No." That's why his parents' suburban house intrigued her. She wasn't judging, she was yearning.

"Helena isn't maternal in the way your mother is." Dimity had obviously picked up his ambivalence. "I accepted years ago that wanting her different wouldn't change anything, so I adjusted my expectations."

You mean you stopped wanting. She was breaking his heart. And their friendship balanced on a knife's edge. One word of sympathy from him and it was over. "That was sensible."

"Uh-huh." Dimity was silent a few minutes, then chuckled. "What's really interesting is that Floyd actually made Mom worry about offending me." There was humor in her voice, a touch of wonder. "I had nothing to do with getting them together and I might end up with a stepfather I actually like."

♪ ♫ ♩

Seth took a long time to get to sleep. As Dimity waited for his breathing to become slower and more regular, she fought her body's yearning for him. *Damn sensory memory.* The hug had been a bad idea. Her motives had been pure until she'd lain against him and felt his heat and the curve of his ass through the carefully tucked blanket.

She considered lust a build-up of tension, easily managed with a one-night stand, a vibrator or her hands. Like crying, you found a way to release the pressure, and moved on.

Turned out it was very hard to move on when the body that had given you so much pleasure lay sleeping next to you. Their friendship had survived one hook-up, but two would be taking a risk of kamikaze proportions. Seth was sad, he was conflicted, he was her buddy...and she wanted him inside her more than she'd wanted any man in her life.

Desperate for relief, she shifted position and tried to think about something else like her plan of attack tomorrow with Zander. But even machinating couldn't distract her. Desire weighted her limbs, buzzed across her sweat-dampened skin.

The heat in Auckland was different from LA—damper, humid, almost sensual. Careful not to wake Seth, she peeled the covers off and freed her legs. The satin shift she wore for modesty slithered against her body as she rolled onto her back. She ran her hand over it, her palm coming to rest on her belly, and listened to Seth's breathing deepen.

This physical reaction whenever he was close had to stop.

She could bring herself off in five minutes, she was so ready. Her core was tight and aching, her breasts felt full and sensitive against the satin. One stroke would do it. Maybe two. Slowly, painstakingly she drifted her fingers farther down her belly and fanned them on her sex, pressing her forefinger experimentally on her clitoris. It was swollen under her touch.

"Are you machinating?" Seth said in the dark, and she froze.

"Uh-huh."

She gasped when his hand covered hers, low over her sex.

"That's what I thought," he said hoarsely.

They lay there, not moving. Suspended between insane and sensible. The silence grew, softened, and his hand over hers was warm and heavy, not quite heavy enough. She resisted the urge to wriggle. There was no need to talk about all the reasons this was a bad idea. Sex once was scratching an itch, sex twice suggested a contagion. Seth was mired in family drama and she needed to focus on saving their world. More importantly, they had to work together.

"Dimity." She heard the doubt, sensed his struggle to do the sensible thing, and was suddenly worried he'd win it.

"If you take your hand away now I'll kill you."

He laughed, low and husky, and it vibrated through his hand, then through her hand and into her pelvis, and made her gasp. He stopped laughing. With a groan he rolled over and covered her body with his own, trapping their hands between them.

They both stilled as a sound came from his parents' bedroom, feet hitting the floor, then a minute later an unmistakable tinkling sound. The toilet flushed, the pipes in the wall creaked. Dimity resigned herself to celibacy. Seth would chicken out for sure, in his place she'd probably do the same—

"No screaming tonight," he whispered in her ear.

"You wish." She started tugging her hand free to give him better access but he was already moving, the bedsprings creaking as he eased down the bed. Dimity lifted her head as he slid her nightgown up to her waist, twisted his fingers in the cords of her G-string, and tugged. The seams gave. This man took far too much pleasure in destroying her expensive clothes. In a whisper, she hissed, "You still owe me for that shir—"

His tongue, rough and wet, swept along her cleft in a bold stroke that sent a jolt of heat spearing through her and would have shot her off the bed if he hadn't been holding her thighs apart.

She'd forgotten he dispensed with preliminaries.

"Shh." His breath was warm against her sex. "We can't make any noise, remember?" She didn't even know she had. Worried, she grabbed a pillow—just in case.

She'd already been primed and ready to explode before he'd touched her, and had no defenses against his onslaught now. His joyful, lusty disrespect of her dignity was the most erotic thing she'd ever experienced. Pinned to the mattress, helpless to writhe or squirm away, with his tongue savoring the wetness of her earlier hunger for him, she blew like a skyrocket within five minutes.

She felt him kiss her inner thigh tenderly, then give it a playful bite. The bastard had the nerve to rub his mouth dry on her three-hundred-dollar slip as he levered himself level with her face and lifted the pillow she'd jammed against her mouth.

"You're welcome," he whispered with a chuckle, and she reached down blindly for his cock, needing to redress the balance that had swung suddenly and dangerously in his favor. Heard his quick intake of breath as she found it. Rock hard.

Grabbing the pillow, she thrust it at him. "You'll need this."

"Yeah?" His whisper rough, dark, shivery…male.

"Oh yeah." Twisting, she took him in her mouth, just as he was, sitting back on his heels, knees spread wide. Greedy to torture him as he'd just tortured her.

He sank farther on his heels, bracing himself on the bed and gave himself up to her, the pillow scrunched under one fist.

She licked up the column of his throbbing cock, flicking her tongue around the head, and felt the mattress dip as he tensed. She worked him hard, wetting him with her tongue, using her hand to pump as she sucked, squeezing his balls. He arched and tried to move her as he came but she tightened her grip, milking him dry, swallowing every last spurt. Wiping her face against his heaving chest, she rose triumphant and took the pillow away from his face.

"You're welcome."

They sat on their heels in front of each other, like two yogi masters, and even in the dark she saw the suggestion of white as he smiled.

She smiled back.

CHAPTER 11

SETH PROPPED HIMSELF UP ON one elbow and looked at Dimity sleeping. She lay as far away as possible from him in the bed, but under the sheet one toe touched his calf. When he moved his leg, she murmured, and then her toe found him again. It was oddly…sweet.

"You can't hurt me, Seth, I'm not made that way," she'd assured him as they'd resettled to sleep. He believed her. But there was that toe. Blonde hair tangled, face clean of war paint, her smooth, bony shoulder hunched protectively under his gaze. Even deeply asleep the woman was defensive.

And from what she'd revealed of her upbringing, he could understand why. Gently, he stroked her shoulder through the sheet and it melted like snow.

He had no idea what he and Dimity would do next, and it didn't matter. There was something freeing in being with a woman for the adventure of it, unbound by expectations on either side. He hadn't realized how Mel's expectations had been weighing him down. Or maybe they'd only gotten heavy when he couldn't make her happy. Dimity would never devolve responsibility for her happiness onto someone else.

Next door his parents rose—it must be six a.m. The shower ran, the toilet flushed, the wardrobe backing the wall between them rattled in a ritual that he recalled from his childhood. Silence fell over the house as they went downstairs. When he was little, it was a signal to jump out of bed and follow—there was too much space left without their solid presence.

Lying on his back, he put his hands behind his head. It had been years since he'd remembered that. Dimity muttered something in her sleep, and he dropped one hand on her shoulder again until it relaxed, in no hurry to leave this bed.

Relationships in the rock world tended toward casual. None of the Rage crew would bat an eye if he and Dimity had an affair, though some of his female fan base wouldn't like it. Too bad.

He'd already disappointed a few by ditching celibacy. A month after his breakup with Mel he'd gotten tired of being the victim, and accepted a couple of the many offers he'd got to party. Sex had helped, at least until Mel blindsided him with news of her engagement.

Now that he'd figured out why he'd taken the news so badly—thanks to the woman beside him—he could refocus all his energies on getting right with his father. And then—his spirits rose—immerse himself in his career and his music without guilt. How good would that feel?

Dimity stirred, her ass brushed his thigh, and his daydreams fell to earth and got dirty. Seemed a shame not to take advantage of the fact that his parents were downstairs.

Rolling over, he spooned her and tuned his tone to earnest. "So, are we going steady now?"

She woke in a panic and would have fallen out of bed if he hadn't already hooked an arm around her waist. He cracked up laughing.

"You bastard," she hissed, pushing her tight ass against his groin as she reclaimed her share of the mattress. "Don't scare me like that."

Tightening his hold, he rolled onto his back, taking her with him so she lay on top. "I'm not scaring you, I'm teasing you."

"Some things aren't funny." But she adjusted her position to make room for his hard-on. "Your parents…"

"Are downstairs."

He loosened his grip around her waist and smoothed down her hair where it was tickling his chin. "I want to keep doing this with you." Sliding his hand down her collarbone over the swell of her left breast, he palmed it lightly, feeling her nipple harden. "What do you say?"

"Sounds too much like being taken for granted." But her tone was distracted.

He moved his attention to her other breast. "Only a fool would attempt to domesticate the mighty Honey B."

She reached behind to touch him but the angle was wrong, so she raised her arms above her head. Her searching fingers found his cheekbones, then his nose and lifted to his hair. Tangling her hands in it, she tugged but Seth barely noticed because her movements had shoved her breasts into his palms.

She tugged harder. That's right, she liked rough. Lightly, he scraped her nipples and she arched. "I'm interested," she said. "As long as it's just sex."

"It's not just sex." He nudged his leg between hers, encouraging them open. "It's friends with benefits."

"Ugh, too cutesy."

He slid his hand down her ribs to the indent of her belly button and circled lightly. "What would you call it?"

"Fuck buddies," she suggested, opening her legs wider. For a woman who looked like spun glass, she had a mouth on her like a hard rocker when she wanted to keep things simple. "Only while we're in New Zealand," she clarified. "But we keep it secret from Zander and Elizabeth…the Rage crew."

"No." He widened his touch circle around her navel, teasing her, and she dug her fingers harder into his scalp. "Our phony relationship was a crazy idea that caused nothing but trouble. No more lies."

"It made your mother happy," she wheedled. "And Kevin."

He punished her by sliding his fingers close—so close—to where she wanted attention, bypassing at the last moment to caress her inner thigh. His cock throbbed painfully. He could spend hours torturing them both. "If we're doing this, we're doing it openly. Like grown-ups." If she wanted him, she owned it, publicly. "That's my deal-breaker."

"No, that won't work." Lowering her arms, Dimity used her elbows to lift just enough to rub her butt against him. "I have a brand, an image as a tough bitch, and even a casual relationship with you will undermine that."

He tightened the arm around her waist so she couldn't move. "Because I'm the band's nice guy?" He kept up the gentle caressing of her inner thighs, stroking everywhere but where she was slick and wanting.

"Partly." She started tickling his shin with her big toe. "We want to keep your brand wholesome with your fan base, at least until we're out of this mess." He stopped caressing and she made a small sound of protest. "But mostly because everyone in the music industry knows I have a rule about not mixing my personal and professional lives. I don't get hit on, and I'm treated as one of the guys."

"Okay." Holding his temper, he removed his hand from her lower belly. "I can respect the last part of that." He slid her body off his and she landed with a small oomph on the mattress.

Confused, she looked at him. "We could still have sex now. One for the road?"

"Nope." Cupping his aching groin, he got out of bed. "I'm protecting my brand."

"Are you *sulking*?"

"No, I'm pissed." He pulled on pants. "You want to keep your rule, fair enough. But don't tell me who I have to be." Grabbing a change of clothes, he headed for the main bathroom down the hall. "I didn't jump out of one box to be put in another."

♪ ♫ ♩

"I'm sorry." Dimity rolled the apology around her tongue, savoring it and not particularly liking the taste. And yet it felt necessary. Re-packing her bag, she hesitated, then made the bed, untangling sheets and puffing up the pillows until it was hotel perfect. "I'm sorry," she said again. It was getting easier, possibly because she meant it.

She'd hit a sore spot telling Seth his place, and she'd done it deliberately to test a theory. He had too much heart to treat an affair as lightly as she needed him to. Guys like Seth were forbidden fruit to someone who fetishized *normal*. Well-adjusted, centered, sensible... these were her temptations. It wasn't that she was afraid of him falling in love with her. Only afraid of wanting him to.

She was a fighter, not a lover, with all the corresponding lack of social skills that implied in her private life. These strange longings for intimacy would pass. She just needed to be busy again, crazy busy. Working. She needed Zee to be working.

"I'm sorry." She had to say it now because she didn't want to say it later to Seth. Couldn't give him an opening to try to change her mind. Already he had an uncanny ability to hack through her thorns with a smile and a joke.

She breezed into the kitchen in her highest heels, dressed for business. Seth turned from the coffeemaker, his face impassive but Gayle's eyes lit up when she saw her. "I do love your shoes."

"Thank you." They were her lucky stilettos, the ones she always wore to war.

"That dress last night was gorgeous." Gayle glanced through the open door into the dining room and returned to stirring scrambled eggs on the stove. "Seth said you were both wakeful last night with the change in time zones. I didn't hear snoring though…that remedy worked?"

"Seemed to," Dimity said brightly.

"Janey and Tom are still in bed." Gayle glanced in the other room again. "They always take the opportunity to sleep in when they're here. Frank is walking to the shop for the paper. It's his token exercise."

"Go sit down at the dining table," Seth invited without turning around. "I'll bring coffee through." Dimity knew banishment when she saw it.

Wandering into the adjacent dining room, she stopped short. Em was in some kind of harness hanging from a spring in the doorway to the living room. Seeing Dimity, she chortled and bounced off the floor.

"Um…the baby's in here," she called over her shoulder.

"Don't worry," was Seth's dry reply. "She can't escape."

Gayle laughed, thinking he was joking. Reluctantly, Dimity pulled out a chair and sat, watching Em bounce on her sturdy little legs, pivoting toward any surrounding toy that caught her eye. When she stopped moving, she swung in a slow spiral to face the other way. The back of her head didn't look happy about it and a squawk confirmed it.

Dimity hesitated and looked toward the kitchen. Okay, this was ridiculous. She could help out a trussed baby, for God's sake—as long as she kept her hair away from those grabby little hands. She walked over before she could chicken out and turned the harness to face the dining room. Em looked up and gurgled, delighted to see her again. Emboldened, she bent to touch the baby's cheek with the tip of her index finger. Petal soft. There, that wasn't so hard.

Em started bouncing, surprising her into a laugh. Impulsively, she caught the crazy jumping baby in her arms and held her close—just for a moment—to smell her, heart beating wildly at her own daring. Releasing her into the wild, Dimity turned around and gasped. Seth stood in the doorway with two coffees, watching.

"Addictive, isn't it?" he said casually. "Just one sniff…and you think, yeah, I can take or leave it. And then somehow you find yourself wanting another." He put the coffees on the table. "I can take her out of the jumper if you like."

"No." There was no way to spin this, so she didn't try. "That would be too scary." If this was a way back into his good graces, she'd take it. "I'm guessing you probably want a litter, eventually."

"My future wife might want some input into that decision."

His confidence fascinated her. Admitting he wanted a wife, kids? She could never do that. Assume she'd settle down and live happily ever after. "I'm surprised you still want to get married after what you've been through with Mel."

"What, so I just give up?" he said, amused. "Why can't I expect a better outcome? Or say that I want kids in the next five to ten years?"

She shook her head, unable to answer him, unable to imagine anyone loving her enough to make the offer. She wasn't the kind of woman who inspired forever. It was hard enough living with *herself* sometimes. She had no experience of intimacy. Her parents certainly hadn't patterned healthy behavior.

"Do *you* see kids in your future?" he asked.

"C'mon, me?"

He had to be teasing. But his eyes were perfectly serious as he stood in the sun streaming through the window.

"Sure, why not? You're a multi-tasker, you like a lot of projects going at one time. Kids, family could be one of them. Yes, I can imagine it. You'd probably be one of those annoying women who make it look easy."

She liked his confidence, even if she couldn't share it. "I'd have to actually hold a baby first."

"Want me to teach you how to approach wild animals?"

Shaking her head, she stepped away from Em, smiling.

"First, you act confident, like you know what you're doing." He walked toward them, his gaze on the baby. "You smile, you soothe, you talk sh—nonsense so they get used to your voice, decide you're friendly." Em burbled nonsense at him. "And when they're comfortable, you make your move." Turning, he cupped Dimity's cheek. "Hey, Honey B."

"Very funny." She moved away from his hand.

As she went to walk past, he blocked her way. "Then you herd your honey badger into a confined space..." He backed her into the wall, one arm braced against it to prevent her escape.

"Having fun?" she said acidly.

"Oh yeah." Dropping his hand from the wall, he stepped in closer and began to nuzzle her neck. "You smell pretty good, too."

"I should." She resisted the urge to turn her head and give him better access. "My potions and lotions are expensive."

"Mmm, sass, chili and sugar."

"None of those have scents."

"Warmed they do." He ran his palms down her bare arms and up again. "I owe you an apology for overreacting earlier."

"No, I'm sorry. I was talking bullshit and you called me on it. But...I can't do this. Please understand."

"Okay, lose me to another woman." Stepping away, he scooped up the baby. "I'm not going to pressure you into anything, Dimity, that's not what we're about." He hesitated. "And if it helps Zander's cause for me to be branded the nice guy, then hell, brand me the nice guy. But only until the band's on the road again."

"Thank you," she said through a tight throat. Told herself it was gratitude that she could rely on him to be a team player. Not regret they weren't having an affair. "Do you think you can drop me by the ferry terminal this morning?" The sooner she got to Waiheke, the sooner she could start fixing this for everybody. And if she stayed here another night, there was no way she'd keep her hands off this great guy.

"I'll run you in when I drop Dad at work. But eat first or I'll sic the baby on you." He held Em up and she beamed at Dimity.

"Why does she like me?"

"She's used to being adored, and you mostly ignore her."

Dimity reached out and patted Em's head. "That's it," she said. "That's all you're getting."

The baby chuckled, waved her baby arms. Gently, Seth lowered her to the floor, where she started bouncing again.

They were sitting at the table eating scrambled eggs with Gayle when Frank came into the dining room, and dropped the morning newspaper by his wife's plate. Nodding acknowledgment, he buttoned his business jacket and checked his watch. "I'm surprised Jeff hasn't arrived yet."

"I told him at the party that I'd drop you into work today, Dad," Seth said so casually that Dimity looked at him across the table, sensing a cunning plan. He winked at her, confirming it. It had become clear last night that Frank was trying to avoid spending time with him. "It gives me a chance to say hi to everybody who didn't make the barbecue," he added.

Dimity smiled at him. *Color me impressed.*

"Don't bother," said Frank. "I'll drive myself."

Gayle put down her fork and eyeballed her husband. "You won't," she said. "Seth is taking you." Some silent message passed between them.

Frank sighed. "Fine. When will you be ready to leave?"

"Ten minutes. Okay if we drop Dimity off at the ferry terminal en route?"

"Of course." Frank smiled at her politely. "I would like to be at work for nine, though, a customer's coming in."

"No problem." Dimity stood. "I'll collect my bags."

She didn't like Seth's father, and liked him even less when his son was buying her ferry ticket and they were left waiting by the car with the luggage for a few minutes. Frank Curran struck her as a man who'd founded a small kingdom and confused that with a divine mandate to have his own way all the time. And somehow, Seth had been brainwashed into thinking that *not* wanting to become a chip off the blockhead was something to feel guilty about.

"What is it exactly that you do for Zander Freedman?" said Frank politely, but there was a whiff of condescension in his tone.

"Whatever he needs to keep his twenty-year, multi-million-dollar, global business running in a volatile market."

"Sounds impressive. What does that mean?"

Dimity examined her nails. "Longer hours than nine to five."

Frank bristled. "I've only recently pulled back my hours. I used to average sixty."

"I pull up to seventy during a tour."

"I once worked eighty to meet an order."

"Look at you two bonding over who's the worst workaholic." Seth returned with her ticket.

"Oh, sure." Dimity smiled at that bitter, old man. Seth wasn't going to win him over. His father had soured all the way through. "Thanks for your hospitality, Frank." *And if you reject your son, I'm coming for you.*

"You're welcome." Oblivious to the danger, he stepped into the car.

Seth pushed her trolley into the terminal. "Tell Zander and Elizabeth I look forward to catching up this weekend."

"I will. Good luck." Impulsively, she hugged him, felt his surprise and covered her lapse with a wave toward the vehicle. "Your dad's watching, I figure I have to do the girlfriend thing."

Seth glanced over his shoulder at the same time as his father looked up.

Nice save.

Breathing a small sigh of relief, Dimity took over the trolley. "See you, then."

"One more thing." Seth caught her face in his hands and kissed her, something she would have objected to, had she been able to speak. As it was, his tongue did all the talking, playfully persuasive, a continuation of their interrupted foreplay this morning.

"What the hell was that?" she demanded when he released her.

"A mind fuck since I'm not allowed any other kind." His audacity was breathtaking. She wasn't used to it, didn't expect it from him.

"You said you wouldn't break my rules!"

"Just reminding you that *you* can."

She stepped away from his infectious grin with a frown. "Is this where you say, 'Hey, baby, I know you want to'?"

"I do now," he said cheerfully.

Dimity narrowed her eyes. "Goodbye, Seth."

He let her go fifty yards. "Hey, Honey B."

She turned.

"Think about it."

Exactly what she was trying *not* to do.

CHAPTER 12

SETH WALKED BACK TO THE car feeling more optimistic than he had in a long time. A weight had lifted off his mind last night. He and Mel had reached an understanding, he and Dimity were working toward one, and even his father's impatient glance at his watch wasn't going to dampen his optimism that good things happened in threes.

"Finished making a spectacle of yourselves?" said Frank.

"For the time being," Seth answered affably. The next move was Dimity's. Hopefully, he'd piqued her curiosity. The hug had been a strategic error on her part—it told him she was intrigued. They could have a lot of fun if she bent the rules. And fun had been seriously lacking in their lives over the past few months.

"I shouldn't be surprised that you replaced Mel with a trophy girlfriend," Frank remarked, when Seth didn't bite.

"Get to know Dimity before you judge her, Dad. There's a whole lot more to her than looks." He tried to think of something his father would be impressed by. "I've never met anyone who works harder."

"For God's sake, don't you start."

"Didn't you just have a love-in over your workloads?"

"Never mind, just drive."

The atmosphere at the offices where Seth had interned through his engineering degree and worked after he'd graduated was warm and friendly, despite the air-conditioning always dialed a couple of degrees too chilly. His father softened when he walked into the place. Seth had forgotten that.

He noticed immediately that the pot plants were fake. Yvonne the office manager told him she'd threatened to quit if the live ones weren't given to a good home. "You were the only one who cared about them," she said, when they were standing in reception. "I felt like they died a little every time I went near them. It got too depressing."

Through the slimline blinds of his old office he could see Jeff, wearing a suit and tie, on the phone. Looking harassed, he waved hello before returning to his call. *There but for the grace of rock 'n' roll go I.*

Seth had enjoyed the job in an I-trained-for-this kind of way, but he'd ripped off his tie every night. It had always got tighter over the course of the day. And overtime had felt like a jail sentence.

When he thought of the hours he put into the band, a forty-five-hour week at Curran Engineering seemed like a walk in the park. He'd caught maybe five hours sleep a night on tour and still bounced out of bed every morning. *I made the right choice.*

As soon as Yvonne announced he was in the building, Seth found himself besieged. He spent half an hour in the staffroom looking at recent family photos on people's phones, having selfies taken and signing autographs. Everyone was delighted that "one of our own" had gone on to glory.

His father slipped away after five minutes. Otherwise, nothing had changed. The coffeemaker still made god-awful coffee, the fridge was still full of lunch boxes with name tags, and he could still match every mug to its owner.

He loved seeing everyone again, but also felt as if he'd walked into the land that time forgot. So much had happened to him in the interim and some of these people were still quibbling over who'd left their mug in the sink instead of stacking it in the dishwasher.

When he returned to reception looking for Frank he saw him in the meeting room, the only space that was kept spartan and uncluttered, talking to a woman Seth didn't recognize. They were both poring over papers spread out around the table.

"New employee?" he asked Yvonne.

"The valuer," she confided in a low voice, "here to count teaspoons. I told her she better not include my mug in the chattels."

"Valuer?"

"Changes ahead." She beckoned him closer. "I'm trying to take a positive attitude in front of your dad. He's finding all this hard enough. Keep it to yourself, the other staff don't know yet."

Of course she'd assume he was in the loop.

The reception phone rang, and she excused herself to pick up. "Curran Consulting, how may I help?"

Mind reeling, Seth stuck his head into the meeting room. "Dad, what's going on?"

"Excuse me a minute, will you, Carol?" Frank led the way to his office and closed the door. "I'm getting an independent valuation before I put the business on the market."

"You're selling?" *Impossible*. "But this business is your whole life."

Frank said bitterly, "I don't have a choice."

Seth was still struggling to get his head around it. "Why didn't you tell me you were in trouble?"

His father folded his arms. "You made it very clear that you weren't interested in being part of this company."

"In working in it, but I can still be an investor, a silent partner! Shit, Dad…" Seth grabbed his father's elbow. "If it's a capital injection you need, I can put in a hundred thousand." Reckless to offer so much with his future uncertain, but if his father needed help…

"All cash and no responsibility?" Frank snorted as he moved to his desk. "No thanks."

That stung. "Yeah, the money really came easy to me. Supportive family, loyal girlfriend and an audition process that was nothing like *The Hunger Games*." Old rockers nostalgically recalling the bad old days for documentaries had a lot to answer for. "For God's sake, don't cut off your nose to spite your face, Dad."

"If only life was as simple as you think it is," his father snapped.

Seth stared at him. "Really? That's your only takeaway from what I just said? That my life's simple? I spent sixteen months scaling Everest—without *any* Sherpas in support—and had maybe five minutes at the top to enjoy the view. If Zander's voi—reputation doesn't recover, it's back to the foothills to start the climb all over again."

His father made an impatient gesture. "You made your choices. And why I'm doing this is no longer your concern, so—"

He couldn't believe what he was hearing. "We really can't have a conversation anymore, can we? Even when I offer you my life savings, I'm still in the wrong, still the disappointment. Tell me this, Dad. If there's no way I can ever make it up to you, then why the hell am I even trying?"

"Don't be a such a drama queen," Frank said scathingly. "You're not in Hollywood now."

Seth left before he said something he'd regret.

♪ ♫ ♩

Lighter by a substantial fee, Dimity stood amidst her luggage at the bottom of the steps leading up to Zander and Elizabeth's rental property and watched the Toyota sedan's tires churn on the rough track as the taxi bumped and rattled its way out of sight. The driver hadn't been happy at the state of the driveway.

The engine backfired—possibly channeling his annoyance—startling birds from a stand of dense native bush. So much for the element of surprise.

She hadn't told Zee that she was returning. Ambush was their modus operandi in complex negotiations—catch people off guard, start them on the back foot. And if she had any shot at changing his mind, she needed every advantage.

Ruefully, she glanced to the house, but no one appeared on the decks through one of the many French doors. The house was ridiculously modest for a rock star, a board and batten rectangle weathered to a silver gray with a black corrugated iron roof. If it wasn't for the panoramic sea views and the number on the letterbox at the end of their perilous driveway she'd have sworn she'd been dropped at the wrong address.

Leaving her suitcases, she shouldered her laptop and handbag and climbed the stairs. With the cab gone, every sound had intensified—the rustle of wind through grasses, the trill of birdsong, and the nibbling of sheep eating grass in an adjacent field. An unwelcome suspicion growing, she tried a few doors and found them locked. No one home.

Now what?

She headed for the outbuildings, hoping to find one open—it was a warm day and she wanted shade for her laptop at least—but even the large rusty-roofed barn was padlocked. So, too, was the separate two-bedroom sleep-out and a small shed.

Peering through the window, Dimity saw it had been converted to a writing retreat. Elizabeth's laptop sat on a desk, surrounded by manuscript pages. A lot of people would pay a lot of money to get their hands on it. Dimity stopped being annoyed that they locked their doors, when they lived in the middle of nowhere.

Returning to the main deck, she was digging out her cell to break cover when she spotted a solitary figure, with Zander's distinctive white-blond hair, fishing from the beach.

Pay dirt. Stowing her laptop and handbag under an outside table, she followed a zigzag trail down the hill to the beach, taking off her war stilettos halfway down. This bloody island was going to ruin every good pair of heels she'd packed.

His back to her, Zee was fishing from a rocky outcrop at one end of the beach, wearing faded jeans and a Grateful Dead T-shirt in psychedelic colors. Possibly why she experienced such a sense of the surreal as she picked her way along the seaweed-strewn foreshore, taking care to stay out of his peripheral vision. She was used to seeing him surrounded by people, or center stage in an arena in Milan, Singapore, Buenos Aires, not on a rock with a rod, alone in the middle of nowhere.

All because a Kiwi woman saw him as an ordinary man.

No, that was unfair. It was Zee, the passionate extremist, who was insisting on giving up everything for love. Why the hell couldn't he have taken up a harmless obsession like coconut oil pulling or kundalini yoga?

But she had to keep her frustration out of this. Play smart. Disarm him with the last thing he'd expect after yesterday's verbal assault— conciliation. Lead him gently to the realization that becoming mortal could never work. Find out his plans and then stymie them. If anything, all this was *her* fault. He had no real idea of the consequences of his actions because she'd made so many go away. That stopped today.

The rocks were covered in barnacles, impossible to navigate in bare feet. With a pang of regret, she stepped into her heels, comforting herself with the thought that Caesar had probably sacrificed a few pairs of Roman sandals through his campaigns.

The odor of sun-ripening bait drifted toward her, and seagulls skulking for scraps squawked loudly to keep away.

Shush, you idiots. Zander turned to look over his shoulder.

His laser-blue gaze narrowed as he waved acknowledgment, possibly because of the glare of the sun. More likely his clever brain was assessing her mood.

Smiling, she returned his wave. *And so it begins.*

"Good timing, I'm catching lunch," he commented when she arrived. Glancing into the cooler beside him, she saw a small snapper.

"That wouldn't feed Diamanté."

"Patience, woman. I have a bigger one on the hook." The rod in his hand jerked and he reeled in some line. "If you'd phoned ahead, Elizabeth could have given you a ride." His conversational tone confirmed he knew *exactly* why she hadn't given him warning. "She's in Oneroa, picking up supplies."

"I figured the next move was mine."

The line yanked hard and he started reeling in earnest. "I'm just grateful you're here. And safe."

Since Elizabeth had come into his life, he'd started throwing out the occasional "caring" comment. Dimity wasn't sure how she felt about that.

"I'm sorry for overreacting yesterday," she told his profile. This was her second apology today, she really had to knock this bad habit on the head. Though it had the desired result. Zee nearly lost his grip on the rod. Inwardly, she smiled. "I've had a chance to calm down, and while I can't pretend I'm happy about your decision—" *because you won't buy it* "—I respect your right to make it."

Adjusting his hold, he eased back the rod, making it bow alarmingly, and reeled in more line. "I'm sorry, too. I could have broken the news better." He added ruefully, "Or at least locked the car doors before I told you."

She had *no* intention of rehashing her embarrassing meltdown. "Is the fishing rod meant to bend like that?"

"Yeah," he grunted, biceps straining. "When it's a big fish."

She stepped to a safer distance in case it was a shark. "I've bitched about you not confiding in me in the past, so I really appreciate the trust." *Ugh, too much?*

"I appreciate—" he braced his legs wide, taking the strain of whatever monster was on the other end of his line "—that *you* appreciate that."

This touchy-feely bullshit was embarrassing both of them, so she changed tack. "I haven't told Seth the truth."

"I never thought you would." Because he trusted her. And she could no longer return the favor.

A large fish broke the water, tail flapping, scales gleaming. Not a shark, thank God. Another snapper, twice as big as the one in the cooler.

"Are *you* going to? Tell Seth the real story?" She didn't know how long she could skirt around the truth, and she didn't want to outright lie.

"Because it worked so well with you?" He swung the snapper over the rocks and killed it with a practiced blow under her appalled gaze before she could close her eyes. "Everyone will find it easier to move on if they believe my voice is the issue." Handing her his rod, he crouched to remove the hook. "Look at it as the most humane way," he said gently.

It took everything she had not to snap his rod in two. Instead she said calmly, "Man can't live by fish alone—what are you going to do for income? Because if the insurers won't pay out, you're going to be broke. Or are you expecting Elizabeth to support you?"

He frowned as he dropped the fish in the cooler. "I am not. Rage disbanding will be big news. Nostalgia will revitalize sales of the touring album, which will make the distributors happy—right now they're writing it off. My label recorded and produced it, so that will put dollars in the bank."

Picking up the bait bucket, he tossed the slimy contents into the sea, causing a frenzy among the gulls. "The other guys have written or collaborated on new songs on the album, and that means royalties for all of us, which should help keep them afloat until they make headway with a new band."

He rinsed his hands clean in a nearby rock pool. "And I have no doubt my old labels will release 'Best of Rage' albums. I won't be able to keep Elizabeth in opulence, but we'll do okay."

"That's a relief," she lied.

Zander picked up the cooler, his tackle box, and the bait bucket, leaving Dimity to carry the rod. "I thought you'd fight me to the death on this," he admitted as they walked across the rocks.

"Don't get me wrong, I'm gutted." She adjusted the rod over her shoulder. "But I can see how serious you are—and I'm saving myself more angst by helping you make this work. A lot of people are going to be impacted by your decision."

"That would have been the case if my voice hadn't recovered—"

"But it *has* recovered." She softened her tone. "I'm not trying to make you feel bad, Zee." *I'm trying to make you feel terrible.* "I just want to make sure we tackle your exit properly, so everyone's taken care of."

"I've already been working to soften the blow. I'll still need bodyguards in the States, at least until my haters run out of steam. And I've told Luther we'll go all-out with security when Elizabeth starts promoting her book."

Death threats were still rife on social media from those who considered he'd committed treason by lip-syncing the national anthem, and he'd already told Dimity how deeply concerned he was that

Elizabeth's memoir might make her a target. "You'll have plenty to do while I'm selling assets and fighting the insurance company. Elizabeth wants you handling all her promotion so she can concentrate on her own projects again."

Dimity had fallen behind, so Zander stopped to let her catch up. "The rest of the band still have a bright future. They're writing great songs, and I'm not the only one who thinks so. There are a couple of producers interested—"

"That's fantastic," she said, "but it will still take a good six months to get a new band off the ground."

"About the same time it would have taken to get Rage touring again," he pointed out. Damn his logic. "Jared and Kayla are downsizing their house in the New Year to give themselves a financial buffer."

Dimity sighed. "I just hope the pressure of starting a new band isn't…never mind, you don't need to hear it."

"Tell me."

"I hope the pressure isn't going to tip them into divorce."

Zander stopped to face her. "I thought they'd resolved the problems they had on tour."

"No, they *recognized* their problems on tour. If they split up—" *over my dead body* "—Jared will need to earn enough to set up *two* households, at least until Kayla can find a job. Which means Rocco and Madison will go into daycare." They'd reached the soft sand of the beach. She took her time removing her ruined shoes, giving him time to conjure up their innocent faces.

"I didn't know that," he said slowly.

Dangling the straps over her wrist, she pressed her advantage. "Moss will play it cool, but Rage is all he has." To her surprise, her voice caught on the words. *Him and me both.* Zander glanced over, and she concentrated on re-balancing the pole against her shoulder.

"I'll still be around to keep an eye on him," Zander said as they started walking again. "We all will. If anything, Rage's disbandment will keep him alive longer. He won't be able to afford as many drugs."

"That's cold."

"Addiction is like a security blanket. Eventually you have to grow up and give it up if you want a bigger life. Only Moss can save Moss. But he's a smart guy. It shouldn't take him as long as it took me."

"You've never been an addict, Zee." He'd come close with alcohol and coke, but he was too driven to risk losing control.

"You're wrong. I'm a fame-aholic. Adulation was my crack for seventeen years. That's why I can't go back." His eyes were very blue, very determined. "My newfound conscience is still a ninety-seven-pound weakling and I can't risk screwing this up."

"This, being your relationship with Elizabeth?" So *that* was his fear.

"And with my mother and brother. You have no idea the shit I put them through to stay at the top."

The sand turned cold underfoot as they walked in the shade of pohutukawas.

"If you're worried about addiction I'll watch out for you, like I always have." He was a phoenix, always capable of rising above his limitations through charisma, willpower, and sheer bloody-mindedness. "Besides, Elizabeth won't let you fall."

Stubbornly, he shook his head. "It's not enough that she's good for me. It has to work both ways."

She was silent as they climbed the narrow path from the beach through the native bush, trying to understand what he was telling her. Zander Freedman was *afraid*? It threw her.

He stopped at the top of the hill. "Let's catch our breath."

"I'm fine." What could she say to reassure him?

"I meant our mental breath."

Trying to hide her impatience, she glanced over the cliff's edge, and the sea sprawled out before them like a fallen sky. Another day it might be beautiful, today all she could focus on were the jagged rocks at the bottom of the cliff and the surge of surf choking and smothering them. *We don't have time for this.*

"I used to pity people who told me to stop and appreciate the view," he said astutely. "If you're alive, then you should be in motion. And what do I know about being still? And yet there are moments, hours even, when I am. At peace. I knew I'd be happy with Elizabeth. What I didn't expect was the ability to enjoy my own company."

For a moment Dimity got a glimmer, a firefly spark of what life could be like—and doused it. He'd never thought about the greater good, and he wasn't thinking about the greater good now. It was still all about him.

If he wanted to sacrifice himself for love, then he could do it for the band family he'd created. The one he'd made them all believe in.

"You want a better work-life balance, I get that." *Not at all*. She returned to her agenda. "Which makes me worried for Seth. He gave up everything to join Rage…his girlfriend, his stake in the family business. His father still hasn't forgiven him for it." She hated sharing details of Seth's private life, but this wasn't the time to be squeamish. She was fighting for their lives.

Zander looked stunned. "Why did he never tell me?"

"Not *every* rock star wears his heart on his sleeve."

"Nice dig. But Seth has his head screwed on. He's the *only* one I don't worry about."

So he *was* worried about everyone else? Her spirits lifted. She was getting to him. Now to give his newfound conscience more weight than it could carry.

"Have you thought about what Robbie will do?" Robbie had been Rage's manager for eighteen years.

"He told me when I was in hospital that if Rage disbands he'll retire. I talked to him yesterday. He hasn't changed his mind."

"Did you tell him it's over?" she said sharply.

"I'll tell the band first—tomorrow—then Robbie, then all our key people. I want to give everyone time to get their heads around it before I make a public announcement."

"You can't do that." She tried to keep the panic out of her voice. "I know I'm the Wonder Woman of administration, but I can't possibly lay the groundwork for a roll-out of this magnitude in twenty-four hours."

"Is there much work?"

"Oh my God, come with me."

They reached the deck, still no sign of Elizabeth. The moment they were inside Dimity opened her laptop and started pulling up staff records, split-screening them on the monitor. Zander was a big-picture guy and she was going to bury him under minutiae.

"I estimate you have upward of fifty employees who have worked for you longer than five years." Painstakingly, she went over every single one of the staff records, belaboring the theme of loyal and faithful servants until *Downton Abbey*'s crew looked like a bunch of slackers, and her spreadsheet was littered with human sacrifices to his selfishness.

"It's not like we can afford a redundancy payout or long-service bonus, but at the very least we can present them with a glowing

reference when you tell them. I'll also help them update their resumes."
As she talked, her voice grew hoarse. She hadn't realized how much
these people had come to mean to her; how much she knew of their
lives through the little things she'd done for them.

Researching the best deals on christening bracelets for Steve the
roadie's first grandchild; organizing an emergency flight to her father's
funeral for Cal the lighting tech. Negotiating a better price with a
wedding venue for Consuela the cook's niece. She paused on a picture
of Zander's executive housekeeper, an Englishwoman in her early
forties. Dressed like a punk rocker with the plummy vowels of the
Queen, Philippa epitomized their family of talented eccentrics.

By the time she'd finished Zander was looking dazed. "You're
right," he said. "I haven't thought this through."

Her pulse leapt. "You haven't?"

"I'll take another look at my financial statements over the next few
days, see if we can squeeze some money from somewhere for a long-
service bonus. This empathy stuff is new to me, so I really appreciate
you pointing it out."

Disappointment crushed her.

"Clearly, I need to work out how to do better by my staff. All my
staff." He hesitated. "Seeing you so upset yesterday—"

Dimity squirmed. "Let's not go there."

"I want you to take the rest of the week off."

"What?" It was the last thing she expected him to say.

"Do some sightseeing around New Zealand, go to a spa…whatever
you want. I'll cover all costs. Why should the lawyers and real estate
agents get all my money?"

She was shocked. "Zee, you can't manage without me."

"I can handle the critical stuff for a week, and everything else can
wait. I'm serious, I want you to take a break."

The timing of his magnanimity couldn't be worse. She couldn't
change anything if she was sitting in a spa in Queenstown. It was the
equivalent of Nero fiddling while Rome burned. "But—"

"No, don't argue. Let me show how much I appreciate all you do
for me. I know you missed your mother's wedding because of your
workload."

As Dimity racked her brain for a good reason to refuse, Elizabeth
walked through a side door wheeling one of the suitcases Dimity had
left on the driveway. "Thank God you're back."

Her relief would have been ego-boosting, except Elizabeth was always nagging her to take a break, and was bound to side with Zee.

How the hell was she going to talk her way out of this with *two* people ganging up on her?

CHAPTER 13

Seth drove the long way home needing to simmer down before inflicting himself on the rest of his family.

He couldn't believe that a thirty-year business had gotten into trouble so quickly. He thumped the steering wheel. *Shit, shit, shit.*

Legacy had always been an important motivator for his dad. With no one to build an empire with, to pass the baton to, had he lost interest, let things slide and misread key economic indicators?

"Yeah, because it's all about you, rock star." He had to stop shouldering the guilt, assume this was his fault. It wouldn't help him come up with a solution.

Every business had customers who were slow payers. Maybe one of the company's major clients had gone into receivership owing them a lot of money?

These were questions he should have asked his father, but the news had come as such a shock, then Dad's knee-jerk rejection of help— He slammed the brakes on when the car in front stopped for a red light that he hadn't noticed.

He pulled over into a side street and phoned his old office extension, feigning surprise when Jeff answered. "Sorry, Jeff, I thought I was phoning reception. It's Seth. Yeah, old habits I guess. Before you put me through, how the hell are you? We haven't managed much of a chat yet."

By the time he hung up he knew that the company wasn't subject to a hostile takeover, Jeff thought the valuer was an auditor, and he had no access to financial accounts. Seth could talk to Yvonne about bad payers and whether a major client had gone bankrupt and was dragging the firm down, but his ignorance would also reveal his estrangement with Frank, and he wasn't prepared to wash that dirty linen in public.

Which led him back to Frank—*I have no choice*—Curran, who didn't want to sell but was being forced to. The signs led to a financial disaster. So why not at least *consider* Seth as an investor?

Does he hate me that much?

He didn't want to go there, so he nursed righteous anger, which at least kept the cold dread at bay. A couple of blocks from the house he saw Janey power-walking toward him, pushing what looked like the Mars Rover. As he drove past, he blasted the horn to get her attention, did a U-turn and pulled up alongside.

The Mars Rover turned out to be a hi-tech stroller.

Removing her iPod's earbuds, she opened his driver's door and smiled at him. "Hey, want to come walking with us?"

Seth wasn't in the mood for smiles.

"Why didn't you tell me that Dad was getting ready to sell the business?" he demanded. *That it was in financial distress?*

"Really? That's fantastic." Janey's smile broadened. "Mum's been trying to talk him into retiring since…for months. She hasn't mentioned it lately. I wonder if she knows?" Tightening her ponytail, she glanced into the stroller where his niece lounged like a suburban princess, one fat leg slung over the rim and a bottle clutched to her chest.

The teat popped as the baby broke the suction and gave Seth a milky smirk, which he was too distracted to return.

"Yeah, I'll walk with you." Locking the car, he crouched by the stroller and greeted Em properly, then wiped her away her drool with a bib that read, 'These fools put my cape on backwards.'

"Has Dad mentioned how the business has been going lately?"

"Are you kidding?" Janey set the pace with a long stride. "After you left, work was the *last* topic I brought up. It fell under 'don't mention the war' category."

He was startled. "As bad as that?"

"Dad would start venting about your ingratitude, I'd defend you and then get the 'everything I've done, I've done for my kids' speech."

He had no idea. "I'm sorry I left you with the fallout."

"Don't be. It's bullshit. Dad works obsessively because he loves it."

That's what Seth had always believed, but now he wondered if his father worked so hard because he had to. Except…he'd seen the balance sheets when he'd worked in the business, and they were healthy. Which meant the business *had* gone downhill after he'd left. He felt sick. And it would be just like Frank with his pride to hide a fall in fortunes from his family.

"I've been thinking about our childhood a lot since I've had Em." They reached the park and turned into the entrance, taking the perimeter track. "Not once did Dad come to a single netball game of mine, or make a 'meet the teachers' evening. Mum did all the school camps, all the ferrying around to after-school activities. Did he ever go to any of your football games?"

"No," he said, only half listening. Should he tell his sister what he'd learned?

"Let's face it, the only reason you two got so close was because you took the same interest in his work that he did."

Seth stuck out a hand and slowed the stroller. Janey was feeding her anger into her stride. "Don't get bitter," he said, talking her down. *I am not letting this family implode more than it has.* "Dad has that old-school mentality—the father provides and the mother nurtures. But he loves you." *Me, I'm no longer sure about.*

No wonder Frank was so sour and unforgiving. Yeah, he was responsible for what was happening with the business, but Seth *had* left him in the lurch by resigning so abruptly. And he *had* let his father believe he'd take over the family firm, until the Rage opportunity arose. Guilt started riding him hard again. "He helped you and Tom out with the deposit on the house when you moved back to New Zealand, and the first thing he did when Em was born was set up a bank account for her."

More reasons why he needed to persuade Frank to accept his offer of a bailout.

"And that's supposed to compensate for ignoring us?"

"Dad might not tell you how he feels, but he sure as hell tells everyone else. All his business associates used to ask after you." They'd told him, too, how proud Frank was of him. He remembered his response to Dimity in The Comfort Zone when she'd suggested he spill his guts to her therapist.

I'm a Kiwi bloke. We suffer stoically, and die of heart disease brought on by repressed feelings.

It summed up his father to a tee. *But not me,* he thought. *I am my mother's son.* He would fix this, not out of guilt, but because he loved the old bastard.

They reached the lake at the center of the park. "Let's walk around so Em can see the ducks," Janey said. "I brought bread." They changed direction. "I really want Dad more involved in his granddaughter's life," she said. "If he sells the business and retires, then maybe he will be."

As long as they have enough money to enjoy that retirement.

"Seth, why are you frowning?"

"Just wondering if having him around full-time will drive Ma crazy. And you know what they say about workaholics quitting the daily grind. Their adrenaline levels drop, and they keel over."

Janey stopped walking. "Don't even *joke* about that stuff."

"Sorry." Em squawked a protest from the stroller and Seth took over pushing to get them moving again. Janey was still looking anxious. She'd always had a vivid imagination. As kids, he'd used to scare the spit out of her with bogeyman stories.

Putting his gnawing anxiety aside, he worked to coax a smile out of her. He wouldn't tell Janey anything yet, she'd only worry herself sick about how to repay the house deposit. "They'll find plenty to do in retirement. Mum can take Dad to yoga and meditation, sign him up for salsa dancing."

Janey grinned. "They can follow Rage on the tour circuit, and stay at your bachelor pad in LA."

"Yeah, I can see Dad partying with Moss. They can get stoned together and get a piercing."

She was laughing now and an answering chuckle from the stroller only made her laugh harder. He made himself join in.

"Silly Uncle Seth," Janey said to her daughter.

"You can't choose your family, kid."

"I think I lucked out with my brother." Janey butted his shoulder with her head. "I missed you."

"I missed you, too." He had to convince his father to take money, for all their sakes. "Is that a coffee stand? Let's get one."

"Sure."

As they waited for their order he said casually, "Don't tell Mum that Dad's getting a valuer in. Let's not get her hopes up in case he changes his mind about selling."

"Okay." She was crouched in front of the stroller, keeping Em entertained. "I was sorry to miss Dimity this morning. When will we see her again?"

"Not sure. She's in work mode now." He paid for the coffees and they resumed their trek to the ducks. The lovely lightness of this morning had disappeared as though it had never been.

"I like her," Janey said.

"Yeah, me, too." It occurred to him that Dimity was the only person who knew his two worlds and could move comfortably between them. They reached the area where a dozen mallard ducks congregated, in and out of the pond, and picked a course around the duck poo to the water's edge.

"I wasn't sure at first," his sister confided, "but she's such a character and totally in love with you. So yeah. I approve."

He couldn't help but be amused by her blessing. "We're just having fun, sis." He unbuckled Em from the Mars Rover, hoping Dimity's day was going better than his. What would she do in his place?

She'd fix it. *So I'll fix it.*

"Totally in love with you." Janey stressed, unpacking the bread.

"Uh-huh… So when does this baby brain thing wear off?"

His sister threw a crust at him.

♪ ♫ ♩

"Why is your PA looking in need of strong liquor?" Elizabeth said accusingly. She'd taken one look at Dimity's face and turned to Zander.

"Because I embraced my caring side and offered her a week's holiday. What you're seeing on her face, my love, is joy."

If Dimity wasn't so *winded,* she would have rolled her eyes. But she needed all her mental energy to dig herself out of this unexpected hole.

"*Now?*" Elizabeth suddenly looked as sick as Dimity felt. Elizabeth's fingers tightened convulsively on the handle of the suitcase. Then she smiled. "That's really thoughtful."

"Isn't it?" Zander looked as proud as if he'd just ridden a bike without training wheels for the first time.

"How about I show you where you're sleeping?" Before Dimity could argue, Elizabeth had caught her arm and was marching her outside, moving so fast that Dimity's pink suitcase bounced from deck to ramp to the shell path leading to the sleep-out.

Elizabeth stopped the moment they were clear of the main building.

"Please say no," she pleaded. "Zander might be able to do without you for a week, I can't."

And there is a God. "I don't know…"

"I swear I'll make it up to you, but I need your help. The publisher wants to reshoot the cover after feedback from the big accounts. Apparently it's too—"

"Esoteric?" She'd tried to tell Max that when she'd first seen the concept. An unmade bed, Zander's famous Stetson on the bedpost and a pair of reading glasses on the pillow to denote the nerdy academic. Elizabeth didn't even *wear* glasses. "Intriguingly significative," the art department called it.

"Tame and boring," Elizabeth said darkly. She, of course, had loved it. "Max wants to reshoot the cover with me lying under rumpled sheets. He's even suggesting 'No Rest for the Wicked' as a subtitle."

Dimity shook her head. "How crass." She wished she'd thought of it.

Elizabeth might have thought she'd given up her privacy by writing this memoir, but she hadn't yet comprehended that there were degrees of exposure. Exactly what Dimity been trying to explain to Seth when she'd turned down an affair. There was a big difference between first- and third-degree burns. But Elizabeth clearly didn't need to hear that analogy right now.

"I haven't even shipped the manuscript yet and the publisher wants a naked cover shoot?" Elizabeth raked a hand through her red curls. "I know it's a big ask to defer your break, but I need you to stall Max, at least for another couple of weeks until I finish the damn book."

"Of course," Dimity said magnanimously. "Though it's odd that Zander didn't factor that in when he offered me a holiday." And why was it suddenly a *damn* book? Wasn't it a labor of love?

"Zander doesn't know," Elizabeth admitted.

"I don't know what?"

Zee strolled into the back garden carrying the cooler and a sharp knife.

"Oh, God," Dimity said. "Really? In addition to watching you kill my lunch, I now have to watch you remove its guts? This is taking your wild man reputation to ridiculous levels."

He wouldn't be diverted. "What don't I know, Doc?"

Elizabeth looked hunted.

"She's running behind schedule." Dimity gave him the truth—just not all of it. "She wants me to defer my holiday and handle Max while she gets it done."

"Tell him you need the deadline extended," he suggested with the unconscious entitlement of the very famous.

His lover rallied. "No, I always meet my deadlines. And they're rushing the book to print so there's no wriggle room. Having Dimity around to handle extraneous stuff would really help."

Zee looked torn. "Just when I was getting the hang of empathy," he muttered. "So who do I worry about now? You or Dimity? I can only manage one at a time."

"Neither," they said together, caught each other's eye and smiled. And in that moment, Dimity realized she'd been using her arguments on the wrong person. Zee listened to Elizabeth, *she* could change his mind.

But first Dimity had to change hers.

♪ ♫ ♩

When he returned from feeding the ducks Seth phoned his accountant and re-familiarized himself with his investments. Being brought up alongside the business had made him savvy with money and he'd invested most of what he'd earned.

As he'd suspected, he'd be penalized on a couple of fixed term investments by pulling cash out early, but there wasn't anything he could do about that.

And if Curran Consulting needed more?

Calculating the time in LA—It was ten-thirty p.m.—he texted Moss. Five minutes later, he was looking at Rage's axe-man via Skype.

"You're lucky you caught me, I'm just about to head out for the night." Wearing black jeans, an unbuttoned red shirt and towel-drying his wet hair, he was clearly just out of the shower.

"Best time for vampires."

"With this tan?"

Mongrel, Moss called himself—black-haired, olive-skinned, green-eyed. A product of invader/invadee genetics, he'd told Seth once when they'd got drunk together. The lore from the show was that he'd been living in his car at the time of auditions—it was actually a converted Volkswagon Combi. But as Zander said at the time, "Why ruin a good story?"

"I was talking about your nocturnal habits."

"It's nice to have the choice," Moss countered. "Between Jared's kids training him to be up at six a.m. and your inability to break nine-to-five habits, I'm making the most of this downtime while I can." He picked up the tumbler beside him and the ice rattled. Rum and coke was his poison.

"Is this a social call, or…?" His voice was perfectly level, but Seth sensed him bracing himself.

Before he could reassure him, a woman came into shot behind him, naked. Reaching over Moss's shoulder, she took his glass from his hand and sipped from it, bending to bite his neck, as she returned it to him. With a little wave for Seth, she walked away, curvy ass swaying.

"I hate to ruin the mood, but any chance you and I can have some alone time?"

"Sure. Hang on."

Moss picked up the laptop and carried Seth into the living room. In the dark, the ceiling was dappled with the reflection of the lap-pool's lights shining through the water on the other side of the glass wall. The two of them shared the lease on this living-the-dream, Santa Monica mansion. Moss switched on some lamps. "You've got news on Zander's voice, haven't you?"

"All I know is there's been some kind of setback in his recovery."

Their captain had provisioned their life raft as best he could with food and water should he fail to return—but the music industry was akin to the Bermuda Triangle. They were well aware a new band could disappear without a trace.

"Fuck." Moss ran his fingers through his damp hair. "This is worse than waiting for a pregnancy test."

Seth was momentarily distracted. "Have you been doing that?"

"Not for a while."

Sometimes it was impossible to tell if he was joking or not.

Born Aiden, his nickname had nothing to do with the color of his eyes, despite what his female fans believed. He'd become a rolling stone at sixteen to escape foster care after the death of his father.

He'd pawned his dad's guitar many times, Seth knew that much. Stolen it back at least once, when he couldn't find the money.

"Don't panic. Dimity insists all hope is not lost."

"Well, she'd know. How are you doing?"

Neither of them saw any point in wasting emotional energy on conjecture. *Expect the best, prepare for the worst.* They'd already discussed finding cheaper digs if the worst happened with Zander's vocals.

Seth told him what he'd discovered about his father. "If I clear out my savings—which looks likely—I wanted to give you a heads-up in case you want to find another roommate. I could end up sliding further down the property ladder than you need to go."

"Don't be an idiot," Moss said. "Who the hell else would live with me? And we can always buy another Combi."

"That gives me an idea for a new band name." Humor was how they kept this crazy waiting game manageable. "The Combi Brothers."

"Or the Downsizers," Moss countered.

Seth grinned. "We could riff off the small house movement…The Small Band Movement."

Moss shook his head. "Sounds too much like a bowel movement."

So far nothing beat Zander's suggestion—Freed at Last, though Jared's four-year-old was still lobbying hard for The Fairy Dragons. Jared himself wanted Orphan Three, and Kayla had suggested The Snicketty Lemons.

Seth was laughing at Moss's suggestion when Gayle poked her head around the door. "Ready to go, sweetie?"

He grinned over the screen. "Give me two minutes."

"So it worked out with Mel then?" Moss asked.

"That was my mother. But yeah, things worked out with Mel. Turned out I was more homesick than heartsick." *Thank you, Doctor Dimity.* "I'll fill you in some time. Right now, I'm taking my parents out to dinner."

Moss grinned. "Off you go then, sweetie."

"Fuck off," Seth said kindly.

"That is in my plans, yes…good luck with your dad."

"Thanks, I need it."

His mother had her 'going out' perfume on, the one that smelled of gardenias. It gave Seth a pang seeing her excitement. As far as Gayle was concerned her husband and son were well on their way to reconciliation, and he didn't have the heart to tell her any different.

He thought of what Janey had said earlier. It was true, his father was always at work—even tonight, he was meeting them at the restaurant—and yet Seth had never felt his absence through their childhood. His mother's enthusiasm and support filled any gap. Made him believe he had two loving and involved parents. Had he? He pushed the thought aside for another time.

"You look nice, Mum." From a Kiwi son, that was an effusive compliment.

She beamed. "You told me to dress up."

He'd pre-booked the best restaurant in town from LA a couple of weeks earlier, figuring that if parents could try to buy their kids' love, it could work the other way with his dad. After today's events, that plan now seemed incredibly *naïve*. So he wasn't the least bit surprised when his father bailed with a text as Seth was feeding coins into the parking meter. If anything, he was relieved that they wouldn't have to pretend everything was fine in front of Gayle.

"Frank says he's too tired to go out." She looked up from her cell with a worried frown. "I hope he's okay. Maybe we should postpone?"

He ruined my day, he's not ruining our evening. Taking his mother's arm, Seth steered her toward the brightly-lit bar and restaurant precinct. "Dad will be fine after an early night, and it will be more fun with the two of us." *The world does not have to revolve around Frank Curran.*

He asked for a table outside so Gayle could people-watch and when she excused herself to go to the bathroom, he ordered a bottle of champagne, determined to spoil her.

Through the restaurant's French doors he glimpsed his mother on her cell near the hostess stand. Of course she'd phone Dad to double-check he was okay. He hoped his father appreciated his luck.

As he waited for her return, Mel walked past with an armful of groceries. She'd mentioned at his party that she'd moved to an apartment around here.

She laughed when she saw the champagne bucket. "How the other half live!"

"Stay for a glass," he invited.

"I don't want to ruin your hot date. Where *is* Dimity?"

"Waiheke." He experienced a strong urge to tell Mel the truth about his 'girlfriend'. Keeping secrets from the people he cared about made him too like his father. "Mum's my date tonight and she doesn't mind threesomes."

Chuckling, Mel shook her head. "Kevin's waiting for ingredients."

Screw it, he was going to come clean. They could laugh about what an idiot he'd been. "Before you go, I need to confess something. Dimity and I haven't been dating. We pretended she was my girlfriend because…well, the reasons don't matter now."

"You're lying."

He took a second to register her response. "What?"

"Remember the night you sent me all those texts about Dimity? Later you pocket dialed me."

"I'm not following."

Color tinged Mel's cheeks. "*Home-baked cookies* ring any bells?"

"Should they?"

"What about *raw beefcake*?" She waited.

"I have no idea what you're talking about. Menus?"

"Dimity was baiting you. And then you said—" She faltered.

Memory hit like a freight train. *I will fuck you, unless you tell me no.* Heat suffused his face. "We were drunk and it was…" He hesitated, unwilling to call it a mistake.

Messy, sure. Complicated, hell yes. But Dimity been there for him when he'd needed her. And that hadn't happened in a very long time.

"I need to ask you a question. Answer it honestly." Mel lifted her chin. "Were you faithful to me before we broke up?"

"What? Yes!"

She gave him a considered look and said coldly, "I don't believe you." And walked on before he could respond.

Incensed, Seth jumped the railing and followed. "So I have to believe your relationship with Kevin never went beyond friendship while we were together, but you won't give me the same benefit of the doubt?"

"Don't yell at me in public. *I'm* not the one caught in a lie."

"It's not as simple as—" He started to explain and then stopped, sick and tired of always being the one in the wrong with her.

She'd ended their relationship months before he'd slept with another woman. What had Dimity said? *She doesn't have the right to your business anymore.*

"You know what? I've dealt with enough bullshit for one day." Maybe Mel hadn't cheated on him with Kevin, but their attraction hadn't come out of nowhere. While Seth was being loyal and faithful and trying to make their long-distance relationship work, she'd been flirting with—and falling for—another guy. "You don't want to believe me? Fine. Walk away."

And damn it, she did.

Astonished, furious, he was still staring after her when his mother called his name.

He took a deep breath and pinned a smile on his face before returning. "I thought I might have left the car lights on."

"Oh, it would have beeped when you tried to lock it."

"Yeah, I figured that out." He jumped the railing and poured her a flute of champagne. "How's Dad?"

She laughed sheepishly. "You were right, he's fine."

The waitress arrived with menus and Gayle glowed when she asked for Seth's autograph. Her maternal pride bought an unexpected ache to his chest. It can't have been easy living with his disappointed father these past months, but never once had she complained. It had always been, "Do what you need to, darling, I'll handle your dad."

Mel should have been more supportive of his dream. He'd always supported hers. Their lives had revolved around her five a.m. swim training. He could recall only two weekends when she'd said, "Screw an early bedtime, I'm watching you play a gig."

Encouragement went both ways. With that reminder, he shoved his disappointment in Mel aside and concentrated on showing his mother a bloody good time.

"Crayfish," he told the waitress.

"Oh, sweetie," Gayle protested. "Isn't that expensive?"

"Very expensive." Leaning forward, he kissed her cheek. "But you're worth it."

Finishing their main course, she said out of the blue. "I know your father's difficult. I'm sorry, honey."

"Don't take this on yourself, Ma." He dug the last morsel of white meat from the crayfish tail.

She pushed her plate aside. "I could have tried harder to make him see reason."

"Hey, Dad and I will work this out. You don't have to be the intermediary anymore. I'm all grown up." *And it's my turn to look out for you.*

"Yes, you are." A mischievous look replaced her frown as she rinsed her fingers in the finger bowl. "Dimity's smitten."

Seth laughed, imagining Dimity's face if she heard this. The women in his family were crap at reading people. "I'd say she likes to keep me guessing."

"Which is as it should be." Gayle was silent as she dried her fingers on a napkin. "I'm glad you didn't end up with Mel," she confided.

"You're kidding?" They'd been together for so many years he'd thought both their families considered them as good as married.

"I love her to bits, but she's not the right woman for you, not long term."

"As events have proved," Seth said grimly. He hated the thought that their relationship had only worked so well for so long because he'd been easygoing. "But why don't *you* think we're suited?"

"No chemistry," she said simply. "You acted like an old married couple and if you do that when you're young, then God help your sex life by the time you hit your thirtieth anniversary." She smiled into her glass. "That's one thing your father and I still have going for us."

"*Okaaay*. I'm not totally comfortable with this subject." He'd forgotten his mother was a lightweight with alcohol.

"Stop being a baby and listen. I'm giving champagne wisdom here."

"Yeah, I picked that up."

The waitress delivered the dessert menus and he was grateful for the reprieve.

"The spark isn't just confined to sex," his mother continued, accepting the dessert menu. "There should be sparks in other areas as well."

Ignoring Seth's groan, she smiled at the waitress. "Give us a couple of minutes, sweetie."

"Um…sure." He noticed she stayed within earshot.

"The best relationships have their own kind of alchemy." Unconcerned, Gayle opened the dessert menu. "That's why I think Dimity is a better choice for you. You've got to have a partner who'll challenge you to grow to your full potential. Or what's the point?"

Despite himself, he became fascinated. "Does Dad do that for you, Ma?"

She gestured for the waitress. "We're ready to order now."

So just the sex then.

After they'd ordered a crème brûlée for Gayle and an affogato for Seth, she leaned forward. "I am challenging your father to change," she confided. "Your leaving, while painful, will probably be the best thing for him. He needs to retire so we can start spending some of that hard-earned cash on *us*."

"Good for you, Ma." Seth toasted her, before making another silent one to his father.

Dad, you're going to take my bloody money if I have to ram it down your throat.

Chapter 14

It was terribly important to get this meeting right, so at noon the next day Seth dressed like the businessman he used to be, in a gray suit, white business shirt, and striped tie. He'd dug them out of the closet where he'd asked his mother to store them, dry-cleaned and protected under plastic. Relics of a previous life, and, with hindsight, a back-up plan if music didn't pan out.

It still might not pan out, but the days of second-guessing himself were gone. He made a mental note to drop the suits off at a charity shop before he left New Zealand.

He hadn't seen his father since their heated argument yesterday. By the time he and Gayle had rolled home, slightly the worse for wear, Frank was in bed.

He'd heard the murmur of voices when his mother retired though, and his father's wariness as he wondered what Seth had divulged to Gayle…

Nothing. This was between them.

He'd sent Dimity a text before he brushed his teeth.

Think of me when you're machinating tonight.

Her reply came when his mouth was still full of toothpaste, and he nearly choked laughing—a shot of a crazy-eyed, razor-toothed honey badger in full snarl mode.

After rinsing his mouth out, he responded. *Stop sending naked pictures.*

She'd replied instantly. *Pervert.*

I love it when you talk dirty.

She'd stopped then, obviously realizing she couldn't win.

Climbing into bed, he heard his mother giggle next door and

recalled her comment that sex still worked for her and his dad. He slept with a pillow over his head. It smelled of Dimity. Strangely addictive.

First thing this morning, he'd phoned the office and asked Yvonne to block out some time after lunch so Frank had no excuse to cut their meeting short. He had also requested she not divulge that he was the one-thirty appointment. "It's a surprise."

She'd assumed he'd meant a good one. That was up to Frank.

He printed his financial statements on his mother's printer and borrowed one of her plastic manila folders, feeling like a kid about to do show-and-tell in class. "See, Dad. I did good."

The tough part would be getting Frank to reciprocate with the company's current financial accounts, but Seth wasn't throwing his savings away. He had to know if the downturn was due to a management issue. If his father had dropped the ball, then they'd need to employ a fixer. Another fun conversation to have after this one.

He arrived ten minutes before Frank was due back from lunch and settled in the meeting room opposite the reception desk, deliberately leaving the door open. When Frank saw who his one-thirty was, he pivoted, only to meet Yvonne's smile as she glanced up from the counter.

"Just like old times, isn't it?"

Got you, Seth thought. Appearances had always been important to his father.

Reluctantly, Frank re-entered the meeting room, taking in Seth's suit and the manila folder lying on the table, the documents neatly lined up in front of him. "Haven't we done this already?" he demanded in a low growl.

"I'm here to represent Mum's interests." Seth gestured to a chair. "Why doesn't she know the business is in financial trouble?"

"For God's sake." Hastily, his father shut the door. "You haven't told her that, have you? She didn't say anything last night."

Seth gestured to the chair again, waiting until Frank sat. "Not yet…not ever if I can make you see sense. Isn't it better to let me invest than sell it at a loss? And for what, Dad, pride?"

Frank went to speak and Seth held up a hand. "I'm not finished. I know we don't see eye-to-eye but we're still family. Please. Let me help, for Mum and Janey's sake, if not your own. I had my accountant prepare some financial statements." He pushed one of the documents across the table. "I can go up to two hundred grand."

"I don't *need* your money." Impatiently, his father pushed it back. "The business is doing great, better than ever."

Seth slammed his palm down on the table, making him jump. "Don't bullshit me. You said you were being forced to sell."

"No, I said I had no *choice.*" Frank was silent a moment, as though weighing his next words. "I had a health scare a while back. A transient ischemic attack—TIA, they call it."

"A *stroke*?"

"Not as bad," his father blustered. "A clot blocks blood supply to the brain, but only briefly. That's why I'm not driving. I'm on a stand-down period for six months because it happened while I was behind the wheel."

"Jesus, Dad." So *that's* why Jeff was giving him rides to work. "Are you okay?"

Frank swatted his concern aside. "I'm fine as long as I keep my blood pressure down. Eat healthy, exercise, reduce my hours—all the boring stuff."

Other puzzle pieces fell into place. All Bran, not pancakes, the morning walk to the shop for the newspaper.

"When I thought I was on my deathbed I foolishly promised your mother I'd sell and she's holding me to it." Frank scowled.

"Wait...back up." Seth was struggling to process. "*When* did this happen?"

"May." And it was November.

"But...no one phoned me."

"I told them not to." Frank shrugged, looked at his hands. "I didn't want to make a fuss."

"Dad, you thought you were on your *deathbed.* That means it was serious."

"You were busy in your new life." There was a note in his voice that was almost triumph.

The final puzzle piece fell into place. *And you were punishing me.* He knew it as clearly as if Frank had set the words to music. Discordant, clashing, ear-splitting music. "And if it had been a major stroke?" he challenged. "If you'd died? Well, that would have shown me, wouldn't it, Dad?"

His father's gaze slid away from his. "Don't be childish."

"I had a *right* to know. I resigned from the job, not being your son."

Still, Frank couldn't meet his eyes. "Now you're being melodramatic."

Seth stood, his anger compressing and solidifying into something impervious and hard. "And all the family knew," he said slowly. Mum. Janey. Dad's brother and sister. Seth's cousins. The whole goddamn family. And no one broke rank and called him.

He gathered his documents and replaced them in the manila folder, neatly and precisely. "You talk about loyalty, but where's your loyalty to me? From the moment I chose a different road you've blanked me." He felt nothing except a kind of bitter relief. "Congratulations, you win."

"What's that supposed to mean?"

"You're a smart man." He loosened his tie and ripped it off, dropping it on the boardroom table where it coiled like a venomous snake. "Work it out."

Seth caught a cab home and packed, then began scrawling a note for his mother who was out shopping, then scrunched it up and gave her the courtesy of a phone call. Gayle was upset when he told her why he was leaving and full of excuses.

"Frank made me promise in the ambulance that I wouldn't call you. Made everyone promise. He was agitated, we needed to calm him down."

"If he'd died, Mum…"

"It became clear within a couple of hours that it was a TIA, not a stroke. And you were in Europe, at least thirty hours away. If it *had* proved a life-and-death situation, you wouldn't have made it."

"And that makes it okay?" He felt so betrayed his voice shook. If you're lucky, you have people in your life you can trust absolutely. Today, he felt like he'd lost two of them—his mother and Janey. His father he didn't give a damn about anymore.

"Sweetie, I'm sorry. I felt *terrible* lying to you, but I didn't want you blaming yourself, either, thinking your leaving brought on his hypertension. The doctor said your father's family history, and his workaholic lifestyle, made an episode inevitable. Really, the TIA was a blessing, because he's making changes."

Frank Curran will never change. "Well, I'm relieving him of one of his stressors by leaving for Waiheke Island."

"Seth, please don't put all the blame on your father for this. In the end it was a family decision."

"Yeah," he said. "That's what hurts the most."

He thought of his efforts to firewall his estrangement with his dad

and keep Mum and Janey in a functioning relationship with Frank—
defending their father to his sister, staying at home to save his mother
distress, hiding his loneliness and disappointment all these months. "I
thought I was part of this family."

♪ ♫ ♩

"Dotterels, huh?" Dimity looked at the sign that said *Don't crush us!*,
above a picture of cartoon baby birds about to be stomped on by a large
hiking boot. She wiggled her toes inside the ones she'd borrowed from
Elizabeth. They were too big, and she wore thick wool socks to bulk
them up.

"How could you not own practical shoes?" Elizabeth had exclaimed.

"Because then I'd have to come to places like this." Nature was
unfamiliar to her, and she was happy to keep their acquaintance to a
casual wave from the window of an air-conditioned vehicle.

"If these birds are dumb enough to lay their eggs on a beach covered
with white shells, then maybe they deserve their near extinction. Didn't
they learn anything from the dodo experience?"

She'd spent the morning unpacking her files and setting her laptop
up in Zander's office, a plywood-paneled room on the shady side of the
house where light wasn't an issue for computer screens. He or
Elizabeth had softened its spartan woodiness with a Persian rug from
Zander's LA house. Dimity had taken off her heels and wriggled her
bare toes in its soft silkiness, intensely homesick for the mansion, her
cat, her life.

The homesickness was not helped by discovering how much work
he'd done behind her back, in transitioning to his retirement. He was
actually doing a fair job of putting out feelers for staff. Half the roadies
had back-up job offers touring next summer with Zee's 'mates' The
Stones—the opportunistic bastards.

Even now, Zee was industriously going through the long-service
names she'd flung at him yesterday, trying to figure out where he could
place them. She needed to get back and supervise before he started the
diaspora; equally, she needed to bond with Elizabeth. "Why are we
here, exactly?"

"Because I knew Zander wouldn't want to come with us."
Elizabeth paused to un-snag a strand of her crazy corkscrew hair from a
low-hanging branch on the narrow path leading to the beach. "I've

dragged him here so often since I've developed an interest in bird-watching."

"Aren't you nerdy enough?"

Elizabeth laughed.

Dimity followed her past the second sign—*Diversion Avoiding Dotterel Breeding Area*—to the track wending through clumpy grass behind the beach.

"If we're patient, we might spot them sitting on their eggs." Elizabeth dug in her rucksack and pulled out binoculars. "They're virtually invisible when they're still." She offered the binoculars to Dimity, who waved them aside.

"Okay, Doc Doolittle," she said. "What's going on with the book? More importantly, why aren't you sharing it with Zee? Aren't you two one mind, one heart and all that crap?"

"I can tell he's secretly worried about me signing up for this project." As Elizabeth spoke, she stopped every dozen paces to scan the beach through the binoculars. "If he knew how much I was struggling with this whole experience, he'd feel even worse."

Secretly, really? Zee already had his guard dogs in place—Luther, for her physical safety; Dimity to steer publicity; with Zander poised to do something outrageous to divert attention if Elizabeth was taking too much heat. Between them, they'd protect her from the paparazzi and shit-eaters out there.

The crazies.

Maybe he hadn't told Elizabeth all his save-the-day measures because he didn't want to scare her with what could lie ahead?

But of *course* Elizabeth understood the possible consequences. On tour she'd seen firsthand the downside of fame. And had her own taste of being tabloid fodder when she'd started working for Zee. A photojournalist with a long lens had snapped her trying on a bathing suit, the accompanying caption asking whether Zander would be interested in screwing "an under-endowed PhD" instead of his usual double Ds. Because that's how nasty the media could get.

Elizabeth lowered the binoculars. "Zander's dealing with enough challenges without me burdening him with mine."

Dimity had the full picture now, and it was kinda sweet. Zee was trying to protect Elizabeth without alarming her. And Elizabeth didn't want to worry him by sharing her anxieties. Both of them putting on a brave face to each other and sharing their fears with Dimity.

She opened her mouth to set Elizabeth straight, then closed it. Better to remain their only confidante. For now. It would help her cause.

Elizabeth had resumed her scan of the foreshore. "Naked covers, a proposed world tour for the launch next year...next Max will be suggesting I conduct interviews from bed, to mirror the title. It's no wonder I'm having trouble writing the damn book!"

Filing another great marketing idea away, Dimity opted for reassurance. "I told Max we wanted to pitch alternative cover ideas. I'll sort something out." Subtly, she reminded her friend she was on her side. "Now what's this trouble you're having writing the book?" Writers—always so dramatic on deadline.

"There could be an issue when I deliver the manu—there!" Thrusting the binoculars at Dimity, she pointed a direction.

Dimity took a look, and saw a speckled bird with a head not dissimilar in shape to a seagull, with black eyes and bill and tawny coloring on its breast. "That's it?"

"They probably look like plovers to you."

"I don't know what plovers are."

"Now that's just sad," Elizabeth said. "Did your parents never take you outside?"

"Of course they did. We had ski holidays, resort breaks." Dimity watched the bird, waiting for it to do something interesting.

"I mean, into nature—camping, hiking."

"Not their thing...they were city-limits people."

"Well, I think that's terrible. Let me be your guide."

It was a novel experience to be told she'd had a deprived childhood. "Thanks, but I don't think I've missed much." She was about to drop the binoculars when the bird finally moved. "It's hurt." Instinctively she moved to its aid.

Elizabeth grabbed her arm. "No, it's a con, we must be near its nest."

"Are you positive? It looks like it's trailing a broken wing."

"Let's move away and you'll see I'm right."

They walked another twenty yards down the beach. Sure enough, the bird reverted to a normal gait.

"Now *that*," Dimity said, "is seriously cool." Then she remembered they were here for business and returned the binoculars. "You were saying there might be a problem when you deliver the manuscript."

"An *issue*," Elizabeth corrected. She started wrapping and unwrapping the binocular's strap around her index finger. "*In Bed With A Rock God* might not be as sexy as the publisher is expecting."

"Haven't they already approved the first three chapters?"

"I put the foreplay stuff up front. First meet, sexual tension. I can write sexual tension. I think readers would prefer the sex implied." The strap was so tight around her index finger it was turning bright red.

"And the success of *Fifty Shades* was what? An aberration? Women will buy the book to find out what it's like to have sex with a rock star, specifically *your* rock star."

"Then there are plenty of others they can ask," Elizabeth snapped. She released the strap and her finger regained its normal color. "*My* point of difference," she said reverting to her usual calm tone, "is that I'm the only one who knows what it's like to be loved by Zander Freedman. Now that's something special."

"Very touching, but you pitched a nerd-out-of-water-falls-for-a-hot-rock-star, humorous, tongue-in-cheek, behind-the-scenes boinkbuster. Not *Sense and Sensibility*."

Elizabeth looked furtive. "Does it count if I'm stripping Zander Freedman bare in a *metaphorical* sense?"

"Oh, God." Dimity felt the need to sit down. "*Please* tell me you haven't written a *love* story." The book was vital to Zander's reintegration into the rock world she was determined to return him to.

"I tried not to," Elizabeth said in small voice.

Dimity forgot about being her only friend. "This is *not* the time to screw up Zander's reintegration into impolite society! This book will seriously help the rehabilitation of his brand."

The other woman rallied. "You think I don't know that? At the time I pitched it to Max I knew I had to burn bridges to shock Zander into seeing me. So I closed my eyes and jumped into the flames, thinking I'd deal with the burns later." The fight went out of her. "Now it's later." Her voice got smaller. "And that's not the only problem."

Dimity threw up her hands. "I don't need this." Between trying not to sext Seth last night, and plotting today's tactics, she'd hardly slept a wink.

Elizabeth whispered. "It's sentimental."

"Fuck."

"I'm so ashamed." The award-winning literary biographer put her face in her hands. "I write clean, sharp prose that dissects my subject's flaws and strengths and gives both equal page space. Yesterday I wrote three pages of how I feel when he walks toward me across a crowded room."

Desperately Dimity tried to think of a spin. "Were you looking at his hot body?"

"No." Elizabeth bowed her head, as if under a guillotine. "I was looking into his *eyes*."

We are so screwed. For a moment neither spoke. The waves splashed against the shore, dotterels chattered, and the breeze carried the scent of dank seaweed.

Elizabeth looked up. "Ordinarily, I'd be honest with the publisher, return the advance and bow out of the contract. But I can't do that—"

"No, you can't!"

"Didn't I just say that? If I get this right, I can do Zander's reputation an enormous amount of good. And if I don't—" she wrapped her arms around her lanky body "—I'll have failed him when he needs me most." She took a deep breath. "Which is why I need you to read it. You have an instinct for the zeitgeist. *You* can judge its marketability. Maybe it's not the crap I think it is."

"Why haven't you asked Zee? He's got the best instincts of anyone I know."

"Are you kidding, I'm not giving him that crap."

The two women looked at each other.

"If you don't deliver what they want," Dimity said evenly, "they're within rights to cancel the contract and ask for the advance back. And you and Zee need that money right now. Not only will it augment the scandal, you're screwing one of the big five publishers—and they talk. It will negatively impact future contract negotiations of your own books."

Elizabeth said, "I think you have the whole picture now. No way can I jeopardize either of our careers."

Dimity didn't need another crisis—she had too many already. *Seriously, God, what have you got against me?* "Give me a minute," she said. "I'll think of something."

"I already have," Elizabeth said. "Which is why you *really* need to read it. Like I said, you've got an instinctive feel for the zeitgeist. If you say it's crap, you help me rewrite it. If not..."

She waited for Dimity to catch the ball.

"I help you sell the new concept to Max." *Either way, proving myself invaluable, predisposing you to my cause, and putting you in my debt.* "Yes, that will work."

"Okay," Elizabeth said. "We're agreed. Let's head home. I'll clean up what I have and leave it on your desk for tomorrow."

They started the return walk. "So we've sorted out my issue," she added. "Let's try to sort out yours."

"Mine?"

"Ignoring all my actions relating to this bloody book, I'm not dumb. You haven't accepted Zee's decision and you're looking for an ally."

Jesus, this woman was sharp.

Dimity took a deep breath. "I truly believe Zee's making a huge mistake. Will you keep an open mind while I tell you why?"

"You're my friend, we both love him. Of course I will."

She let the love thing slide. Affection, respect…hell, did they have to label everything? "His life needs to change—I don't dispute that," she began. "We both saw the burn-out. But he's got the two of us now to make sure it doesn't happen again. That it doesn't take the same toll on him."

Elizabeth listened attentively, and Dimity's hopes rose as she made her case. "Zee says you changed him for the better. That he's worried he might revert to bad habits. But he's forgetting how many he'd already dropped." *Drinking, drugs, press-baiting.* "He'd already made positive changes before you came onto the scene. He's not giving himself enough credit for that."

If she could just get this woman onside, then together, they could change Zander's mind.

Slyly, she threw in a personal angle. "As a writer you know that creativity isn't something you *do*, it's something you *are*. It's where you find your joy." That's what this job meant to her, something she'd created from nothing, a world, an empire, an identity. It wasn't art as Elizabeth and Zander understood it, but to Dimity it was everything. "Performing is oxygen to Zee, he needs it to breathe."

By the time she'd finished her pitch they were climbing the track to the house and she was almost breathless from the weight of hope. "What concerns me is that he's burning bridges." Deliberately, she finished by echoing Elizabeth's earlier phrasing. "It will be so much harder for him to start again in a year or two. He can return now and still have a balanced life. It doesn't have to be all or nothing."

They reached the top and wind buffeted them as the ground fell away on all sides. "So what do you think?"

Elizabeth was silent until they reached a huge, gnarled tree twenty yards from the house, then she stopped to pick up a fallen leaf stem, turning it over in her hands. Its leaves were dark green and glossy, clustered in sets of five, like fingers. "Here's what it comes down to for me. I love the man. And the man doesn't want to be a rock star anymore."

Disappointment kicked strategy to the curb. "Zander could never be happy outside Rage," she said sharply. "He'll miss it too much. Wasn't I right last time I gave you advice? After the lip-syncing when the press was baying for his blood, I said, 'Don't go to him. Let him protect you.' If you'd rushed to his rescue, he would have rejected you out of hand. Now it's your turn to protect him from making the worst decision of his life."

"My job is to protect his heart, and his heart's not in this anymore. I'm sorry. I can't side with you on this."

"It's not about taking sides…" Even as she said it, Dimity thought, *No, it is coming to that. I'm the lone voice of reason.* "It's about safeguarding all our futures. You've spent the past six months researching his history. You know that in everything he does, Zee acts first and thinks later."

"He follows his instincts."

"Same thing. Your best shot at a happy-ever-after is keeping him where he belongs. In the band. He'll be miserable living out of the spotlight." They could have it all, why couldn't Elizabeth see that?

"Once he's tired of playing house…once the novelty wears off, he's going to regret this choice." Dimity hated spiking Elizabeth's anxiety levels, but she needed to hear the truth. "He may even blame you. It'll be unfair, but that's how it goes."

"If he does, I'll remind him this was his choice. I can't let my fears for the future derail us before we've even started. I have to trust his commitment."

"Like I did," Dimity said bitterly. "Good luck with that."

"I understand you're having a hard time with this, but Zander hasn't made the decision lightly. He tells me he knows what he's doing."

"And you believe him?"

"I believe in him. When you love someone, it's as simple,"

Elizabeth smiled wryly, "and as complicated as that."

I believed in him, too. And suddenly he's converting to another faith. One she had no access to. Dimity remembered the way Zee had smiled at Elizabeth this morning as they'd left for their walk, as though she held his heart in her hands. For a fleeting moment Dimity had even wondered what it would be like to love and be loved like that. To trust someone that much. Her imagination conjured Seth. *Gah, this shit is catching. We all need to get off this island ASAP.*

"I'll say one more thing," Dimity said, "and never raise the subject again. Zee said he's not doing this for you, but I don't believe that's true. He loves you and wants to make you happy. And he thinks this is the only way to do that. The question you need to ask is, would he be choosing differently if you weren't in his life?"

"I think a more important question is, what does Zander need from me right now? And that's my unconditional support."

"Okay." Dimity held up her hands. "We're done here."

Elizabeth's gaze was searching. "Are we still friends?"

Dimity managed a smile. "Of course we are." *Which is why I'm going to save you both from making the worst mistake of your lives.*

Working with Zee had taught her that failure didn't count unless you quit trying to achieve your goal—however impossible that goal seemed to other people. Every success they'd had together had been built on that philosophy.

"For the record," Elizabeth said as they approached the house. "History has shown Yoko was grossly misjudged."

Dimity laughed. "I got you with that one, huh?"

Inside, she was satisfied. She'd sown seeds of disquiet and truth would make them grow. However calm Elizabeth appeared, she would think about Dimity's arguments—she was too smart a woman not to. Zee only needed to *sense* that Elizabeth had doubts about his actions to start questioning the rightness of his decision—the biographer was that important to him.

The man they'd been discussing sat on the deck. He must have finished his errands early and forgotten his key. Catching sight of them, he stood and walked out from the shadow of the porch, where sunlight sparked red in his hair. Not Zander.

Dimity's heart skipped a beat, and she told herself it was annoyance. She wasn't in the mood for playing, not when she was trying to save their world.

"Seth," Elizabeth called delightedly "We weren't expecting you until tomorrow."

"I hope you don't mind me showing up early. I needed time out from family obligations."

"Of course not." She hugged him. "It's wonderful to see you. Stay as long as you like."

"Let me get back to you on that." He turned to Dimity and she braced herself, but above his easy smile, his blue eyes were bleak.

He wasn't here to pick up where they'd left off——he was seeking refuge. "Honey B, I almost didn't recognize you in those sensible hiking boots."

What happened? She bit back the question because if he'd wanted to tell them, he would have done it already.

"Even more amazing, I've been bird-watching," she said, recalling the bird feigning a broken wing. This man was broken and pretending to be fine.

And even though she still had at least half a dozen Herculean tasks ahead of her, she couldn't stop herself touching him, taking his arm. "Come inside and tell us what you've been up to."

CHAPTER 15

FIVE HOURS LATER, DESPITE HER best efforts, Dimity still had no idea what the hell had happened to Seth.

The atmosphere around the green baize card table where the four of them sat playing the Kiwi version of 500 and drinking whiskey reminded her of a circus performance she'd seen as a child.

Her father had paid top dollar for their seats, positioning them so close to the action—beaming clowns on a tricycle on a high-wire—she could see the sweat and grimace of effort under the grease-paint. Her eleven-year-old self had become uneasy. Something about them reminded her of her parents. Two days later, her father left them.

She had the same sense of impending doom watching her card partner, who was laughing, joking and betting recklessly. And could not seem to sit still.

Between hands, Seth kept getting up—to refill his whiskey glass, pace the room, or walk to the French doors to stare out at the night sky, as he was doing now.

"Deal ten cards," Zander reminded her. Returning her attention to the table, she saw she'd stopped after five. "Sorry."

These apologies had to stop. Now Zee was looking at *her* as she dealt out the extra cards.

Picking up his hand, he bid. "Eight diamonds…Seth, you want to join us?"

The drummer returned to the table and downed the contents of his whiskey glass. "This one, I'm going to win."

As he sorted his cards, she, Elizabeth, and Zee exchanged glances. "So I'm guessing the helping-Seth-get-his-girlfriend-back thing isn't going well," Zander had said when Seth was unpacking. The others were in the kitchen preparing dinner, and Dimity was setting the table.

"We dropped the idea." She sifted through the cutlery drawer, grateful that the task meant she didn't have to meet his eyes. "He decided they're better off as friends."

"Zander said Seth's having a terrible time with his father," Elizabeth commented as she stuck a knife into the roast potatoes in the oven, checking if they were cooked.

Dimity dropped the napkins. "Can we keep that between us?" Kicking herself for saying anything, she retrieved them from the floor. "Seth is a private person."

Infuriatingly so. She hadn't managed to get a damn thing out of him as to what was wrong. "If you keep trying to be alone with me, Honey B," he'd told her on their third 'unplanned' encounter, "I'll think you want me."

The only good thing about his shutdown was that he hadn't asked for an update on Zee's voice. And she hadn't had to lie to him.

Now, as Elizabeth considered her bid, he tapped out a nervous staccato beat on his thighs. "I need another whiskey." Abruptly he stood up again. "Anyone else want one?"

"I'd love a cup of tea," Dimity said, hoping to slow his drinking down. Alcohol was only making him more restless. She felt like a doctor waiting for her patient's fever to break.

"Coming right up." He disappeared down the hall leading to the kitchen.

Elizabeth was still considering her cards. "You haven't taken your eyes off Seth since he got here. What's going on between you two?"

"Nothing. He's my card partner and I'm reading his signals." Nonchalantly, Dimity pushed back her chair, seeking an escape route. "I'll see if he needs a hand."

"It'll be the only decent one he's had from you since we started playing," Zander commented dryly. "And since when do you drink hot tea?"

Since Elizabeth started noticing my interest in Seth.

Her cell rang, enabling her to ignore his question. Caller ID showed Janey's number. Maybe Seth's sister could fill in the gaps.

Excusing herself, she started walking away for privacy. "Hi, Janey. Nice to hear from you."

Behind her, Zee said to Elizabeth, "And why have *you* been staring at me all night, and not in your usual, 'I can't wait to rip your clothes off' kind of way, more like a 'Let me imprint your adorable little face in my memory' kind of way?"

Dimity's steps faltered. She knew why. The seeds were starting to germinate.

"Is my brother with you?" Janey recalled Dimity to her surroundings.

"Yes, he is." She walked on.

"He's not answering my calls and I really need to talk to him. Would you get him for me?"

"Of course." Dimity headed toward the kitchen. "What's going on?" It wasn't like Seth to ignore Janey.

"He found out we kept something from him." As she listened to Janey's explanation—and excuses—Dimity came to a dead halt.

"Dimity, are you still there?"

"Yes." She tried to keep her voice neutral.

"I know we stuffed up." The defensiveness in Janey's voice suggested Dimity hadn't succeeded in corralling her disgust. "Please help me."

"I'll try."

Seth wasn't in the kitchen. The kettle was boiling, steam billowing from its spout in a small cloud. As she entered, the auto switch clicked off. The back door was open. She found Seth standing on the porch, forearms resting on the rail and head bowed. He straightened as he heard her footsteps.

"Just checking the view."

It was cloudy, but she didn't challenge him, only said, "Phone for you." Then she passed over her cell and returned inside, pausing on the doorstep.

"Janey…yeah, I got your messages." His tone was impossibly weary. "Uh-huh. Sure, I'll listen."

Dimity continued inside to finish making the tea. As she picked up the kettle she noticed her hands were trembling. Which was crazy, this wasn't her crisis. God knows she had her own to— "He put you in a difficult position. You made the best decision at the time, I get that." The low rumble of Seth's voice grew clearer. He must be pacing outside the kitchen window, left partially ajar. "But you and Mum could have told me later, when he stabilized. You could have told me any time these past six months and you didn't. You treated me like an outsider. You let the bully win."

She put the kettle down and reached across the sink to close the window, but the catch was too high. Seth's voice grew indistinct as he moved away. Needing a task, she looked for teabags, lifting the lids of two pottery jars before finding them in a third.

"I can't even talk about how betrayed I feel. I'm absolutely gutted that you and Mum kept the truth from me."

Okay, he needs privacy. Abandoning the tea-making, Dimity hurried toward the living room.

"Are you sure about leaving Rage?" Elizabeth said. "*Really* sure?"

"Don't you start. I finally got Dimity to accept it, and—wait…has she said something?"

Dimity retreated into the hall, but Elizabeth didn't betray her. "You know I don't kiss and tell…except for a vast amount of money. Answer the question. *Would* you be choosing differently if I wasn't in your life?"

Dimity held her breath.

"I'd already realized that being an asshole egotist wasn't making me happy." Zee's tone held a touch of impatience—suggesting he'd tired of the subject? "You were the intervention, the divine intervention, but if you hadn't come into my life some kind of intervention was still necessary. Would I have known what changes to make? No."

Yes!

"As long as you're making the *right* changes."

"I need you to trust me." No question that he was impatient now. "Why are you having second thoughts about my ability to make this work?"

"I want you to be happy. I want to protect you—"

"I don't need you to protect me. I have this under control."

"Well, at least your yelling voice has come back," Elizabeth said mildly.

Dimity's own feelings were anything but mild. Triumphant. Uneasy. Ever so slightly nauseous. This was the first real breakthrough she'd had. Was it wrong to feel such relief? She didn't wait for Zander's response, quietly retracing her steps. Seth's voice stopped her.

"I can't talk to you about this right now, I'm too angry." He must have walked into the kitchen.

With crises happening on both sides she had no choice but to press against the wall and stay hidden.

"I love you and I'll see you in a couple of days," Seth said curtly. "No, not Dad. I bent over backward to make peace with him over this and frankly I'm all out of giving a damn. If he wants me in his life, he's going to have to make the first move... Yeah, I don't see that happening, either. I have to go."

She had to move before he caught her skulking. She escaped into the living room. "Elizabeth, I didn't ask if you wanted tea?"

Her friend turned her head. Her color was high, her eyes bright with anger, but she answered calmly enough. "Love one, thanks. Milk, no sugar."

Zee didn't turn around. "Mind giving us a couple of minutes?"

Okay you two, have an epiphany that I'm right and I'll ease up on the pressure. "Of course."

Reluctantly, she returned to the kitchen and collided with Seth coming the other way. "Have you finished making the tea? Elizabeth would like one, too. I'll help if you like."

He looked at her blankly for a moment. "Right. Tea. Do you take milk?"

"No, and make it weak." It was the only way she'd be able to drink the stuff. She added casually, "Want one, too, or are you still on the whiskey?"

"No, why risk a hangover?" He looked like he already had one. "I'll have tea, too."

He grabbed another couple of mugs while she re-boiled the kettle and tried not to stare at him anxiously. "Are you finished with my cell?"

"What? Oh yeah, sure." He dug in his pocket. "How does Janey have your number?"

"I texted her a link to an online fashion store I use. She said she couldn't get hold of you—your cell must need charging. Is everything okay?"

She caught his sharp look in her peripheral vision and kept her expression impassive as she added the teabags.

"Do you know what happened today?" he said quietly.

She broke into a sweat. She was tempted to lie, but enough people had betrayed his trust. "Yes." Finally, she could look at him directly. "Do you want to talk about it?"

"No."

Okay, not ready to be looked at. "It doesn't have to be me." She poured the water into the mugs. "What about Mel? She could have some advice."

Seth's laugh was bitter. "Mel isn't interested in being my friend anymore. She thinks I cheated on her while we were still dating."

"With who?"

"You." He gave her the details, and she was outraged.

"How could she not believe you?" Honesty, loyalty, and fidelity were the bedrock of Seth's character. If Mel truly loved him, she'd know he could never lie about something so important.

He opened the fridge and got out the milk carton. "I don't care anymore. Who takes milk?"

His defeatist attitude frightened her. Seth was the optimist, the guy who said, "We'll find a way."

"Everyone but me," she said. "I really think we should talk this through."

He added milk to two mugs. "Not even you could come up with an excuse for Mum and Janey that I haven't already dredged up myself."

She bled for him. "They didn't know how much it would hurt you?"

"Well, they should have known." He slammed the milk carton on the counter. "I know what hurts them. I'm making peace with Dad mostly for Mum's sake. I've kept Janey from taking sides because I don't want her suffering the fallout. All my life I've been the buffer because I can handle disappointment and pain better than the people I love. Well, not this time. I'm hurt and bitter and rising above it is beyond me."

Dimity couldn't bear it. She made a move toward him. "Seth—"

Zander walked in. "I'm here for Doc's tea," he said. "I need to grovel."

"What did you do?" Seth passed him a mug.

"Overreacted," he said. "Hard to believe, I know." His volatility was infamous in the industry, but Dimity hadn't seen it since she'd arrived on the island and put doubts into Elizabeth's head. She felt like a snake in the Garden of Eden. Events were spiraling beyond her control. Short-term pain for long-term gain, she told herself. *Hold your nerve. It's working.*

In the living room, Zander gave Elizabeth her tea and she raised her face for a kiss. It was tentative, tender, missing their usual passion. Their commitment was still so new, Dimity had to be careful not to do real damage. Could she be going too far? She glanced at Seth, lost and lonely, to strengthen her resolve.

No. She had to keep trying to save Rage, for all their sakes, even if it meant shaking foundations. For some of them, the band was all they had.

Seth looked at the card table and remained standing. "I hate to be the buzzkill but I need an early night. Mind if we finish the game another time?"

"That suits me," Elizabeth said, standing. "I want to print my manuscript. Dimity's agreed to read it," she told Zander.

"That's great." Zander looked at Dimity. "I guess we could put in a couple of hours, too." Because that's what they did. Worked.

"Not tonight," she said. Conscious that she could be setting herself up for a mighty fall, she walked over to Seth and held out her hand. "Bed?"

He looked at her. "Is this a pity fuck?" His voice was low, low enough so only she could hear it.

"You expect *me* to distinguish between empathy and sympathy?"

His mouth twitched. "Good enough."

He took her hand. "We're dating," he said, leading her toward the sleep-out.

"It's not serious," Dimity clarified over her shoulder. "Don't make a big deal of it."

There was absolute silence in their wake.

Outside, he stopped on the path that led to the sleep-out's second bedroom. Squeezing her hand, he released it. "I love sex with you, Honey B, but I'm not on my game tonight. Can we take a rain check?"

He'd said yes, so he could say no in private. Even at his lowest ebb, he'd considered her pride.

Maybe she could find the guts to forget hers for him. Because she wasn't leaving him while he felt so alone.

"Or I could take a turn at guessing your sexual fantasy."

"My sexual fantasy, Honey B, was to make you scream, and—"

"If you say mission accomplished, I'll make *you* scream...and it won't be pleasurable."

"For future reference, S and M is not my thing. You might have picked that up from my wimpy reaction to the hurty hand I got hitting Luther."

"And then some."

"So if you were planning on tying me up…?"

"Stop fishing." Every quip he made reflected his courage. Did he have any idea how that unraveled her? "Wait, do you want to be tied up?" she added.

"Hell, yeah. But not tonight. Tonight?" He sighed. "I need to be alone." Leaning forward, he kissed her lightly. "I hope you understand."

"Totally." She recaptured his hand, tangling her fingers through his. "You want to hole up and brood. Pull all the hurt and the pain and the loneliness inside until you've made it your ally. Something that reminds you why it's easier not to give a fuck every time you're tempted to give anyone the benefit of the doubt." Tightening her hold, she started tugging him toward her room. "I'm not letting you do that. There are too many of us in the world already."

"Yeah?" He dug in his heels, forcing a standoff. "How are you going to stop me?"

"I'm going to do something for you tonight that I've never done for any guy."

He stopped trying to loosen her grip. "Okay, I'm intrigued. What's that?"

She took a deep breath. "I'm going to be tender."

Chapter 16

SETH HONESTLY HADN'T THOUGHT HE had a glimmer of real amusement in him tonight, but holy hell, Dimity found it. He laughed.

Her earnestness faded and she dropped his hand. "Fuck you."

"I'm sorry." He tried to look contrite.

"This is a big deal for me, you should be more appreciative."

And wasn't that a trigger word for the anger simmering inside him. "I'm tired of being appreciative," he said bluntly. "Tired of being grateful. And bloody tired of considering everyone's feelings while they stomp all over mine…" He ran a hand over his face. "Honey B, I'm not in a good space for this."

"You want to be the one taken care of for a change," she said.

"Hell, yeah."

She raised her eyebrows. "That's what I'm offering."

"Tenderness?" If he was up for sex tonight, it would be for the sex she preferred. The savage marauder kind. He felt rubbed raw and so angry.

She shrugged, awkward suddenly. "I'm not saying I'll be any good at it," she said. "But I'm willing to give it a try."

This was hard for her, but she was concerned for him. Concerned enough to go public. Cared enough to offer what she thought he needed. Who the hell had done that for him lately? Perversely, he resented having to consider anyone else's feelings tonight. He wanted to brood over his family's sins and pick at the scabs. But this was a big deal for her.

"I am appreciative," he began.

"Good." She reclaimed his hand and continued to her room.

He went because he couldn't be that much of an asshole.

Her bedroom, like his, was all about the view but the overcast night had removed it. The picture window reflected the room, whose spartan bareness was enlivened with kitschy seaside-themed touches.

Dimity's laptop sat on the battered dresser which had drawer pulls of rope, artfully tufted on the ends. A lifebuoy hung above the double bed and shells lined the sill.

It was easy to see what stuff was hers and what wasn't. Clothes lay scattered in heaps of silk and expensive fabric on the seagrass matting, indicating someone used to a housekeeper. Creams and lotions in fancy bottles crowded the bedside table, gold and silver chains and rings glittered on the bedside table.

"I thought we'd start with a massage," she said.

Maybe this could work. His neck and shoulders were knotted with tension. He stripped off his T-shirt, took off his watch, and placed both on the floor. "Where do you want me?"

Dimity picked up a small tub from the dresser. "Sit on the end of the bed and I'll scoot behind you. We don't want coconut butter over everything…wait, let me move this."

The bed cover was a pretty quilt made of colorful fabric squares, and she folded it carefully to one side. He sat.

Cloudy, the night sky was so black he could see Dimity clearly reflected in the window. Hitching up her floaty dress to mid-thigh, she knelt behind him—and the view of her smooth knees either side of his jean-clad hips changed the direction of his thoughts.

Sex with a beautiful woman wasn't the worst way to end a shitty day.

She opened the jar and hooked out an opaque glob. The scent of coconut butter filled the room as it melted on her palm, but her first touch made him shiver. "Your hands are cold."

"Uh…sorry." Briskly, she rubbed them together. "Let's try this again."

It occurred to Seth that she was nervous. She went to work, her strong fingers finding the sore spots. The massage hurt like hell but he could feel his tight muscles uncoiling. And at least pain kept him from thinking. Her thumbs dug into the hollow at the base of his skull and suddenly there was pleasure in it. "How do you know how to do this?"

"I get tension headaches…this always works for me."

She dipped her fingers in more coconut butter and reached over his shoulders, gliding her hands over his collarbone, from his pecs to his belly. Her reflection sat back. "I don't want to get oil on this dress. Can you take it off for me?"

"I can do that." Things were definitely looking up.

Twisting, he eased it up and over her head. The heat of her skin was still in the silk. She wore a scarlet lacy bra and matching panties. His body responded. "Want to share some of that massage oil?"

"No." Planting her hands on his shoulders, she faced him forward. "You don't get to touch. This is all about you."

"So I can't take control of my own fantasy?"

"No. Stop trying to turn around."

Amusement bubbled through the primordial mud of his black mood. "I'm not hearing much tenderness."

Dimity's reflection rolled her eyes but her tone was sweet. "Please?"

Another bubble. "Or feeling it either."

She leaned forward. He felt a careful kiss on his neck. Frowning, her reflection wiped off the excess oil with the back of one hand.

"That's nice," Seth encouraged. "Do it again." Maybe he *was* into S and M.

But she was too smart for that. "Why don't you lie down?" she suggested in honeyed tones. "Make it easier."

And he'd really liked where her hands had been heading. "I wouldn't want to mess up the sheets."

"I'll get a towel." Climbing off the bed, she went into the adjoining bathroom.

He grimaced at his reflection. *Serves you right, smartarse.*

She returned and laid the towel over the sheets, patting out the wrinkles with all the fastidiousness of a nurse delaying giving an old geezer a bed bath.

Seth said with the sincerity of God, "I'm loving all this tenderness."

A muscle around her left eye twitched.

He had to bite the inside of his cheek hard to keep a straight face.

For a second, he considered adding, "I can't wait to kiss and cuddle afterward." But that would give the game away.

"Lie down," she invited. Propping herself on her elbow, beside him, she palmed the day's light stubble on his jaw, less a caress and more of a carpenter testing woodgrain before sanding it.

Dimity kissed his temple, then peppered some staccato kisses along the curve of his cheek to the corners of his mouth before lifting her head. "Am I doing this right?"

"Maybe more here." He touched his finger to his mouth. "Lots more."

She planted one on his lips.

"A little lighter, Honey B. We're not date-stamping an envelope."

"You really like these wimpy kisses?"

"Oh yeah, but if you're not into it…" He sighed.

"It's your fantasy." She kissed him again—lighter—and Seth noticed how very soft her lips were when they weren't firm with resolve. Her mouth moved against his, slippery with a trace of coconut butter, and he opened his mouth before she slid off altogether.

Dimity's tongue touched his, withdrew as if uncertain before touching again.

Slowly, very subtly, what began as a kiss of counting steps changed and became smooth and fluid, Fred Astaire and Ginger Rogers, perfect. And Seth stopped wanting to laugh.

Her sweetness invaded him, pumping through his blood like a drug.

She started trembling. Her arms had to be tired, holding her weight above him. He opened his eyes to change position and saw hers wide with panic.

"Hey," he touched her cheekbone. "What's going on?"

With a despairing expression, she flung herself onto her back. "I'm crap at this tender stuff!"

This woman was gifted in so many ways—he wouldn't let her give up on the softer emotions. He tucked a loose strand of blonde hair behind her ear. "What's my name?" he asked.

Confusion entered her blue eyes.

"Because you've made me forget it."

"Idiot." But some of the tension left her body.

"Yeah." He brushed his thumb across her lingering frown, then stroked her lids shut and kissed them.

"Kissing eyelids, really?" Her tone was indulgent.

"Really." He did it again and her long eyelashes tickled his nose. "I could use your eyelashes on my snare drum."

"They're extensions."

"I figured." He rubbed his nose against hers to get rid of the tickle. "This is also a traditional Maori greeting to visitors." He did it again, solemnly this time. "It's called a *hongi,* and by exchanging the breath of life we're confirming that we're friends, not enemies."

Her eyes opened and stared into his, mere inches apart, cautious and curious. Their breath mingled. And he experienced the strangest sensation, as though there really was something vital and sacred about this moment.

He understood suddenly why she preferred her sex combative, why she liked to be taken. She only let herself feel if she could pretend there was some element of coercion. She didn't want to need touch and closeness and tenderness. It broke his heart. "Honey B," he whispered. "We can do this."

Tilting his head, he captured her mouth, returning the sweet tenderness she'd given him. And she let him. Welcomed him. Responded to him. Her fingers massaged his scalp, careless now of the oil.

Time fell away under dreaming, narcotic kisses, each one savored and lingered over. They stopped kissing only long enough to remove each other's clothes, and there was no other foreplay. All their bodies wanted was to replicate what their kisses were already doing, creating magic. They flowed together like water and their energy had a peace to it that was balm on Seth's bruised soul. He had enough experience to know that what they were creating between them was extraordinary. Dimity probably thought of it as heartburn, which made him smile, want to kiss, protect, and shake her. All at the same time.

As he eased into her welcoming body, he couldn't stop smiling. She smiled back, easy and wide, surrendering to the intimacy, and something shifted and changed in him forever. As they made love, she kept her eyes open, fearless, and he drowned in them.

Dimity would never love him back, never let him close probably. She was a complex, contradictory woman, casually cruel, implacably kind, blisteringly honest, and the queen of denial. She'd put up a wall a mile high between them tomorrow. She might even be ashamed of what they'd shared tonight. It was dangerous and foolhardy to fall in love with a woman who knew a thousand ways to leave a man.

And he did it anyway. Knowingly, instinctively, deliberately. With no regrets.

He loved Dimity because of who she was—vibrant, unpredictable, fierce and vulnerable.

He loved her because she needed him to, because someone had to be man enough for the job.

He loved her because she left him no choice.

He loved her without conditions, or expectations…hell, she wouldn't meet them anyway. Likely didn't consider herself capable of meeting them. With her history, he'd choose safety, too.

He fell in love with Dimity for the same reason he'd turned his back on his old life and joined Rage—because he had to answer the call.

And let that be enough.

♪ ♫ ♩

"This bed is too small for two," Dimity said, thirty minutes after the bravest and most dangerous sex of her life. "Maybe you should go back to your own room."

"Okay." Seth rolled away from her and swung his legs off the mattress. His back still gleamed with coconut butter, and the sheets were fragrant with it.

He pulled on his boxers, then his jeans, picked up his T-shirt and shoes, and she watched him with a hunger she couldn't understand, given how thoroughly physically satisfied she felt right now. He turned to face her and she pulled up the sheet, suddenly self-conscious. She must look a mess, a greasy, sticky mess. Her hair was so tacky it stuck to her shoulders.

"Goodnight." Seth bent forward to kiss her and she tensed. "I'm all oily and needing a shower."

Ignoring her, he nipped her lower lip. Hard.

"Ouch. What was that for?"

"I'll tell you when you do it," he said, so casually she figured it for a joke.

"So, we're playing this cool, remember?" she cautioned as he walked to the door. "No mushy stuff in front of the others. Friends by day, lov—boink buddies by night. I don't mix work and pleasure. Don't expect touches or hugs or kisses…and no looks."

She didn't much like the one he was giving her now—it had too much resigned stoicism about it. As though she was predictable.

"I'll respect your boundaries," he said. "As long as you respect mine. I don't want you contacting my father, or trying to fix this for me. My family is my business. Promise me."

His 'don't-fuck-with-me-on-this' intensity made her squirm and turned her on at the same time.

"Your mother and I had a lunch date tomorrow." Gayle wouldn't let her leave the house without committing to another get-together.

"Cancel it."

"Sounds like she might need some reassurance, Seth."

"I don't care." But she could already hear his conscience in his voice.

"Let me have your back," she said. "I can buy you another day's peace."

He shook his head. Forgetting her nakedness, she climbed out of bed and wound her arms around his neck, pressing her body against his. "I swear I won't try to fix this. Your mom and I are meeting in town, I won't even see your father." *The bastard.* There was manipulation for good and there was manipulation for evil, and Frank definitely fell into the latter category. "I'll reassure your mother you still love her, then change the subject."

"And if she wants to talk about it?"

"I'll say you're out of bounds."

"If you didn't need a normal mother," he muttered.

"It's true," she said. "I'm crushing on your mom. And her screw-up in not telling you only makes her more accessible."

To Seth, Gayle might be all too fallible, but she was still everything Dimity had yearned for as a pre-pubescent girl—warmly interested, even a little interfering. A nurturer. Helena was both more sophisticated and more charming—when she wanted to be—but she'd forever be a child in an adult body.

"Stop lobbying. We both know I'll forgive Ma—"

"Only not yet," she said gently.

"I'm so fucking tired of being the understanding one."

"I know."

He leaned his forehead against hers. "Fine, meet her. But first, give me that promise."

"Scout's honor, no interfering." Resisting the impulse to drag him back to bed, she released him. "See you in the morning."

He left, shutting the door quietly behind him. She showered, stripped the oily towel off the bed, turned the pillows over, and burrowed under the sheets on the side Seth had just vacated.

She'd been as limp as a piece of overcooked spaghetti immediately after sex, but now her whole body thrummed. She didn't want to think about what she might have revealed to Seth; didn't want to remember how much she'd needed what he'd given her.

She tossed and turned until five, then rose, dressed and switched on her laptop, grateful that in much of the northern hemisphere people were up and working. As she waited for it to boot up, she saw Seth's watch on the floor by the bed and placed it on the bedside table, to give to him tomorrow.

Sitting cross-legged on the bed with the laptop, she responded to a couple of scheduling requests for Elizabeth and brooded over the fight she'd walked in on earlier. Like the clowns on that tightrope years ago, she was full of public bravado while privately feeling the strain. And very, very conscious of walking a fine line.

Or was exhaustion making her pessimistic? The only time she'd slept well in months was with Seth in her bed—not that she'd tell *him* that. But she wouldn't be encouraging sleepovers. If she detected any hint of dependency in herself, she'd have to give him up. And she wasn't ready to. She returned her attention to the task at hand. Zander had as good as admitted tonight he wouldn't have made this choice if Elizabeth didn't exist.

Having spent time alone with them both, it was obvious neither had any sense of self-preservation when it came to each other. Only fools would jeopardize their careers for someone else. Elizabeth wasn't a fool and she was doing it anyway, with her eyes wide open. As for Zander, he'd more than proved he'd lost his mind. Someone had to stop the lunatics from taking over the asylum.

Ditching her laptop, she climbed off the bed and found a piece of paper and a pen. Whenever she was really stuck, she resorted to handwriting her options. Looking at the blank sheet, she asked herself the critical question. *How far am I prepared to take this?* The first thing to do was review the success of her game plan.

1. Talk Zee out of it.
Well that didn't work. Dimity crossed it out.

2. Get Elizabeth to help me talk Zee out of it.
Another cross-out.

3. Play on Elizabeth's fears to convince her to talk Zee out of it.
She wrote in brackets beside it.
(Still in play).

4.

She chewed the end of her pen, unable to fill in the logical next step. The one she kept suppressing like whack-a-mole, because her strategic brain made no moral judgments in the options it threw up. *It won't get to that.*

Clinically and dispassionately, she reviewed the facts.

Zander was doing the wrong thing. It would screw up everything for many, many people. It would make him miserable. Ultimately his misery would alienate Elizabeth—if he didn't push her away first.

Rage was the only family Dimity had. All Seth had, all Moss had. Recognizing emotion creeping in, she beat it away.

I have to protect my tribe. Whatever it takes, whatever the cost. No one else has the skill, or the will.

She forced herself to fill in the blank and stared at what she'd written.

4. Break them up.

She calmed her breathing by reminding herself that this was a hypothetical, last-resort-only-if-all-else-fails option. She'd started leading them along the path today, but at any time they could take a detour, a side road. *One of you, please, have an epiphany soon.*

She returned to number three and put two exclamation marks after *Still in play.* Underlined it twice.

If it was still in play, then she wouldn't have to take drastic measures. Not yet.

CHAPTER 17

DIMITY HAD BEEN IN THE office for two hours, reading comments on Rage's Facebook page and fan sites and monitoring Zandergate chatter on social media, when her boss strolled in. "Good *morning*."

Refusing to show self-consciousness—the last time he'd seen her, she'd been leading Seth to her bedroom—she didn't glance up from the screen. "Hi…that weirdo I blocked is using another IP address to send more abusive threats. I'm wondering if we should forward them to Luther, get his take on whether we should contact the poli—" A mug of steaming coffee and a plate with two pieces of wholemeal toast and mashed avocado landed on the desk beside her.

"Doc and I thought you might be starving."

Glancing up sharply, she met an innocent blue gaze.

"Thank you." She narrowed her eyes at him—a warning never hurt. "So, the threats of violence."

"Last night when you and Seth dropped the we're-dating bombshell and you said don't make a big deal about it, you meant…?"

"Let's not ever discuss it."

"That's what I figured." Zander settled in his chair—a Captain Kirk Starship Enterprise number—leaned back with his arms behind his head, and crossed his feet on his desk. "On a completely related subject, I didn't expect to see you at your desk so early."

"Work comes first, always," she said, trying to concentrate on it.

He ignored the hint. "So, where's Loverboy now?"

"I have no idea," she returned coolly. "I'm not his keeper."

"Well, I hope you left him with enough energy for our run later."

"If you think you're being funny…you're not."

Chuckling, he dropped his feet to the floor and sat up. "Okay, I'll stop teasing, but if you want my opinion—"

"I don't. Not in my personal life."

"—you'll be good for each other," he continued, unruffled.

"We need to work," Dimity said. "I've got business in the city later."

"Eat your breakfast," he said, finally turning to his computer. "Have you started Doc's manuscript yet?" he asked as he keyed in his password. Time zone differences meant most of their US emails started flooding in overnight.

"No." She picked up a piece of toast, careful not to get the slathered avocado on her fingers, and took a bite. She *was* hungry. "I hope to get to it this afternoon." Which reminded her of a question she'd been meaning to ask him. Spinning around in her chair, she gave him a quizzical look. "Why haven't you read her book yet?"

Busy scanning an email, he answered absently. "Because it doesn't matter."

"And I thought *I* was callous."

"If the book's crap and causes people to burn effigies of me, it doesn't matter. Nothing Doc does will change how I feel about her. Not now, not ever."

It should have been touching, but instead she found it dispiriting. Suddenly the toast didn't taste as good. *How the hell can logical argument counter such passion?*

But it had to. The first thing she'd done this morning was make a paper airplane of her list and fly it across the room. Night terrors. In daylight she acknowledged the truth. She'd gone soft.

Breaking them up wasn't an option.

"No one's bulletproof, Zee…which brings us back to this internet troll who's making death threats."

He rose to read it over her shoulder. "'Dear cowardly piece of shit,' yada, yada." Sadly, they were getting blasé about the hate mail, but this guy was persistent. "'You think you can stop a patriot exercising his right to free speech, asshole? You disrespected our flag, you spat in the faces of the brave men and women who have given their lives for this great country. You can't hide from me in cyberspace or on the ground. Watch out motherfucker, I'm coming for you.'"

Her chair squeaked as his hands tightened on the backrest. "Yeah, forward it to Luther," he said with his usual casualness. "We need to identify all these nutcases before Elizabeth goes on her book tour." He returned to his desk. "So what's on the agenda today? Or are you too busy starring in your own lov—"

"Finish that word and I'll come for you myself." Baiting each other dissipated the lingering malevolence in the air. Gave a two-fingered salute to the haters.

Grinning, Zander returned to checking his inbox. "One from our chief counsel…the insurer has made an offer to settle. Low, as expected."

"How much?"

He told her and she snorted. "See you in court, assholes." While their offer would clear the cancellation costs associated with the next tour leg, it wasn't anywhere close enough to reimburse Zander for the money he'd personally paid to the small contractors who'd go under if they had to wait for the court case to settle—the truckers, the caterers, the local sound tech firms.

Zander had mortgaged everything to go on tour and skimped on tour insurance. If his voice hadn't given out, the payoff would have been huge for everyone. Now, they needed a full payout by the insurers just to recoup his losses.

He didn't respond, and glancing over, she saw he was pensive.

"You can't seriously be considering that offer, it's far too low. Opening salvo stuff…a shot across the bow."

"Uh-huh. What time is it in New York?"

She did a conversion on her cell. "Three. Why? What are you plotting?" He was throwing and catching a pen, always a sign of deep thought. Today, it made her nervous.

"Nothing. Maybe nothing. That fight Doc and I had last night was our first since becoming a couple."

"Wow, that woman has the patience of a saint."

"Very funny. Something's wrong and I think I know what it is."

Dimity swallowed. "You do?"

"As soon as she started talking about the real world intruding. She's having second thoughts about this book project, isn't she?"

Facing her screen, Dimity tapped the forward icon on the email. "You'll have to ask her." Her tone was completely neutral.

"Yeah," he said, not fooled. "That's what I thought."

She changed the subject. "While I've got you alone, I wanted to remind you of your promise not to tell Seth or anyone you're quitting until we work out—"

"Today or in a few days, there's no miracle happening here. Surely you're not still expecting one?"

"I'm thinking of the timing for Elizabeth," she said tartly, entering Luther's email address. "She's got enough pressure meeting her deadline."

"So I *am* right," he said. "This is tough for her."

Dimity kept her eyes fixed on the screen. *Should we be worried about this?* she typed, asking herself the same question about Zander. His newfound empathy was making him dangerously unpredictable. To her note, she added: *Please tell me the threat's benign.* Stared at what she'd written.

Aloud, she said, "Any message for Luther?"

♪ ♫ ♩

Amid the lunchtime bustle of a harborside restaurant, Dimity looked across the table at Seth's mother and said, "You're a cheap drunk, you know that?"

She'd nearly canceled this lunch, reluctant to leave Zander to his own devices after their conversation this morning. But helping Seth—and Gayle—was important, too.

Her lover's mother propped her head between her hands. "I've always been a lightweight with alcohol," she admitted.

On the bright side, getting tipsy *had* improved Gayle's mood. She'd been round-shouldered with remorse when they'd first sat down at the Viaduct for lunch—ironically at the same restaurant-bar where Seth had found Dimity drowning her sorrows.

"It might have helped if you'd told me this before I ordered a bottle of wine, Gayle."

"Yup, but I figured if I got you drunk you'd talk about Seth." Gayle picked up the wine bottle to refill Dimity's glass, discovered it still full, and swung it toward her own empty one.

"A cunning ploy." Dimity confiscated the bottle before Gayle could pour and raised her hand to catch the attention of the waitress. "May we have some water, please?"

She turned back to see Gayle stealing her full wineglass. She grinned at Dimity over the rim, her eyes as mischievous as her son's. "So tell me—"

"I told you. I promised Seth I wouldn't discuss—"

"Yes, yes." Impatiently, Gayle waved her glass, then licked the spilled chardonnay off her knuckles. "You have the right to remain silent et cetera, et cetera. So let's talk about how *you* feel about my son."

"It's just sex," Dimity assured her, then wondered if that was how normal people talked to mothers.

Gayle appeared unfazed. "I see, how interesting." Her smile was positively enigmatic and Dimity squirmed.

The older woman's smile softened to maternal. "Tell me about your family, sweetie. Do you have any brothers and sisters?"

"Only child." She sketched in her upbringing. Normally, her precocious brat anecdotes got people laughing, but when she'd finished a story about being twelve and trying to pay a plumber who'd fixed a blocked toilet with a bottle of Dom Pérignon—it had been a cash job and her mother had forgotten to go to the bank—Gayle reached across the table for her hand.

"Did you have a pet at least, growing up?"

Her earnest enquiry amused Dimity. "We traveled too much. And now *I* travel too much, which is why I timeshare a cat in LA." She told Gayle about Diamanté. "Cats are independent so I'm confident she doesn't miss me too much. But if I ever stay in one place I'll get a Jack Russell terrier—tan face, white muzzle and body."

"That's very specific." Gayle hadn't removed her hand.

"When I was six, we lived in Paris, and I walked past a pet shop on the way to school. My nanny and I would stop and pat all the animals. There was a Jack Russell puppy who was always so pleased to see me. She took so long to sell, I started thinking of her as mine. I even gave her a name—Madeline, after the books."

"Wonderful children's books," Gayle said. "Janey had the whole set."

"I begged my parents to buy her but they said we moved too often, Madeline would spend more time in quarantine than at home with us." *You wouldn't want that for her, would you, darling? That would be too selfish.* "They were right, of course."

Gayle's hand tightened, reminding Dimity it was there. Her nails weren't manicured and the roughened skin identified her as a fanatical gardener. "It wasn't all bad," Dimity assured her. "They gave me a soft toy—a Jack Russell—for my birthday, which I pretended was real for years." Smiling at Gayle, she slid her hand free and picked up her water glass. "I still have it."

She hadn't meant to add that, but the older woman simply nodded and lifted the wineglass.

"To bitches," Gayle toasted.

Inexplicably, Dimity felt tears prickle. She picked up her water glass. "To bitches… We're talking dogs, right?"

"Whatever works." They chinked glasses.

Gayle took a sip and yawned widely. "Oh boy, this lunchtime alcohol has made me tired."

There was no way this woman was fit to get behind the wheel. "How about I drive your car home," Dimity suggested. "I can catch a taxi to the ferry from your place." With Frank at work there was no danger of breaking her word to Seth.

"Would you? That's so sweet."

Gayle gave directions when they left the parking building but it still took all Dimity's concentration to stay on the right…left…hand side of the road. It was fortunate she recognized Seth's "landmarks" because his mother was asleep when they reached his neighborhood, only waking when the car stopped.

"Oh dear, I'm making a fool of myself, aren't I?"

"You were probably due."

"Come in, I'll make you coffee."

"Thanks, but the ferry leaves on the hour. I just need the number of a local cab company."

"I'll do better than that, I'll phone them for you." Gayle unlocked the front door. "Frank, I'm home."

Oh, no. "He isn't at work?"

"Half day."

So much for your fabled work ethic, Frankie.

He walked out of the living room, and looked about as pleased to see Dimity as she was to see him.

"Hi," she said cheerfully. "Gayle had a couple of wines on a restless night's sleep and no breakfast." *And we all know who's responsible for that.* Dimity didn't say it—she was keeping her word to Seth. "She's feeling a little under the weather, so I drove her car home."

He put an arm around his wife. "Honey, are you okay?"

"I will be after a lie-down. Will you call Dimity a taxi, Frank?"

"Of course," he said politely.

Gayle hugged her tight. "Thank you for your company, sweetie, and we'll see each other soon. Tell Seth I love him."

"I will." Over Gayle's shoulder, Dimity glared at Frank. Not using words, not breaking her promise.

"Are you sure you don't want me to help you upstairs, honey?" he asked his wife.

"I'm drunk, not infirm," she grumbled.

"Okay, then." His gaze followed Gayle as she walked upstairs and Dimity was startled by the concerned tenderness in his expression. Frank caught her watching and his lips compressed.

"I'll phone a taxi." He gestured to the sofa. Please. Have a seat."

After he'd made the call, they sat in a silence Dimity was determined not to fill with small talk. After a minute, Frank cleared his throat.

"When do you return to LA.?"

"End of next week."

Is Seth going with you? She could see the question in his eyes. But of course he didn't ask. Instead, they sat in that warm, friendly home in a chilly silence while everything she longed to say burned inside her. "I'm Switzerland," she chanted silently. "Neutral."

"Gayle didn't mention you were the lunch date," he commented. "I didn't think you'd have a lot in common."

Even Switzerland had an army for self-defense. "Out of interest," she inquired nicely, "is there something about me personally that offends you, or do I just remind you of the lifestyle your son chose over this one?"

Frank looked at her a long moment. "I haven't decided. Do you talk to your own parents as freely?"

"God, no! My mother and I have never had an honest conversation in our lives. And I don't get beyond small talk with my father. We only see each other once a year."

"You surprise me," he said dryly.

She continued as though he hadn't spoken. "After their divorce when I was eleven, my mother made me choose between them. We got out of the habit of each other, I guess."

Frank shifted awkwardly. "I misspoke, I'm sorry."

"Apology accepted." A toot sounded outside the house and they both stood with relief and exchanged cursory goodbyes. It took every ounce of Dimity's self-control not to say, "Want me to give Seth *your* love?"

She managed it, though, running through a gusty rain shower to climb into the cab. "Downtown ferry terminal, thanks."

The taxi was reversing down the driveway when Frank exited the house holding an umbrella, and waved at the driver to stop. On a heart-skip of hope, Dimity pushed the down button on her window.

"You went out of your way for Gayle," he said gruffly. "Let me pay for this." He handed her a fifty-dollar note.

Dimity stared at him. "That's it?" she said, before she could stop herself.

"What else is there?"

For a long time, Seth took all the shit you dealt out as though he deserved it, when all he did was follow his dream, not yours. Your son must really love you.

"Nothing," she said. "Forget it." *I gave Seth my word.*

He walked toward the house. The cab started reversing again.

"Wait!" Dimity cried. The taxi jerked to a halt and she scrambled out of the car. Frank had reached the porch and was closing his umbrella.

"I didn't finish my story about my father," she said, standing in the rain.

"What?" he said, confused.

"You'd think I'd miss him less as the years go by but the weird thing is, I miss him more." Pinning his gaze, Dimity dropped her guard and let him see her pain. "I wish he'd tried harder. I wish…Dad hadn't let me go so easily."

Without waiting for a response, she ran to the cab. As she closed the passenger door she glanced up, but Frank had already disappeared into the house.

Another fail. They were piling up now. But she'd kept her word. She hadn't talked about Seth. God, she needed to get a win, needed it so bad. Grabbing her cell, she logged onto the internet and found Swimming New Zealand's training schedules for elite athletes.

"Driver…"

"Let me guess. You want me to turn around."

"That depends on where the Millennium Centre's located."

CHAPTER 18

"SO," ZANDER SAID FROM BEHIND Seth, some twenty minutes into their run. "You and Dimity."

"Yep." Seth jumped a tree root pushing through the trail like a gnarled fist, leading the way to the summit. The surrounding native bush grew so thickly that little rain made it through the green canopy.

Zander grunted as he followed suit. "Serious?"

"For me."

"Shit."

Trust Zander not to sugarcoat Seth's chances. "Yeah."

"Good luck."

Seth was touched. "Thanks, mate."

The trail grew steeper, ending their heart-to-heart as both men concentrated on the climb. Zander stayed on Seth's heels, pushing him hard. Son of a bitch had ten years on him, too. Drumming required physical stamina and Seth kept himself fit, but even so the muscles in his thighs were burning when they reached the clearing at the top ten minutes later. Ignoring the view, he bent double, blowing hard and grateful for the cool rain on his back.

"Show-off," he managed to say.

Chest heaving, Zander grinned. "Always." Shrugging off a small backpack, he unzipped it and tossed Seth a water bottle. The two men moved under the drooping branches of a young rimu. Even with gray skies and sheets of rain blowing across the silver sea, the Hauraki Gulf was stunning.

Seth picked out the shape of islands through the mist—Great Barrier, Little Barrier, Tiritiri Matangi. And all around him the lush native bush bursting with Nikau palms, pohutukawas, kauri, and ponga.

He'd have to bring Dimity up here.

God, he had it bad.

Zander looked surprisingly at home in this rugged setting. He was such a brash showman it was easy to forget that he, too, had roots in this land through his Kiwi mother.

Seth felt that kinship as they stood silently looking at the view. "This would be the place to tell me you're not coming back to the band," he commented.

Zander gaped at him. "Dimity told you."

Replacing the cap on his water bottle, Seth shook his head. "Not a word, but she's been acting crazy since we got to New Zealand. Spending time with you confirmed my suspicions." *You're sad.* He kept that thought to himself. "Dimity's clearly still hoping for a miracle…" He waited.

Zander shook his head.

"That's what I figured." Even though he'd expected this, the confirmation cut deep. But he could mourn his own loss later. "I'm so damn sorry, Zee, that the vocal damage is permanent."

His mentor looked away.

"You probably don't want to talk about it, I get that. But let me just say, it's been one hell of a ride and I'll be forever grateful for the opportunities you've given me. Moss and Jared will tell you the same. I've learned so much from you." If he didn't crack a joke, he'd tear up. "And I can work on four hours sleep a night now."

Zander laughed. "Mate, if you can work with me, you can work with anyone." He dropped a hand on Seth's shoulder. "I'm so sorry."

"Hey, this isn't your fault."

"It's all my fault." Zander started to say something, then shrugged. "Don't you read the papers? And while we're doing the gratitude thing…I appreciate your loyalty these past months. I think you were all idiots—you could have killed your careers if the public turned on you—but on a personal level? Your support meant a lot to me."

"Only assholes would abandon the guy who gave them their first break."

"Yeah, but I was—still am—a difficult son of a bitch."

Seth grinned. "I'm not saying touring together hasn't been… challenging. But you made me a better musician and took my career to warp speed. Most of all, you gave me self-belief." His throat tightened. "I'm following my passion because of you."

"Jesus." Zander caught him in a hug. "I'm welling up."

"American guys." Seth blinked hard. "So fucking emotional."

"Kiwi blokes." Zander released him. "So fucking repressed." Unashamedly, he wiped his eyes. "Any band you three form will be successful. I wouldn't have chosen you if you weren't the best. And I'll keep doing as much as I can to help you." He replaced their water bottles in the backpack and led the way down the trail. "One thing—let me tell Dimity you know I'm leaving."

"Sure."

They started running. "I have to say, you're taking the news more philosophically than she is," Zander commented.

His crucible had been ditching engineering for a music career. "As long as I can make a living playing music I'll be happy. For Dimity, it's different."

"How? She'll still have a job, at least until I run out of money."

"The band is her family," Seth said. "Probably the first real family she's had."

Zander's stride faltered. "I'd never thought of it like that."

They stopped talking and concentrated on running. When they were on the flat, and walking in a warm-down, Seth raised his idea. "We'll need a good manager."

"Yeah, it's a shame Robbie wants to retire. You need a powerhouse who knows the business inside out. Someone with easy access to the right people."

"I have a person in mind...I'm not sure it's fair on you to ask, though."

"I can play a backroom role, but my current reputation won't do you any favors."

"Your fucking ego." Seth grinned. "I wasn't talking about you. But yeah, I am thinking the job could stay in the band family. Dimity."

Zander stopped. "That's brilliant."

"Yeah," Seth said modestly.

"Only...shit. I'd have to let her go. Sooner than I'd hoped to."

"So let's drop the subject."

"No, it's the perfect role for her. It would be selfish to hold her back, and I don't want her staying through a misplaced sense of loyalty."

Three joggers approached and they stepped aside to let them pass.

"Besides," Zander added ruefully. "I can't afford to pay her what she's worth much longer. Neither can you, so include a profit share in your offer. Have you talked to the others about this?"

Seth shook his head. "I wanted to run it by you first. None of us—including Dimity—would consider it unless you're on board. She may still turn us down—she's bound to get other offers. But I don't see Jared and Moss saying no."

"How will it work, with you two being personally involved?"

"Only I'm personally involved," Seth corrected. "And Dimity would never let a little thing like sleeping together interfere with business."

Which was why he didn't mention their affair to Jared and Moss when he set up a video conference on his return from the run to propose the idea. He wanted to respect the boundaries between work and play. And the honey badger would no doubt want to micromanage a 'release strategy'.

Falling in love with her also complicated things. *Ya think?* He needed to bring his raw feelings under control and decide how the hell he was going to handle their relationship going forward.

If Dimity had an inkling of how he felt, she'd dump him. Of that he *was* sure. But if he kept his cool, used his head, then maybe he could sneak into her heart using guerrilla tactics—surprise bedroom raids, sabotaging her communications so she was offline occasionally... A man could hope.

Even split-screened, there was no disguising the disgust on his bandmates' faces, following his suggestion. "You don't like the idea?"

"Stealing our mentor's PA from him if his voice doesn't come back...why would you think that?" Jared said scathingly. Rage's 'soulful' bass guitarist would have scared the shit out of his music nerd fan base right now, his dark eyes furious.

"I guess I should have mentioned that Zander's on board with the idea...if we end up needing a Plan B." Zander's diagnosis wasn't Seth's news to tell. *Thank God.*

He wasn't capable of dealing with that loss yet. Between his family situation and falling for Dimity, he was already at emotional overload and his brain had shut down. *Try again after we've dealt with the feelings we're currently processing.*

"She'd never leave Zander," Moss said. "She's too loyal."

"I agree." And whatever Zander said, it would be a massive sacrifice for him to cut her loose now. He still had huge challenges ahead of him with the insurers and media. "Which is why—if we end up implementing Plan B—we'd work out a job-share arrangement, at least in the short term. There's no way we can afford her yet, either." And Dimity was bound to get better offers once Zander's condition became public knowledge. He wasn't counting his chick just yet.

"A job share could work," Moss said slowly. "There's no doubt that she'll achieve great things for us. And she won't say yes unless she thinks we'll achieve great things for her. Jared?"

"Yeah, sorry." Frowning, the bassist put his cell away. "A text from Kayla. If Zander's okay with it, then I think it's a great idea."

"Everything okay at home?" Seth asked.

"I think so. We're no longer fighting, using please and thank you, having a great time with the kids, regular sex..." He shrugged.

"And?"

"And something's still *off*. Kayla's distant somehow, even in bed."

"I'm always faking it there, too," said Moss.

"I didn't say that," Jared protested, but there was a distance to his gaze, as though he was rerunning a sex tape. He refocused. "And how do guys fake it exactly, Dr. Ruth?"

Moss grinned. "You want to have sex with a big, bad rocker, baby?" He delivered the Clint Eastwood growl perfectly. "Then that's who I'll be for you." His broad shoulders rose in a sigh as he added in a normal voice, "I'll watch *Downton Abbey* later."

Seth and Jared cracked up laughing.

"What makes it funny is that he *does* watch *Downton Abbey*," Seth told Jared.

"It was *once*, asshole." Moss added silkily. "Maybe Jared should work out Kayla's secret sexual fantasy."

"Maybe he should," Seth retorted. Privately, he cursed the night he'd got liquored up with Moss and shared *that* insight. The guitarist was never going to stop ragging on him. Never mind that women loved it. He wondered how quickly he could tempt Dimity into bed again. He had a few ideas...

"I'm starting to think Kayla's fantasy might be starting over," Jared said ruefully, "That advice is no good to—" He stopped. "Hmm, I'm getting an idea."

Seth's cell buzzed in his pocket. Checking caller ID, he said, "Guys, I've got a phone call I need to take. Let's finish this later."

Cutting the connection, he took a deep breath and answered his cell. "Mum."

"Can we talk?" Her voice sounded a little slurred. He wondered how much sleep she'd gotten last night and was ashamed suddenly for letting Frank drive a wedge between them.

She'd been wrong to keep him in ignorance, but her motives had been loving. And Seth knew firsthand how good his father was at getting his own way. "I'm glad you called," he said. "How was your lunch with Dimity?"

♪ ♫ ♩

Dimity associated swimming pools with tranquility. Mirror-still, turquoise water that she sank into slowly as a respite from Los Angeles heat. The only sounds the soft *kadonk* of the filter flaps when she drifted past in a hot pink inflatable chair with her book.

This water was splintered blue crystal, a churning frenzy of sleek bodies torpedoing through the water to a cacophony of shrill whistles and barked commands that ricocheted off the tiles like bullets. Industrial-strength chlorine caught in her throat as she pushed through the double doors.

A whistle blew, shriller than the rest, and swimmers returned to base one after another, their capped heads popping out of the water like seals. It still took her another minute to identify Mel, and only because she spotted her prosthetic lying at the end of a swim lane.

One hand hanging onto the ledge, water glistening on her strong shoulders, Mel was talking to a guy with a whistle and clipboard who had to be her coach. She caught sight of Dimity and frowned, and her coach turned to see what she was looking at.

"No spectators today," he called.

Dimity kept coming. "This won't take long."

"I'm not interested in talking to you," Mel said. Replacing her swim goggles, she pushed off with her one leg, arms slicing through the water with admirable ease as she fast-crawled down her lane.

"It's important," Dimity told the coach, and waited patiently for Mel's return. But Mel didn't stop. Her agile body flipped into a tumble-turn, drenching Dimity in the process, and she set off on another lap.

"Nicely done," Dimity conceded, shaking water off her pencil skirt. "But she'll have to stop sooner or later, right?"

The coach checked his clipboard. "In about fifty lengths." He moved to a swimmer in the next lane.

Hmm. Dimity reassessed her options. Glancing around, she saw a basket of rubber balls next to the kids' pool and fetched one. Next time Mel returned she aimed it squarely at her head. "She strikes! She scores!"

Mel came up spluttering and ripped off her goggles. "What the hell!"

"I'm not leaving until we talk."

"Go away." She hollered to her coach. "Jack, call security. This woman is crazy."

"Seth was faithful to you while you were dating," Dimity said, as Jack hurried over. "Never once did he go home with anyone. I can vouch for that."

"Well, you would say that. And you know what? I don't care." Mel replaced her goggles.

Jack took Dimity's elbow. "She's asked you to leave."

She shrugged off his hand, all her focus on Mel. "Women threw themselves at Seth and he resisted all temptation because he loved *you*. I would kill for that loyalty."

"You need to go," Mel said flatly. She gripped the side of the ledge, preparing to push off.

Dimity stepped away from Jack's second attempt to take her arm and he beckoned one of the lifeguards. "You can't throw away a lifelong friendship for something that isn't true, you stupid cow!"

Mel pushed off from the side. A lifeguard jogged over. In five seconds, Dimity would be thrown out. Stepping out of her heels, she jumped in after Mel. The water was barely heated. Gasping at the unexpected cold, she stretched out her legs, feeling for the bottom.

There wasn't one.

Panic hit as her head went under. She flailed her arms and broke the surface. "Help!" Went under again.

Her movements impeded by her pencil skirt, she kicked, groping blindly for the side, but her fingers couldn't find purchase on the smooth tiles. In desperation, she tried to fling herself onto her back and float, but only succeeded in snorting water up her nose.

"…kidding." She heard Mel's sarcasm as she broke the surface a second time and gasped a breath. "She's a drama que—"

She sank again. She was going to drown surrounded by the country's best swimmers.

Then an arm wrapped around her chest, and she found herself on her back, staring at the ceiling. "Relax," Mel yelled in her ear. "I've got you."

Sucking oxygen into her lungs, Dimity closed her eyes and let Mel tow her to the side where multiple hands reached down and hauled her up and out of the pool. Water streaming off her clothes, she coughed and spluttered thanks.

Mel swung herself out of the pool and strapped on her prosthesis. "You bloody idiot! Why the hell would you jump in the deep end if you can't swim?"

With as much dignity as she could muster, Dimity accepted a towel. "Because I didn't realize it was the deep end, obviously!" Still shocked by her near-death experience, she tugged on her dry shoes.

Only when Mel smothered a laugh, did she register how ridiculous she must look, donning stilettos while she sat dripping like a wet dog. "Okay, *this* makes me a bloody idiot."

Mel lent her a robe and brought her a hot chocolate while a nearby laundromat was speed-drying her clothes.

"You've got to understand," she told Mel, "that in the music industry, being nice is a tool. Something you pick up and put down according to whether it gets you what you want. Actually *being* nice— you might as well write *sucker* on your forehead. When I first met Seth through the auditions, I looked at this nice guy who was so earnest about being faithful to his childhood sweetheart and thought, 'Yeah, good luck with that, Opie. You'll drop those hometown values the second a groupie drops her panties in your lap.' He proved me wrong." He had more strength of character than any man she knew, which was quite a feat considering who she worked for.

Cupping her hot chocolate, she looked at Mel. "He missed you and he did everything he could to keep your relationship alive, even when it was clear to his friends that you'd stopped trying."

The other woman swallowed, but she didn't relent.

"Seth was heartbroken when you ended your relationship and devastated when you told him you'd gotten engaged. Even though I thought you might be stringing him along with all your calls and texts, I offered to help him get you back. Yes, dumb in hindsight, but we *were* very drunk at the time. Which is how we ended up sleeping together."

Now came the hard part. Through the viewing window, she looked down to the pool where the swimmers were still powering through their laps. "Seth would deny it, but I still feel I took advantage of him," she admitted. "And in the spirit of full disclosure, we are sleeping together now."

"I was never stringing Seth along," Mel said quietly. "I kept phoning and texting because I *was* worried about him, and because I didn't want to lose him as a friend."

"Well then, your timing was selfish." Dimity wasn't going to let her off the hook. "You should have been thinking about what was in *his* best interests, not yours."

"Maybe you're right," Mel mumbled.

Dimity cupped her ear. "What was that?"

"I believe nothing happened between you two before he and I broke up, and will tell him so."

"Still not hearing you."

Mel sighed. "Fine, I'll apologize."

"Thank you."

The brunette collected their empty mugs. "You're in love with him now, though."

"Please." Dimity scoffed. "I'm just helping out a friend."

"A friend you're having sex with."

"On a very casual basis. Do I look like the kind of idiot who'd fall for a guy on the rebound?"

"As opposed to the kind of idiot who jumps in a pool when she can't swim?"

"As opposed to *that* kind of idiot," she conceded. "It's pretty simple really. I just want Seth to be—" She froze, feeling the blood drain from her face.

"Happy?"

I just want him to be happy. Horrified, she stared at Mel, who patted her hand.

"Shall I get the defibrillator?" she said kindly.

CHAPTER 19

DIMITY SPENT THE FERRY RIDE home convincing herself that Mel was wrong. She *wasn't* in love with Seth.

She disembarked reluctantly. Home—Zander and Elizabeth's home, Seth's current home—wasn't a refuge. It was a place where challenges kept piling up on each other, each more difficult.

She was losing her edge, losing her touch…losing every which way she turned.

In the parking lot, she sat in the Land Rover she'd borrowed from Zee and Elizabeth and reminded herself that she was a strategist. No matter what shit went down, some part of her brain remained in the war room, composed, in control, and focused on the big picture. The goal. In the heat of battle other people might get disorientated. Not her. And her goal remained saving all their livelihoods.

Her chaotic emotions calmed.

Mel *was* wrong. Dimity wasn't in love with Seth. They were in lust, pure, simple—and acceptable. She was a break from the nice girls he dated and he was the nice guy whose wild side she enjoyed uncovering. Neither of them had to be 'on' with each other and they both found freedom in that. The fling was that simple.

Starting the Land Rover's rumbling engine, she drove home.

Zander had texted that he and Elizabeth were visiting his mother, who lived on the other side of Waiheke, which freed the afternoon for Dimity to start reading Elizabeth's memoir. Hopefully, she'd find an insight she could use to bolster her cause.

She heard drums being played in the barn when she turned off the ignition. *Excellent, they've been delivered.* The first thing she'd done in the city was hire a drum kit for Seth. She wanted to remind Zee exactly what he was giving up, and Seth could use the musical therapy.

Dimity opened the car door. No wonder the sheep in the adjoining paddock had decamped to the far side of the field. He was really tearing it up.

Halfway to the house, she detoured, compelled by the cathartic quality of his playing. One quick peek wouldn't hurt.

Even in the cavernous space, the drum beats reverberated through the rafters. It took her eyes a few seconds to adjust to the gloom. Engrossed in performance, Seth didn't notice her standing at the open doors.

He'd set up the kit in the middle of the barn. Zander had allowed the neighboring farmer to store winter feed here, and behind Seth hay bales were stacked two deep almost to the roof, blocking the light from the only window. A wide plank nailed to the internal framing acted as makeshift workbench and held rusty farm implements, coils of wire and an oil can. Otherwise the space was empty.

The only drums she'd been able to hire at short notice were entry level—bass, toms, snare, hi-hat and one cymbal, with none of the extensions of Seth's own kit. If anything, the basic set highlighted his talent as he spun his frustrations into gold with bright, bold beat improvisations. As she listened, a frenzied staccato segued to a slow, sultry swampiness, as musical in the pause as it was in the beats.

His sleeveless T-shirt gaped at the side every time he moved to reveal tantalizing glimpses of his pecs and the column of lean muscle tapering across his ribs. His hair was damp with sweat and feathered around his face.

The beat pulsing through her body, Dimity watched him and desire rose fast and hot inside her. *Yes, it's just lust.* She moved on the feeling, crossing the hard ground in half a dozen quick strides. Seth stopped playing and the cymbals shimmered into silence.

Tangling her fingers in his tawny hair, she pulled his head back and he looked up at her, his blue eyes amused and curious. She bent to lick the salty bead of sweat at his hairline and then traced her lips down his cheek and over the raspy stubble at his jaw, down the strong column of his neck. The pulse there jumped against the tip of her tongue.

A powerful reminder of the transience of life.

She shoved aside the snare drum between his knees and knelt between his open thighs, sliding her fingers down the armholes of the gaping T-shirt. Clenching her fists in the thin cotton, she said, "For my shirt," and ripped.

The corners of his eyes crinkled in that way she loved as he grinned. Resting his hands on his muscular thighs he opened his legs wider, silently surrendering to whatever she wanted to do to him.

And she wanted to do a lot.

She opened her fists and the remnants of his T-shirt dropped to the ground. Leaning forward, she kissed and licked and caressed her way down his naked torso, tasting and savoring every damp delicious inch of heated skin while he sat like a king and submitted.

Her panties were damp by the time she'd reached the metal fastener of his jeans. It was cold to the touch as she flicked it open, her other hand closing on his cock, warm and oh, so hard under the worn denim. Lightly, she closed her teeth over his erection through his jeans, and he gripped her shoulders.

Freeing the head of his cock, she circled it teasingly with her thumb. "Sit on me," he said hoarsely.

"Not yet."

Working her way up his body, she traced the sinew of his inner forearm, suck-biting each knuckle on his callused fingers and lingering over the smooth flat nipples on his muscled pecs. She wanted him to moan and he did, his hands busy under her light sweater, pushing up her bra to palm her breasts and return the torment.

She kissed his face, relishing the texture of his skin, the rasp of beard on his jaw, the smoothness of the skin over his cheekbones. Everywhere but his mouth. This was all about sex. When he tried to kiss her, she said, "Wait." Stepping away unsteadily, she reached under her pencil skirt to pull off her panties.

Retrieving a condom from her bag, she gave it to him while she hiked the tight skirt up to her waist before straddling him. His hands cupped her bare bottom, steadying her while she wriggled to take him inside her. But with Seth sitting, she couldn't free his cock enough to do more than taunt them both. The stool swiveled every time she adjusted her angle. Her frustration built. "I can't..."

"Hang on, lover, I've got this."

She tightened her legs around his waist as he stood and carried her to the wall, bracing her back against it. He shoved down his jeans, cupped her ass, and thrust into her. This was what she needed, hard, rough, fast. The iron creaked behind them, the wooden post snagging the soft cashmere of her sweater, his callused hands cupping her ass. Flesh slapping flesh, sweat and slick heat.

She gave herself up to sensation, knowing he wouldn't let her fall, even when her own legs loosened around his hips and she came like a bitch in heat. Wanting it that way, needing it that way.

His fingers dug into her ass as he found his own release with a shudder and she forced herself down from her high to watch, clinical, detached. Making this all about the sex. Her exquisite relief was more than physical. *Mel's wrong.*

As soon as it was over, she said, "You can put me down now." Resisting any impulse to linger in the moment or keep him inside her.

He eased her down his body and rested his head against hers. "You're determined to kill me, aren't you Honey B?"

"You wanted to be my—the affair." Knees unsteady, she grabbed his ruined T-shirt and used it to clean herself up. "Right," she said briskly, after they'd straightened their clothing and disposed of the evidence. "Back to work."

He laughed and hooked his arm around her waist. "First, tell me what got you all fired up. I'm guessing alcohol at lunch."

"I only had half a glass," she protested. "Your mother got a little drunk though."

"I know. She phoned me burbling all kinds of random stuff from how much she loves me to demanding I buy you a Jack Russell puppy."

"That *is* random." Nervous, Dimity hid her face against his chest. *Had Gayle mentioned Frank was home?*

"I had to swear I'd forgiven her before she let me off the phone." Seth stroked the tense muscles either side of her spine. "Thanks for the drums. They've been great for releasing angst."

"I heard." Surely if Gayle had talked about his dad, Seth's body wouldn't feel so relaxed?

"Mel phoned, too."

She tried not to stiffen. "Oh?"

Pushing her hair aside, he nuzzled her neck. "Said you bumped into each other."

Literally, when she was hauling me out of the pool.

"And that after talking to you, she realizes she overreacted to our LA hookup."

"Good," she said weakly. "Anything…else?"

He pulled away to look at her. "Why do you sound guilty?"

"I'm not!"

"You're hiding something. What tactics did you use—intimidation, blackmail?"

"I asked nicely."

"Okay, now I'm *really* suspicious. Does Mel still have her other leg?"

Dimity broke free of his hold. "That is unbelievably insensitive. How can you joke about that stuff?"

"Because she does. Her amputation happened when she was three after she got away from her grandmother in a parking lot and ran in front of a car. It's something we've grown up with."

She already knew that—she'd asked Mel. "Anyway, how could I intimidate that woman? She's an Amazon."

"You'd have to cheat," he said, and waited expectantly.

"Ass...I corroborated your story and offered extra witnesses if she didn't believe me. And before you get mad that I went behind your back—"

"I'm not," he said, taking the wind out of her sails completely. "Thank you. You're a good friend."

There was no self-consciousness in his eyes. Evidently, Mel hadn't shared her cockamamie theory with him. Relief helped Dimity ignore a twinge of disappointment.

"Have you talked to Zander yet?" he asked casually.

"No, he's out with Elizabeth. Wait, did you let me ravish you thinking they could wander in at any minute?"

"The entire population of Waiheke Island could watch and I wouldn't have stopped you," he said huskily, and she knew he was going to kiss her.

She stepped away from temptation. "Duty calls...I'll see you at dinner."

"Yes, ma'am."

"Oh, and you left your watch in my bedroom." Confident her boundaries had been reinforced, Dimity headed for the barn door.

"Honey B, wait up, your hair is all mussed." Following her, he smoothed it before giving her a critical inspection. "Okay, you're decent." He dropped a kiss on her lips. It was a simple kiss, nothing passionate or sexy about it, more of a warm, affectionate boyfriend/girlfriend kiss. As she walked to the house she thought idly, *I could get used to that,* and then, horrified, *I* want *to get used to that,* and then, despairingly, *I can't let myself get used to that.*

And couldn't pretend any more.

♪ ♫ ♩

"Are you *crying?*"

Dimity jerked upright. Immersed in the manuscript, she hadn't heard Zee come into his office. "With laughter, sure." Averting her face, she blinked hard and two tears splashed onto the pages and puckered the paper. "This is really hilarious. You should read it."

Elizabeth had said she'd stripped Zander bare, metaphorically, and she had. It was an epic love story, of a woman who saw beyond the pretty and the power, to the man inside the rock icon. A man moving tentatively toward using his big heart, even if it did need jump-starting occasionally to keep it beating on its own. This was exactly why Dimity had to end her affair with Seth. He was making her too susceptible to this stuff. *One more night.*

"Can you put the book aside a few minutes? I want to run an idea by you. I'm thinking of asking the publisher if I can buy out Elizabeth's contract. Since I'm quitting the band she's moving into the jungle with no real reason to."

She spun her chair around, sending half the manuscript pages flying. "You can't do that! You need the money for—" *touring.* She forced herself to calmness "—your new life." Bending forward, she picked up the scattered pages. "And buy it out with what?" she added reasonably. "It's not like you have piles of cash lying around anymore."

He picked up the loose pages out of her reach. "I could accept the insurers' offer of settlement."

"Zee, no! That's loser talk, and we're *winners.*" Panic coiled insider her like a slowly tightening spring. "Full settlement is the only way we can keep all our—*your*—options open."

"Hear me out. If the case drags on for months, I might spend everything I've got left in legal costs. And still lose. We both know that justice doesn't always prevail or I wouldn't have gotten away with all the shit I have over the years," he added wryly. "Restoring my good name—such as it was—isn't as important as Elizabeth keeping hers."

Dimity's fingers closed on the manuscript. "You love her that much?" It was a rhetorical question. Thanks to this damn book, she already knew the answer.

He looked surprised she even had to ask. "Yes."

Their willingness to sacrifice for each other made her claustrophobic, and a tiny bit envious. She couldn't imagine an equal partnership of give-and-take. More importantly, she couldn't imagine how the hell she was going to keep Rage together in the face of such blind devotion.

"But this isn't just about Elizabeth. If I accept the settlement, I can probably keep the Calabasas house. There might even be a little money for staff bonuses."

"Zee—"

"Let me finish, this next bit is tough for me. You shot me down at the wharf when I said I'd always be there for you, but it's true. You're a high flier, meant for big things. Which is why it would be selfish of me to expect to keep you beyond the next few months."

He waited for her to speak, but she was recalling the last scene from *Gone with the Wind,* when Scarlett asked Rhett where she would go and what she would do without him.

"There is another job that would suit you if you're interested. Seth thought of it—"

"*Seth* knows it's over?" Intellectually she'd accepted that she might fail to change Zander's mind. She even thought she'd prepared herself. The reality shattered her.

"He said something that made me think you'd told him."

"No, I would never break your trust." *Like you've done mine.*

"Since he's up to speed, I think it's only fair I tell Moss and Jared. Tonight."

Fair? Everything she'd relied on to give her life meaning was being swept inexorably away, leaving her alone and desperately adrift. And Zee was talking *fair*?

Choked up with hurt and anger, she couldn't speak. She gave and she gave and he didn't care. Thinking about it, his complete selfishness when she'd met him had probably drawn her to working for him. Another person, like her mother, she could devote herself to serving. Another person who would ditch her once they no longer had need of her. And she hated him for that, even though he didn't have a clue what he was doing to her.

She put down the manuscript before her shaking hands gave her away. "Contact the publisher and make an offer to buy Elizabeth out of her contract. It's a great idea."

Zander looked thoughtful. "You don't think I should talk to Doc first?"

He was still looking to her for advice like her opinion mattered. Even when, as a person, she clearly didn't. *Unbelievable.* She was so angry that it felt as though she was encapsulated in a bubble, removed from her actions. "She'll only say you can't afford it—which is true. Find out first whether the publisher's open to the idea." Whether Max was or wasn't didn't matter, the damage would be done and Elizabeth's trust broken. Independent women didn't accept someone trying to run their life.

He wanted her to support him in his reckless journey, fine. *Deal with your own fucking consequences, asshole. I'm done protecting you.* She knew she should care about what she was doing, but she didn't care. She burned to make him feel what she was feeling. Abandoned.

"You sure you're okay with all this?" he said. "You look pale."

"Of course I'm okay. Why wouldn't I be?"

She'd thought that by building an identity through her career and not personal relationships, she'd be safe. But she'd screwed up and come to rely on Zander, thrown herself into his quest, and now he was throwing her to the wolves. "I need fresh air—a walk. Why don't I take Elizabeth with me? It will give you privacy to make the call. Oh, and it's after office hours in New York so call Max directly on his cell." She found the number and gave it to him. Her hands weren't shaking anymore. "Do it soon, Zee."

"Thank you…and for understanding. But I haven't told you what Seth suggested—"

"Let's talk about this later." She couldn't think about Seth now. Seth, who didn't know her at all if he thought a new job would make everything better. Surely he'd seen how much *this* one meant to her? The small slices of happiness she'd allowed herself to savor with him were over. She was reverting to an intimacy-free diet.

CHAPTER 20

DIMITY FOUND ELIZABETH IN THE converted shed she used as her writing retreat, sitting at her desk staring trance-like at the copy on her screen.

"Let's go see the dotterels and discuss your manuscript." She'd even dressed for it. Exercise pants, sensible shoes.

"Five minutes." Elizabeth started typing furiously. "Let me just…" Her voice trailed off. Her fingers flew across the keyboard.

"I'll wait outside." Her anger still pulsed so hot, she'd combust in such a small space.

She paced outside the shed. Some deluded idiot—the owner?—had planted sweet peas against a trellis facing the wind-blasted cliff and their slender stems had tumbled into a fragrant heap. God, she hated wishful thinkers. While she waited for Elizabeth, she began roughly untangling them and only succeeded in pulling half the roots out. *Dammit!* Throwing them on the ground, she brushed her hands on her pants.

Hadn't her childhood trained her not to rely on anyone? Taught her that the cost of investing in relationships was too high for her?

And now she'd gone and done the same thing in her career, except using Zander as the stand-in for her parents. How dumb was that? Yet, even understanding this was a textbook case of transference, she still couldn't smother the need, the yearning, the hope that *this* time it would work out different. That someone would appreciate her over and above what she could do for them.

As for all her worrying about the Rage family…every member of it was probably more capable of moving on than she was.

Her chest ached so much she had to hug herself for comfort. *Turns out* I'm *the needy one.*

Even wanting Helena to disappear, it still hurt that she'd left Dimity so easily. It drove Dimity *crazy* that she kept wanting nurturing. She was a grown woman, for God's sake.

Carrying her binoculars, Elizabeth appeared, closing the shed door behind her, her hair an orange marigold color against the forest green paint. She took one look at Dimity and blanched. "You hated it. I can tell by your expression."

"No, it's—" *Zee I hate.* "Let's wait until we get to the beach to talk about it. I need to walk." She wasn't ready to re-examine her feelings about the book. Abruptly, she headed toward the cliff path, away from the scene of her crime. *No, not* your *crime.* It had been Zee's idea to phone Max.

They hiked in silence for a while, each lost in her own thoughts. At least Elizabeth probably was. Glancing at her, Dimity saw that she had the intent, inward focus of a writer working out a story problem. While Dimity was trying not to think at all. Numbness replaced anger, as blanketing as a fog, and she welcomed it. Why care about anything?

Elizabeth moved ahead to push aside a branch overhanging the track, holding it until Dimity had passed. "Are you okay to hike so far? You're looking tired."

An understatement. She could barely manage to put one foot in front of the other. "I didn't get much sleep last night." Too late, she remembered her dramatic exit with Seth.

Elizabeth said nothing.

"I know you disapprove. But I have no intention of hurting him, just so you know."

"Why on earth would I disapprove?"

"Remember the middle-of-the-night phone call I made to Zee when my mother remarried? When he told me to go flirt with Luther, you hit him. I figured it was because he's a nice guy and I'm the tough bitch." She shrugged as if it didn't matter. Not just tough, but mean. Setting Zander up for a fall. Even now he was probably dialing Max's—

"I wasn't worried about Luther's feelings; I was worried about yours. He's a tough nut and I don't want you hurt."

"Me?" Dimity stopped dead. "Sensitive? That is fucking ridiculous."

Elizabeth gave her an assessing look. "Okay."

Dimity started walking again. "Let's just look at the damn birds."

"Sure."

This time when they saw one dragging its wing, she didn't immediately try and rush to the rescue. As they backed off to give the nest protector some space, she said awkwardly to Elizabeth. "I sounded harsh earlier. I didn't mean to imply I have no feelings. I do." *Too many I don't know how to manage, which is why I keep them under lock and key.*

Elizabeth squeezed her arm. "Forget it, we all have our bad days. You don't need to apologize."

God, how had Dimity ended up having *nice* people in her life? She seemed to be attracting them like flies to honey. An image of Seth pierced her numbness. *Honey B.* "I wasn't apologizing."

Elizabeth handed her the binoculars. "My mistake."

As they walked along the foreshore, passing the binoculars between them to look at the birds, Elizabeth's tolerance felt like a debt she had to repay. "Your book made me intensely uncomfortable," she offered reluctantly, "which means it had all the feels."

The biographer's face fell.

"That's a good thing," Dimity clarified. "You want to move people. But whether the publisher will accept it? I don't know." *I don't know anything anymore.* "My radar for what works is unreliable right now." Hearing the defeat in her voice, she attempted a weak joke. "Maybe because we're nearer the south magnetic pole or something."

The other woman was studying her in a way Dimity wasn't comfortable with, so she lifted her hand to her eyes and pretended to shield them against the sun's glare. "The last chapters were missing."

"I'm still writing them, only I can't decide the best way to end it."

"Make sure there's a happy-ever-after," she advised. "Isn't that what happens in love stories?" Except there wouldn't be a happy-ever-after because she'd just encouraged Zee to go above Elizabeth's head and screw with her career.

All because you want to punish him for hurting you. He's not the selfish one here. You are.

Just like your mother.

Her body jerked, and she gasped as the full extent of her actions shocked her out of apathy. She was undermining a love that was good and real because she wasn't getting her *way*? What the hell was wrong with her? She felt as though she'd been flat-lining and a medic had just applied the defibrillator. "Oh, God. What have I done?"

"What's the matter?"

She thrust the binoculars at a startled Elizabeth. "I loved it. Don't change a word. We'll fight for it with the publishers." *Only it won't be published if Zander makes his phone call.* "I have to fix this." She started inland.

"Where are you going?"

"Stay there," she flung over her shoulder, "and make sure that bird isn't hurt. *Please.*"

"Okay," Elizabeth sounded bewildered.

Dimity jogged backward. "And if I'm too late, it's my fault. Everything. Don't blame Zander."

"What's your fault?" Elizabeth hollered.

Dimity didn't answer, turning and running along the path, shoving foliage aside. She was a destructive bitch who didn't deserve any nice people in her life. A twig scratched her cheek and she ignored it. Zander would have made his call, but the sooner she got there the faster she could hit redial, explain to Max that it was a joke, a mistake… She'd think of something.

From the moment she'd arrived on Waiheke, Zee had told her the truth, but she hadn't believed it because she couldn't go through giving everything again, and ending up with nothing. *Oh no, you had to keep working out your fucked-up childhood issues through him.*

How could she blame him for not noticing her pain when she'd trained him only to see his fearless, emotionless PA? It wasn't Zee's job to make up for her lousy childhood by being her best bud forever, her mentor, her big brother.

She got the stitch halfway up the hill, and dug fingers into her side, so she didn't have to stop. Reached the summit gasping, she had to walk the last fifty yards.

Seth was sitting on the steps to the deck, wearing an expression more commonly seen on someone nursing a shotgun in a spaghetti western. "I've been waiting for you."

Dimity tried to hobble past him. "I can't talk right now."

He barred her way. "Yes. You can. I went to get my watch and—"

"Seth, this is urgent. Can't we talk later?" She ducked to the other side, he countered.

"No, we can't."

She got impatient. "If this is about not telling you about Zee's decision to leave the band—"

"No." He ground the word out. "It's about this." He held up the paper airplane she'd hurtled across her bedroom.

♪ ♫ ♩

Dimity stopped, her expression first guilt-stricken, then defiant.

Seth's heart sank. So the list wasn't a joke. "You're under a mountain of pressure right now, so I'm prepared to chalk this one up to temporary insanity if you'll explain to me what the hell you're doing."

"Trying to save our jobs is what I've been doing. Trying to stop Zander from making a terrible mistake is what I've been doing." She swallowed an angry sob. "I've gone too far and I need to fix it, so stand aside. You can call me an unscrupulous bitch later."

And just like that, his outrage left him. Seth opened his arms. "Come here, Honey B…nothing is that bad."

"Isn't it?" She backed away from his comfort. "Zander's voice will be fine, Seth."

He lowered his arms. "What?"

"His vocals will heal. He's quitting Rage to become a better man for Elizabeth or some other woolly-headed bullshit. As though someone with Zee's genius could ever be a regular guy. He'll regret it and she'll regret it and we'll all regret it so I've been trying to stop him. Only…I wasn't strong enough to go through with it. And then he took away my job, which is probably *your* fault," she added cryptically. "And I got mad and I encouraged him to—"

"His singing voice will be okay?" He had to repeat it to make it real. And yet he still couldn't process it.

Dimity put a hand over her mouth. "I shouldn't have told you. It was a secret."

"Come with me." Needing answers, he caught her arm and steered her inside. She shook free when she saw their direction. "No. You need to stay out of this and let me fix—Seth!"

Ignoring her, he opened the door to the office. He *deserved* answers. Feet up on the desk, Zander was on the landline. He glanced up. "Can this wait?"

"No. It can't. We need to have a full and frank discussion." Still holding the door, Seth glanced over his shoulder at Dimity, who was hanging back. If it was anyone else, he would have said she was scared. "You, too."

Reluctantly she moved forward, glimpsed Zander on the phone, and sprang to snatch it from his hand. "Max?"

"What the hell?" said Zander.

Her anxious expression eased as she listened. "It's only your mother." Returning the phone to him, she said urgently, "Did you call the publisher yet?"

"I left a message for him to call me on my—"

His cell chimed on the desk and Dimity dived for it, spinning Zander's chair away as she did so.

"Are you crazy? No, not you, Mum. Listen, I'll phone you later." His pale blue gaze returned to Seth, who folded his arms and waited. "Looks like all hell's about to break loose here…yeah, nothing's changed. Bye."

"Hi, Max," Dimity said brightly. "No, Zee's not here, but I can tell you what he wanted to check. Did you get the release form he signed for Elizabeth's book, okay? That's great. Nope, that's it. You take care now."

"You have some serious explaining to do," Zander told Dimity as she dropped the cell onto his desk, her face a study in relief.

"Funny," said Seth. "That's exactly what I was going to say to *you*."

"Zee, you must never interfere in Elizabeth's work without her permission," Dimity said earnestly. "Ever. She'd never forgive you. And I'm sorry I encouraged you to think otherwise. I wanted to break you two up to punish you for disbanding Rage."

Zander's expression darkened. "What?"

"Will the pair of you shut up for a minute!" Seth yelled, and they turned to stare at him. "I'm getting answers first. Got that?"

He took their mute astonishment as consent. "I have only one question," he said to Zander. "You didn't tell your manager, your family, your band the real truth because…?"

"The fewer people who know the truth," Dimity answered hotly, "the less opposition he'll get."

Seth glared at her, and she subsided.

"Well?" he said to Zander.

"That's partly true," his mentor conceded. "People will perceive it as me giving up—"

"And they'd be right!" Dimity muttered.

"Let the man talk."

"I'm not coming back," Zander said. "For a shitload of reasons that can be summed up by one simple sentence. 'For what profit a man if he gains the world and loses his soul.'"

He looked at Seth, who nodded. He'd been a witness after all these past months to the extraordinary pressures on Rage's lead singer.

So had Dimity. Except having worked with Zander since the start of his meteoric comeback, she'd come to believe in miracles. But even Zander's prodigious energy wasn't inexhaustible. If his voice had held, if he hadn't lip-synced, if his bad-boy history hadn't predisposed the world to question his motives... All this passed across Seth's mind, and must have colored his expression, because Zander sighed. "Yeah."

"Go on," Seth invited.

"The decision's non-negotiable, so I'm left with trying to mitigate the damage. Publicly announcing that I'm leaving by choice will only give the haters and the press more ammunition. They'll say it's a tacit admission of guilt—he's quitting because every accusation was true; because he knows he can't come back from this. That could have fallout on the rest of you. So as much as it *kills* me to play the victim card, for the first time in my life I'm going for the pity vote. If the press think I *can't* sing—as opposed to *won't*— then the resulting sympathy will create goodwill for the rest of you when you set up a new band."

"Fair enough," Seth said. "That all makes sense. But I'm still furious at you—both of you—for missing the fucking obvious here. Tell the truth to the people who love you. Stop going it alone. You both spend so much time machinating that you forget you have backup." Jesus, he was so sick of people he cared about hiding the truth from him for his own good. The more secrets a family kept from one another, the more dysfunctional they were. It was Psych 101 stuff.

"I wanted to protect—"

"And that's bullshit, too, Zee. I don't see your choice as desertion like Dimity does. In fact I probably understand it better than anybody." The irony would be funny if it wasn't so gut-wrenchingly painful. "You're leaving Rage for the things I gave up to join the band—love, family, stability."

"In the interests of full disclosure," Zander said heavily. "Cowardice is partly behind my decision to keep this quiet. I didn't want to lose your respect." He included Dimity in the comment but she'd retreated to the window, where she stood looking out, not seeing anything, Seth suspected.

He knew he'd fallen for a woman who refused to lean on anyone, need anyone, because her parents had never done their fucking job and given her security. He'd hoped he might slowly earn her trust over time. But faced with the magnitude of everything she'd been withholding, he realized it had been a fool's hope.

He returned his attention to Zander. "I'm not blaming you," he clarified. "You took me on in good faith, when you had no thought of leaving. I chose to join Rage, and only a candy-assed wimp would delegate responsibility for future consequences. I'm pissed because you think the rest of us will fall apart without your protection. We won't. The trouble with you—and Dimity—is that you're so good at directing and managing that you think you always know better. You don't. You have my respect. If you want to keep my respect, start asking for support when you need it. And tell Moss and Jared the truth so we're all making informed choices."

"Okay," Zander said quietly. "But in person, when I'm in LA in December. Clearly, this isn't news that can be broken remotely. Meantime, progress Plan B."

"Deal." Seth thrust out a hand and they shook on it. Seth held on. "It's okay to change your life. I did, and no matter how tough it gets, I'll never regret it." He held his mentor's gaze, transmitting the reassurance he suspected Zander needed. "Neither will you."

Zander cleared his throat. "Thank you."

Seth faced Dimity. "After you two have talked, come find me."

"Assuming I haven't killed her."

He nodded. "Assuming that."

"What, so you can finish the job?" But her defiance was all show and no substance, and they all knew it.

Crumbling her paper airplane into a ball, he threw it to her. "Find me," he said again.

He walked out of the house to the cliff's edge, where he could suck in enough oxygen to dissolve the residue of anger. At Zander, at Dimity, at his own expectation that people would never disappoint him. That way lay madness. *I chose this life*, he reminded himself. *I chose this love. I chose to live big and no matter how devastating this feels I will keep doing that.* The mantra helped…a little. Just because he was a team player didn't mean he lacked ambition. With Rage, he'd played for one of the best damn teams in the world.

The new band would smash its way into the Big League, he promised himself that.

Elizabeth appeared around the corner of the hill, concern on her face. "Where's Dimity? She ran home yelling some wild words about everything being her fault."

"Forgive her," he said, "she knows not what she does."

"That sounds ominous, and at the same time, quite promising. I thought you two would be a good match."

"I must be insane."

"Let me upgrade that to an excellent match. What's going on?"

"She had some crazy idea of breaking you and Zander up, but thought better of it."

"Good, because it wouldn't have worked anyway." She looked at him more closely. "Are *you* okay?"

"No. I found out he's choosing you over the band."

"There have been comparisons made to Yoko," she murmured.

"They're as bad as each other," he burst out. "They just need to let people in."

"Yeah."

He sighed. "Dimity won't do it, of course. Zander's stubborn but at least he's improving, thanks to you."

"Want a hug from a normal person?"

"God, yes."

She hugged him. "I'm trying to think of something encouraging to say."

"You can't," he said. "Dimity isn't interested in a relationship long term. And it's my own damn fault that I keep choosing impossible mountains to climb. I'll keep trying, but I already know how this is going to play."

She's going to dump me.

Chapter 21

"In my defense," Dimity said into the hostile silence left in Seth's wake. "I have none."

Zander didn't respond to her nervous joke.

"So, is this where you get out your little fish hammer and put me out of my misery?"

Still nothing.

Her throat, already tight after listening to Seth prove, once and for always, that he was too grounded for her, closed up further. "I'm sorry," she managed to say and left the room, the shame she'd been holding under anger finally breaking the surface.

Her boss blew out an exasperated breath behind her.

Seth was waiting for her and she couldn't see him, she just couldn't. If he knew Zee was kicking her out he'd want to help her, be her *friend,* and worse, he'd feel sorry for her—and she couldn't bear to be the object of his pity. Better he think her a bitch for disappearing without a goodbye, than let him see her devastation.

In the sleep-out bedroom, she dropped to her knees and dragged her suitcases from under the bed. She'd pack her bags, leave them for Zee to forward later, and walk to the end of the track to call a cab. The most important thing was to get out of here before she broke down and cried like a baby for everything she'd thrown away today.

"Where the hell do you think you're going?" Zander said from the doorway.

Throwing a heap of clothes into a suitcase, she didn't look up. "I'm saving you the trouble of firing me." If she couldn't get a plane home to LA tonight, she'd find a hotel.

"Or the pleasure."

"That, too," she said in a small voice. She could claim temporary insanity, but really there was no excuse for her behavior. And she wasn't going to try to make one. Backbone was all she had left.

"Unfortunately," Zander said. "My hands are tied when it comes to you."

"I won't sue for unfair dismissal but I will have to stay in the Calabasas mansion, at least long enough to clear my belongings." She suppressed a flutter of panic. "If you can stand it, I'll hang around and bring my replacement up to speed. I'll write out a list when I get—"

"Much as I enjoy the novelty of your newfound humility, that's not the reason. I can't fire you because you're family. And family, as my long-suffering mother and brother have discovered over the years, are people you're stuck with."

"You don't mean that. You're just—"

"What? Being kind? Nice? A sweetheart?" She bit her lip to stop the smile and he said, "Hey, it's me. Your glorious leader. The king of fuck-ups. I guess I can allow you a misstep every once in a while."

She swallowed. "But I tried to cause trouble between you and Elizabeth."

"You'd come around to thinking it was a bad idea."

"What if I'd broken you two up?"

"Then we'd be one of those families that don't speak to each other for twenty years. But don't flatter yourself, if she's stayed with me despite *my* fuck-ups, she's not going to be deterred by your puny attempt."

"Are you trying to make me cry?" she demanded.

"Only you would interpret a joke as sentiment. I know you can't stand mush so I won't embarrass either of us by harping on about how much you mean to me. You've been pivotal to my career. I couldn't have rebuilt my empire—or my life—without you. Which won't stop me telling everyone I taught you everything when you're kicking ass as the manager of the new band the guys put together."

"What are you talking about?"

"Seth hasn't asked you yet? He, Jared and Moss want you as their manager. He talked to the others after our run."

And when Zander had first mentioned Seth had an idea for another job, she'd been hurt that Seth didn't understand her. It hurt even more realizing how much he did. He was such a good man. "I'm pretty sure I've just blown that chance."

"I'm pretty sure you haven't," Zander said dryly. "He's in love with you."

"You're wrong," she said. "It's rebound for Seth, only it's becoming—"

"Serious?"

"Complicated. I'm starting to feel—"

"Scared?"

"Claustrophobic, like he'll start expecting me to—"

"Love him back?"

"Will you stop! I was going to say, be like a regular girlfriend, which I clearly have no aptitude for." She recalled what she'd drunkenly said to Seth about Luther. That she'd liked an honorable man seeing her as decent and full of moral fiber-iness. Her lover was certainly under no illusion now. And yet he'd forgive her, she knew that. It humbled her.

Zander opened his mouth, closed it.

"What?" she said, a little desperately. *If I had any decency myself, I'd free Seth to find a better woman.*

"Nothing. I've reached the limit of my relationship expertise. Talk this out with Seth."

"God, you are hopeless," she said. "A heart-to-heart is the *last* thing I want."

"I've learned that the thing that terrifies you most is usually the one thing you need to do."

Over the years she'd learned to read every nuance of his tone. But only since surrendering all hope of changing his mind, was she able to hear this one. Sadness. "Zee, I'm so sorry," she said softly. "I've made leaving so much harder for you, haven't I?" How could she ever have thought this was an easy decision for him? "I've been so selfish thinking I was doing this for all of us, when really it was all about me."

His eyes were suddenly bright with unshed tears. He looked away and she rose from the floor and went over and hugged him, willingly, for the first time in their history together.

"It's the right decision," he said after a minute. "I know that."

Their empire—beautiful, shimmering, her everything. And no longer right for him. "Yes, it is." She hugged him tighter. "Does Elizabeth know how hard you're finding this?"

"She's got enough on her plate."

"What did Seth say? Tell the truth to the people who love you." She thought about adding that Elizabeth was floundering, too, and decided against it. It was time she stopped interfering in relationships unless they were her own.

"I'll talk to her."

Dimity picked up her suitcase and returned the heap of clothes to the floor. "If I did consider…more…with Seth—and that's highly unlikely—then their band would need to find another manager. Working together and dating wouldn't work for me, which is why I've avoided it in the past."

The fact that she was even *considering* turning down such a challenging opportunity confirmed what she'd spent the day denying. She loved him. Scared didn't even begin to describe how she was feeling. But maybe it was time to take a chance…

"That's a damn shame," Zander said. "You're their best shot at becoming successful. You've got insider knowledge, access, the business smarts, and as yet, no one in the industry knows just how good you are. Think of the deals you could negotiate for them."

Dimity looked up from her suitcase. "Oh hell," she said bleakly. "You're right."

"Everything okay in here?" Elizabeth entered the room and looked at Dimity's suitcases.

I owe this woman an explanation. "Elizabeth, I—"

"Doc, I'm terrified." Zee cut her off. "Not of leaving Rage, but of what I do next. I've been a rock star for twenty years and I don't have a clue how to live a normal life. Until I met you, I never considered failure…but I have to get this right for us. *Us* is the one thing I can't fail at."

Wow. So that's how you jump off a cliff. Dimity looked at Elizabeth.

"Don't be an idiot," she said with a trembling smile. "You can't fail a test you've already passed. But—" she reached out a hand to him "—you're not the only one scared of getting it wrong."

"Doc," he said gruffly, taking her hand.

Dimity rose to her feet. "Ugh, love cooties," she said, blinking hard. "I'm leaving the contagion zone."

Elizabeth touched her shoulder as she passed. "Seth is expecting you."

For once Dimity didn't flinch from the understanding in her eyes, instead taking everything she offered. "Right," she said briskly. "Best get this over with."

♪ ♫ ♩

Dimity tracked Seth to the barn, this time by the melodic harmonies of an acoustic guitar. These chords had a considered, meditative vibe in contrast to his earlier raw improv. He'd pulled the stool away from the drums and repositioned it near the haystack. Shoulders leaning against the wall of straw, his feet propped on a loose bale, he was looking up at the rafters.

"I didn't realize I was in a nursery earlier," he commented softly. Following his gaze, she saw an untidy nest perched precariously off the central beam.

He stopped playing. "Swallows," he said, and she heard the faint sound of cheeping, before he resumed strumming. "I've been sitting here a while and no sign of the parents. My drumming might have scared them off, so I'm trying to encourage them home."

"Why didn't we hear them before?"

"We were caught up in our own world," he said.

And now it's time to rejoin the real one.

"Everything sorted with Zander?"

"Yes…he forgave me."

"He loves you," Seth said, in the same casual way he'd talked about having a future wife and kids. As though love was a commonplace, everyday right that anyone could expect, even take for granted. Their real worlds were very different. For a little while she'd indulged herself by thinking *maybe*. But it had been only an indulgence. Her weak moment had passed.

"I'm the bratty little sister he never wanted." Some of the terrible pressure squeezing her heart eased. Zander wasn't going anywhere.

"You could have turned to me, you know."

"And drag you down with me?" She shook her head. "I don't ever want to be your problem."

If she'd needed a reminder that she was incapable of behaving normally when she was emotionally involved, she had it in the way she'd behaved with Zander and Elizabeth.

"Are *you* okay about all this?"

He didn't answer, his gaze sharpening on something behind her.

Dimity looked up and saw a swallow perched on a rafter near the barn's entrance, head cocked, uncertain. Seth kept playing, a wash of warm sound, as inviting as a blanket. Another swallow joined the first. *Go home*, Dimity admonished silently. *Your babies need you.*

"What are we doing here, you and I?" His question caught her off guard.

"W—what do you mean?"

Still playing, he looked at her, his eyes unguarded, and she started to panic.

"Oh, you mean about the manager offer…Zander told me. I guess that depends whether you still think I'm a fit person for the job."

"There's no question you'll be good for the band," he said, changing chords. The melody developed a haunting quality that made her heart ache.

"It would have to be part time until after Elizabeth's book launch. They still need me."

"Exactly what I was going to suggest. We won't be able to afford you full time for a few months at least." Seth bent over the guitar. "We need to write enough songs for an album, find a new lead singer…a band name…there's a lot to resolve. And you need to think about this carefully. You will get more lucrative job offers once people hear you're available."

"I'm used to working with the best and I'm not lowering my standards now."

There was flash of movement in her peripheral vision. One bird returned to the nest. She and Seth smiled at each other and she imprinted the moment in her memory—this man, russet-haired in a shadowy barn, smiling at her as though they might have a future.

If only she'd practiced intimacy on the idiots she'd been dating so that when Seth came along she had some confidence in her ability to make a relationship work. The same certainty she had in her ability to help him rebuild a career.

"I want to revert to friends," she said calmly. He was too nice to protect himself. So she would do it for him. "If I'm going to manage the new band—and I'd like to—the affair has to end. It's been fun, a time-out from the stresses in our lives, but you know me. Career comes first."

Career is what I'm good at. It's all I'm good at.

"If that's what you want."

Her strength lay in recognizing her limitations and making the hard choices. "That's what I want." Even when it felt like someone had stuck a knife under her ribs and was twisting it.

She had no clue how to make an ongoing relationship work. And if Seth was developing feelings for her, it was better to cut him loose now, before she really hurt him. She loved him too much to mess up his life.

The second bird darted toward the nest and her gaze followed it. "You make the music, I'll make the money. Let's get famous together." He would get more value from her as the band's manager than as his loose cannon girlfriend. Even so, she had to breathe shallowly to manage the pain.

Fortunately, he misread the gesture as awkwardness. "You don't owe me anything, Honey B," he said quietly, putting the guitar down. "You were always clear about what this was. I'm a nice guy, remember? I'm not going to make you uncomfortable."

"Thank you." Forcing a smile, she thrust out a hand. "Shake on it?"

"Let's not get too formal." Bypassing her outstretched hand, he caught her shoulders, drew her close and kissed her. Non-threatening, warm—a friend's kiss. It took all her self-control not to throw her arms around him and beg him not to let her go.

I just want him to be happy. The term wasn't a sappy-sweet, kittens and heart-shaped chocolate box cliché anymore. It was a sword that cut through all the me, me, me crap and made you put the other person's interests first.

"Let's make the transition easy." Seth picked up the guitar. "I'll return to the mainland and stay with Janey."

"Smell the baby for me."

"I will. Dad texted me suggesting we play golf in a few days and talk things over."

"Really?"

"Yeah, I'm skeptical, too. I suspect Mum either stole his phone and sent the text or nagged him into it. Either way, I'm not getting my hopes up." His smile was rueful. "Keep an eye on the news for 'father beaten to death with a nine iron'. Speaking of which, okay if we iron out details when we both return to LA? The other guys need to be involved."

"Of course." *Go. Go now. I can't smalltalk much longer.*

He walked away from her and she let him, watching the swallows dart to and from the nest until she heard Zander's Land Rover fire up, taking Seth to the ferry.

Elizabeth appeared at the barn door, saying nothing. Her unspoken questions lay softly between them. *What do you need from me? How do you want to handle this?* Dimity desperately appreciated the reminder that she was still *capable* of leading. Strong. Resilient. A survivor.

There was such power behind Elizabeth's patience. *How on earth can you be so sensitive and stay sane?* Because the only way Dimity could hold onto hers was to pretend that her heart wasn't pulsing in the dirt at her feet.

"You've turned me into a bird watcher," she growled, indicating the nest. "I hope you're happy."

♪ ♫ ♩

"I've never been very good at apologizing," Frank said as they teed off on the first hole.

He struck the golf ball and it curved left into a stand of Japanese cedar and disappeared. "I'm out of practice," he added, and Seth wasn't sure whether he was referring to his golf or apologizing.

By the time they'd reached the sixteenth hole without his father raising the subject of an apology again, Seth had decided it was the golf.

He let it slide because he was shooting six under his handicap, despite only having played twice in the past year. And he needed the boost of a small pleasure, since the big ones were denied him. The ache for Dimity was constant and he suspected he'd feel it for a long, long time. And that was being optimistic.

She hadn't even considered giving them a chance. It had apparently never crossed her mind that what they had together could have been extraordinary. He should feel humiliated, but instead he felt sad. Sad for himself, sadder for her. She had so much love to offer and she held onto it like a miser.

Frustration powered his next shot and it soared up the fairway, bounced onto the green, and rolled to within two feet of the pin.

Frank grunted. "Good shot."

If Seth wasn't so in love with her, he'd talk the others out of offering her the managerial job and protect his sanity, but he couldn't resist the temptation to keep her in his life.

"Okay," his father's grumble broke into his thoughts. "Enough of the silent treatment. Next time I end up in hospital, I'll let your mother phone you."

An empty promise—both Janey and his mother had already sworn to Seth that they'd never make the same mistake again. "That would be wise, Dad, considering I'll be the one delivering your eulogy."

His father barked a laugh as they pushed their trundlers toward the green. "I hadn't thought of that."

"I have to say I'm surprised you didn't use your TIA to drag me back into the fold."

"Didn't think it would work." Frank gave him a sideways glance. "Would it?"

"I would have come home, but no, I wouldn't have stayed."

"Humph. The thing is, Jeff really *is* better at your job."

"Well, he would be. His heart's in it."

"Humph," his father said again, but it was a softer humph. "Watch your cholesterol levels when you hit your forties, it's a family condition. You'll probably inherit."

On the green, Seth used his club to set up a sight line to the hole. "Good to know."

"You can control it with diet…less saturated fat and more rabbit food."

"Got it." One putt and his ball was in the hole.

Maybe when Dimity had made the band a shitload of money, he could use his share to buy a golf membership at LA's most exclusive club. He'd have to find out what that was.

On the last green of the last hole, his father started to talk. "I devoted my whole life to the business. I wanted to build something to pass on, build a legacy. I missed so much of your lives to do that. When you joined Curran Consulting, well, the only thing that would have made me happier would have been Janey joining the firm, too, but she was never interested."

He didn't look at Seth, concentrating on making his putt.

"And out of the blue, you walked away from it. I thought you understood what I was trying to do, but you didn't."

"Dad—"

"Please, son, let me finish." He struck the ball and it skirted the edge of the hole and rolled away three feet. "And then I got sick, and lying in hospital, I thought, 'What the hell was it all for?' I was going to die and what had I achieved? I felt as though I had lived my life to no real purpose…and I blamed you. It was wrong."

He hit the ball again, and it clunked into the hole. "And it was very wrong of me to ask your mother and sister to keep my condition from you." He retrieved the ball from the hole and stood with it tight in his hand. His eyes met Seth's. "I'm sorry."

"I'm sorry, Dad, that I didn't understand that." It would have made his father's bitterness more understandable. "I didn't leave to hurt you, I left because I'd finally worked out what I wanted to do with my life."

"I still don't get how you can choose the uncertain life of a musician over the security of a family business."

"You don't have to get it, Dad, you just have to accept it." Seth carefully considered his next words. "But you will leave a legacy— Janey and I, your granddaughter. It's not too late to make up the lost time. I know Janey really wants you more involved in Em's life. And I want you and Mum to come see mine."

They packed up their golf clubs.

"Guess I should come to one of your concerts one day," Frank offered reluctantly.

He'd hate it. "Yeah," Seth said ruthlessly. "You should."

"You're not going to let a man with high cholesterol off the hook then?"

"Nice try, but Ma says medication is keeping it under control."

Not a stagnant silence this one, but as gently expansive as an incoming tide. Seth was the first to speak. "It's a damn shame you never saw the stadium shows. It could be five years before we're playing another."

He'd told his family that Zander wasn't able to return to Rage and he, Moss, and Jared would be forming a new band.

"That long?" His father looked surprised. "Janey said Dimity was going to be your manager."

"Good point, make that three years." Given the choice, he would have chosen love over money, but that was a musician for you, all about the emotion. He could almost hear Dimity's incredulous snort. Seth smiled as he and his father walked toward the parking lot. "And don't think you can weasel out of a concert by dying in the meantime."

Frank gave a grunt of amusement. "I'll do my best to stay alive."

"I'd appreciate that." He squeezed his father's shoulder and dropped his hand. "I love you, Dad." He heard a mumble that might have been, "You too."

As they were packing their clubs in Janey's car—Seth had picked Frank up en route—his father said gruffly, "If you need money while you're getting the new band up and running…"

"I'm good, but thanks. Spend it on bringing Mum to visit…have you got time for breakfast?"

"I'll make the time," Frank said.

They walked back to the clubhouse. One door closes, another opens, Seth thought. *The woman I love can't love me, but I have my father again, so it's not all bad.* Given he fully intended to challenge Frank every time he overstepped his authority—*small pleasures*—they were bound to fall out again, but for now Seth enjoyed the moment.

"I was always pretty good on the accordion when I was young," Frank commented as they found a table. "You get your musical talent from me."

"The accordion is *not* in my musical genealogy," Seth said firmly.

His father's laugh boomed around the cafeteria. "You don't have to get it, son, you just have to accept it."

CHAPTER 22

"THE END." DIMITY SLAMMED THE book shut and stared at the four year old who'd requested Sleeping Beauty as her bedtime story. "How can someone who sleeps in a dragon bed like this cra—kind of story. All the heroine has to do is wake up."

"But she's in a tower and she's a *princess*," said Madison, her round brown eyes shining. "An' now they can go and get the bad Queen. With the sword. An' the dragon."

Dimity couldn't recall any dragon in the story. "You mean the prince can," she said dryly.

A bass beat throbbed through the bedroom wall as someone in the living room jacked up the speakers. Jared's impromptu party to celebrate his Grammy nomination was becoming raucous, even separated by several rooms. A few seconds later the volume dropped. Most of the attendees were Rage family, and conscious of his kids sleeping down the hall.

"No, that's why the prince kisses the princess." Madison was looking at Dimity as if she was stupid. "So he can wake her up an' *give* her the sword."

Dimity suspected the prince had the presentation of a different sword in mind, but she preferred Maddie's version. "I'll buy you *The Paper Bag Princess* for Christmas. It's got a cool dragon and a kickass princess."

The little girl scrambled for her present list on the bedside table and gave it to Dimity with a pen to write it down. It was a big list, and included many Barbies under her baby brother's name, which was remarkable considering Rocco couldn't yet talk.

Dimity glanced over to the port-a-cot where the eleven month old was sleeping, wearing headphones to keep him that way, a baby monitor beside him if they didn't. The receiver was being passed between the responsible party-goers. Last she'd seen, Seth had it. She took a big careful breath.

"I'll stay here 'til you go to sleep, okay?"

Madison stuck out her lower lip. "I'm a big girl."

I'm not. "Oh, sure, I get that, only I need a rest from dancing."

It was hard enough seeing Seth when they were both in work mode; on personal time it was agonizing. And she couldn't leave the party because she'd organized it. She stood up and picked up tiny clothes, folding them awkwardly, trying to look useful instead of a big scaredy cat.

"Okay." Madison relented and burrowed into her dragon bed. "You forgot to give me a kiss."

Dimity hedged. "Kisses only wake people up."

"Silly, that's just in stories."

Madison was nearly five and almost domesticated, so Dimity bent reluctantly to do her duty, and was shocked when small arms wound around her neck and held tight. She returned the hug, needing the comfort she couldn't ask of friends or they'd know something was wrong. Neither she nor Seth had divulged their brief affair to anyone on their return to LA two weeks ago. Not by a glance or a comment did he act as though they'd ever been more than friends and colleagues. He was doing everything she'd asked him to, and sometimes she thought she'd explode with the agony of wanting and not being able to have.

"Want Mommy," Maddie murmured sleepily.

"I'll send her in the moment she's home," Dimity promised. Kayla didn't know her house was full of party-goers; she'd left Jared with the kids for a mommy's day out. She and Dimity had shared lunch earlier and Dimity had almost confided her trauma—which would have been the stupidest thing ever. *This is what you wanted, remember? Deal with it.*

She switched off the main light and the soft blue glow of the night light came into focus, spiraling stars on the ceiling. Noticing Rocco had kicked off his blanket, she replaced it gingerly. The talcum baby smell was so lovely, she sat beside the cot, her back against the wall—for a few minutes taking a time out on being strong. Trying to be tender with herself.

Unfortunately, her cell was in her bag in the living room. That left her with nothing to do but wonder who was hitting on Seth in the next room. Sooner or later he'd take up one of the many sexual invitations from women assuming he was a free man. *Because he is.*

She banged the back of her head against the wall—gently, so as not to disturb the kids. Reminded herself fiercely, *And so are you, free.* She'd tried to prove it a few times by going to The Comfort Zone. A hookup would prove she was getting over Seth. Once, she'd even got as far as the manager Antonio's apartment before realizing that she'd be punishing herself with impersonal sex. It wasn't her thing anymore. Unconsciously, she sighed. Most likely she'd end up having a civil union ceremony with her vibrator.

Madison gave a slight snore. Asleep. Still Dimity didn't move to rejoin the party.

It felt as if she spent all day catching and containing *feelings,* only to have them attack her the moment she opened her eyes the following morning. Sadness, loss, doubt. It was getting so she didn't want to sleep, as attested by the dark circles she had to cover with concealer. She yawned, achingly tired. Maybe Sleeping Beauty had the right idea…go to sleep for a hundred years and wake up when the world's moved on.

Shaking off her self-pity, she forced her thoughts to work. Zee and Elizabeth would arrive next week, providing a welcome distraction. Zander would be breaking the news to his core people and signing a renegotiated insurance claim. In the meantime everyone was following Plan B, which included Dimity 'playing' at a managerial role.

The bedroom door opened, and Kayla stuck her head around the jamb to check on her kids. Putting a finger to her lips, Dimity pushed reluctantly to her feet. Party time. She followed Kayla into the hall, mentally donning her Dimity-ness en route. By the time the dark-haired woman pulled the door closed, she was even able to smile when Kayla grabbed her hands and danced her around in an excited jig.

"My husband's a Grammy nominee!"

"And we're going to do everything we can to capitalize on that." Loosing her hands, Dimity began outlining her plans. "First, we want to set up some exclusive interviews. I think—"

"Tomorrow you think." Catching her hand again, Kayla began pulling her along the hall. "Tonight we're having fun."

"Sounds great." *You are Dimity fucking Graham and you do not surrender to feelings, not now, not ever.*

And then Kayla said, "Seth's lined up some shots," and Dimity stopped dead.

"No." Alcohol. Seth. Fun. "I can't do this."

"Don't worry, there are non-alcoholic ones for drivers and teetotalers."

"That's not it." She racked her brains for an excuse. "I've got terrible cramps…period pains."

"You poor thing, I'll get you some Advil."

"No…I'll…can I go home?" Sooner or later she'd have to woman up and cope with spending time with Seth socially. Later sounded do-able.

"Of course you can. Are you okay to drive? I'll—"

"No. I haven't been drinking. You stay. This is a big night for you and Jared. I'll just sneak out."

Somehow she got to the door with her bag and her phone without seeing Seth. *A win.*

Kayla hugged her goodbye. "I'll phone in the morning, and see you on movie night." Since Dimity had instigated it, Girls' Night In had become a social highlight of their friends' calendar. "How about we watch—"

"I've already picked *Gone with the Wind*," Dimity said. Last week it had been *Casablanca.*

"Hmm, I was kinda hoping for something this century."

"You can choose next time," she promised.

There was a hoot of laughter from inside the house. Jared yelled drunkenly, "King of the fucking world!"

Chuckling, Kayla shook her head. "He has the baby monitor. I'd better confiscate it."

"Good idea."

As Dimity unlocked her car, she glimpsed Seth through the kitchen window, playing bartender. Unable to resist the chance to stare at him unobserved, she paused. A carton of juice in one hand, a bottle of tequila in the other, he was filling shot glasses and laughing with Moss and Jared. Biting the inside of her cheek, she got into her car. Even if she *had* been having second thoughts, Seth clearly wasn't.

Literally and figuratively, she'd missed her shot.

♪ ♫ ♩

"So, I have to ask." Zander settled into one of the studded leather couches in the library at his Calabasas home and chinked cognac glasses with Seth. "Why did you wimp out with Dimity?"

Pouring tea from a fine china set, Elizabeth cleared her throat. She sat next to Seth on a couch opposite Zander's. The three of them had enjoyed a quiet dinner before retiring to her favorite room for after-dinner digestifs. Although Zander and Elizabeth had arrived home a few days earlier, this was the first time Seth had seen them privately.

"Doc, we're guys," said Zander. "This is how we empathize."

"He's right," Seth reassured her. "And to be honest, it's a relief to talk about it." These two were the only ones who knew he had a hole the size of a bass drum in his heart.

"I had two choices when Dimity said she wanted to revert to friends. I could beg her to love me, or man up and respect her decision. I manned up. Not that it's done me any good. In fact, I'm not sure we can keep working together."

Zander put down his cognac glass. "What do you mean? What's happening?"

"It's been over a month since she ended the affair and she still can't relax around me." She wasn't home tonight—out Christmas shopping with Kayla—which was why he could be here. Outside business hours he avoided incursions on her home turf. "I told her I wasn't going to make her uncomfortable. I've bent over backward to show there's no hard feelings, and she acts like she has to put a couple of people and five chairs between us every time we're in a room together." He couldn't keep the frustration out of his voice. "Even Moss and Jared have noticed it. We'll be talking band business and Dimity will be her usual snap-chat self, throwing out half a dozen ideas and then she'll look at me, get self-conscious, and suddenly it's awkward."

Neither of his friends said anything. They were letting him rant and he appreciated it. He'd held this in too long. The cognac trailed fire from throat to stomach and did nothing to warm him. "So, I'm wondering…despite my best efforts to play it cool, am I leaking emotion? Does she sense my heart aches whenever she enters the room and I embrace it because it's still better than the numbness when she's not there?"

He shrugged, slightly embarrassed by his raw romanticism, so far removed from his Kiwi bloke roots. Glancing at Zander, he saw a slow grin dawning. Fuck, make that *really* embarrassed.

"Oh, Seth," Elizabeth said softly. Watching her add milk to his teacup, it occurred to him that his countrywoman was literally dispensing tea and sympathy. Zander on the other hand was still smiling. *Yeah, thanks mate. Got the message. Tough it out.*

He accepted the tea from Elizabeth. "It was a mistake to ever sleep together," he said brusquely. "We can't seem to get past it to the easy friendship we had. Dimity's doing great things for the band, but she clearly hates working with me."

Thoughtfully, Elizabeth chewed her bottom lip. "I'd suggest reassuring her again, but it might make her more twitchy. She hates discussing personal stuff."

Zander laughed and the two of him stared at him, incredulous.

"That," Seth said, pissed, "is not sympathy."

Still grinning like a Cheshire cat, Zander shook his head. "I can't believe *I'm* the emotionally savvy one here. It's so obvious that Dimity's in love with you."

Seth groaned. "Not you, too. I've had it from my sister, my mother." Even Mel, when they'd shared a coffee before he'd flown to LA. "It was a fling for Dimity, always was. She made that clear on Waiheke when she dumped me."

"Did she?" Zander said thoughtfully. "Yeah, that makes a lot of sense."

"Not to me."

"Because you don't think like us. By any chance did you tell her you loved her?"

"I was about to, but she shot me down before I even got off the ground."

"Of course she did." Zander nodded sagely. "That would be the scariest thing you could say to her. Then she might have to admit she loves you back, and where would you be then?"

"Happy?" Seth said, confused.

"On a wonderful new adventure?" Elizabeth offered. Seth saw she was smiling at Zander as if he was a genius. Which left him the only person still in the dark.

"You'd be in a *relationship*." Zander was clearly enjoying playing relationship guidance counselor. "Virgin territory where scary beasts like commitment and compromise roam freely. And the unprepared run a very real risk of dying from exposure. I avoided that border crossing for years."

Seth got a glimmer of the big picture, then a glimmer of hope. He wanted to believe, but… "No, that can't be right. Why would she agree to work with me if she's so relationship-phobic?"

"Because she wants you to be successful and she's your best shot at getting there."

"We could have had both," Seth said, incredulous. "How could she not have seen that?"

"Dimity doesn't expect to find true love," Zander explained patiently. "She thinks she's unlovable. I felt the same way when Doc first came into my life."

Seth turned to Elizabeth. "How did you change his mind?"

"I dropped a bomb," she said cheerfully. "Blew away every choice but one. Me—yes or no." She sipped her tea, a fragrant Earl Grey. "That could be your way forward with Dimity."

"Did you know he loved you when you detonated this bomb?"

"Yes."

"And I tried so hard to hide it," Zander commented ruefully. "I wanted her to be sensible. Thank God, she ignored me."

"I don't have your certainty," Seth said to Elizabeth. "I'm not convinced Dimity feels that way about me."

"I can tell you how to get proof," Zander said. "But you'll have to go to war. Your opponent won't surrender until she's fought to exhaustion."

Hope was more than a glimmer now, it was a sunrise. Instinct resonated to the truth in Zander's words, but Seth made a token effort to be sensible. "Take Dimity on? If it doesn't work, it will create an even bigger mess."

"It's a winner-takes-all strategy," Zander admitted. "Is she worth the risk? Or not?"

What had Dimity told him the night they'd hooked up? That he was a covert rebel. *"I'm the only one who sees behind the Mr. Nice Guy facade and wonders what it would be like to let the beast loose."*

Seth leaned forward. "Tell me your plan."

♪ ♫ ♩

Seth was late.

Again.

Dimity strode the service alley outside the south LA production studio, her cell pressed to her ear, waiting for the drummer to pick up.

"Yeah, it's me," said his cheerful voice.

"Wow, you actually answered your phone. I—"

"Leave a message and I'll call you back."

She growled her frustration. "But you don't, do you, Seth? For someone who never answers your bloody phone you sure change your greeting a helluva lot. Is it to mess with me? Because that's what it's starting to—"

Beep.

"Argh!" She kicked the trashcan by the door and the lid bounced off, forcing her to give chase before it rolled into traffic, which took her dark mood into black hole territory.

Mr. Reliable had become Mr. Random. The first time Seth hadn't shown up on time, she'd thought the worst. With fingers shaking, she'd been dialing the local hospital when he strolled in eating an ice cream. "I forgot I was meant to be here."

"But Moss texted. Jared phoned to see where you were—" The two intermediaries she used to keep her distance.

"Yeah, I saw their messages when I got out of the water...I went surfing." He held out the ice cream. "Lick?"

"No!" She wished she could get over the welling up of grief whenever he treated her as a *friend.*

But she was getting over him, she told herself that constantly. And business was looking up. With the help of their lawyers, she and Zee had negotiated a better settlement with the insurers and Zander was in town to sign it. Unofficially, she'd become band manager, becoming official in a couple of weeks when Zee announced his vocals hadn't recovered. Publicly, he was still going for the pity vote. Privately, he'd only told his most trusted friends the truth—to understandably mixed reactions. Everyone was still processing their feelings on that one.

Fucking feelings.

Gently, Dimity replaced the lid on the trashcan, then brushed her palms clean on her pants, remembering too late they were suede. Looked at the smear of dirt on the taupe brushed leather and kicked the trashcan again. Mr. Nice Guy was *still* ruining her clothes.

On the second occasion Seth "forgot the time," Moss said silkily, "Shouldn't you be bitching at him the way you do me when I skip meetings?" They'd gathered in her office in Zander's Calabasas house—the one he was now keeping. Her hidey-hole. Moss glanced over her shoulder. "Instead of researching symptoms of early-onset Alzheimer's?" She slammed her laptop lid shut. "The difference is Seth's not a habitual offender."

He was now. The more correct term was *chronic recidivist*.

And any goodwill his bandmates had for him was long gone. She'd tried to tell Seth that last time he'd showed up late to a key strategy meeting, anxiety gnawing at the edges of her temper. He'd laughed off her concerns. And when she'd lost control and yelled, "What the *hell* is going on with you?" he'd said, "Don't you know?"

She'd backed right off.

"Just promise me you'll make the session on Thursday."

He'd held up his hand, Boy Scout-style. "I promise."

Furiously, Dimity rubbed at the suede, using a hanky out of her Gucci handbag and spit. So why the *fuck* was he thirty minutes late? She rolled her shoulders to loosen them, and returned to the production booth.

The guys were recording a demo of Jared's latest composition, Moss on vocals and a couple of session musicians filling in the sound until they repopulated the band. Both Seth and Jared wanted Moss to take over as lead singer; the guitarist was keeping his options open. The session musicians weren't cheap and neither was the top producer, even with a friends' discount. Zee had come along to give feedback. The very last thing Dimity needed was her mentor seeing her fail to manage the easiest-going guy on the planet.

Mustering excuses, she walked into the booth and stopped short.

On the studio side of the glass partition, Seth sat behind his drum kit, headphones on, tearing it up with the band.

Zander glanced up from his seat beside the producer, who was fiddling with sliders on the console. "Where'd you get to?"

"I had to make a phone call, nothing important."

Moving to stand behind him, where he couldn't witness her relief, she reconciled herself to the torture of watching all that crystallized, powerful focus that would never shine on her again. Closing her eyes when she could no longer manage it.

You can do great things for this band. Deal with it. How many times did she repeat this mantra daily? And she was so lonely she'd even dragged her soft toy Jack Russell out of storage and slept with it.

The drumbeat lost time with the bass line. Dimity opened her eyes to see Seth thwack his sticks on the cymbals in frustration. Moss stopped mid-lyric, and the other instruments petered out.

The producer hit the intercom between rooms. "What's up?"

Dropping his sticks, Seth stood up from the drum stool. "Let's call it a day, Greg. I'm just not feeling it."

Everyone laughed. Jared readjusted the shoulder strap on his bass guitar. "From the top."

"I'm serious." Seth snagged his plaid shirt from the floor and shrugged it on.

Zander said through the intercom, "Are you ill?"

"Nope."

"Sprained wrist, sweetie?" Moss asked.

"Nope. Just not feeling it." He shot Moss a narrow-eyed stare. "Could be your singing."

"I'm not in Zander's league," the lead guitarist agreed, so cordially that the hairs on the nape of Dimity's neck rose. He'd responded to Zee's secret with uncharacteristic sobriety and everyone was treading very, very carefully around him. "But I believe I'm hitting notes." He glanced at the producer, who nodded.

Seth turned to Jared. "Then maybe the song itself is too generic."

Its Grammy-nominated composer frowned. "Yesterday you said it was ground-breaking."

"Which leads us back to me not feeling it." Seth looked at Dimity through the glass. "Can I go now, miss?"

She laughed nervously and bent to the intercom. "Seth, this studio is closed over the Christmas break and these sessions don't come cheap. Sit down and stop kidding around."

"Or what?" he said contemptuously. "You'll fire me?"

"I can't." She tried to lighten the mood with a joke. "Unfortunately we're a democracy."

"You've got my vote," Moss said, stripping off his guitar. "I'm tired of his bullshit."

"Session musicians," Dimity said brightly. "You don't need to listen to family squabbles. There's a great coffee shop across the street. Take a break while we thrash this out... Seth, where are you going?" He was following them out the door.

"Fishing, probably."

"Stay there," she said sharply, and scooted out of the booth. She met him coming through the studio door, and manhandled him into the room.

"Get out of my way, Dimity."

"No." She locked the door. "C'mon, guys, we've all been under a lot of pressure lately. Tempers are bound to fray. So let's all take a few minutes and give ourselves a chance to simmer down."

"Fire him," Jared said. The bassist Dimity had marketed as Rage's soulful poet folded his arms, his stance all about aggression. "We have no leeway on this and I have a family to support. Moss, didn't you say Collision's drummer is unhappy with his band?"

"Yeah. Hear that, Seth? You're replaceable."

Shocked, Dimity looked from Moss to Jared. "C'mon guys, where's your loyalty?"

"Hey, you're the one always lecturing about consequences," Moss reminded her. "And whatever trouble I get into on my own time, at least when we're working, I work. Right, Zee?"

"It's the only way to build a successful, long-term career."

"Butt out, Zander," Seth said. "You have no skin in this game anymore."

Dimity gasped.

"That's it," Moss said. "You've got my vote. Fire him."

"I'd say he's leaving you no choice," Zander said.

This was a nightmare.

"Fine, if no one wants me in the new band." All defiance, Seth faced her, holding up his arms in surrender. "Fire me."

She shook her head, desperate now. *What are you doing? You want this, you need this.* "Guys, he's acting completely out of character. Seth, you can tell us. Have you been taking drugs?"

"I'm not on drugs. You're the manager. Fire me."

This can't be happening. "Could someone have spiked your drink last night?" She knew he'd been clubbing with Moss. She'd spent a sleepless night worried he might take someone home.

He glowered at her. "Get this over with, Dimity. The band always comes first, remember?"

"What about medication for an allergy? Are you taking anything new? Could this be an adverse reaction?" Her eyes pleaded with him. *Help me here. I'm trying to save you.*

Seth shoved the mike stand and it hit the floor with a crash. Everyone jumped. "Will you fire me now?" he said curiously.

"Fire him," barked Moss, a call echoed by Jared. She threw the bassist a betrayed look. In a second honeymoon phase with Kayla, Jared had been generous in his acceptance of Zee's decision. *What happened to peace on earth and goodwill to all men?*

"It's for the good of the band," Zander said impatiently. "What are you waiting for?"

For the guy I love to come to his senses.

"Fire me." Seth picked up Moss's guitar and its owner started forward. "Just joking." Replacing the guitar on its stand, Seth turned and kicked a hole through his bass drum. Looked over his shoulder at her. "Will you fire me now?"

"Stop," she whispered, brokenly. "Please, please stop."

He *smiled* at her. Crossing the room in three strides, he pulled her into his arms and kissed her like no one was watching, a raw, toe-curling onslaught that left her teetering on her stilettos. Carefully, he steadied her on her feet.

"Forgive me for playing dirty," he said huskily. "But I had to win."

And she got it.

"You son of a bitch." He ducked as she swung for him. "You *played* me?"

"How else could I confirm you loved me? You sure as hell would never admit it."

"I'm not admitting it now!"

Moss and Jared were smiling, so were Zander and the producer. She swung around to glare and each and every one of them, and they stopped. "Were you in on this?"

"Save yourselves," Zee advised, and they were all gone within five seconds.

"Why are *you* still here?" She poked Seth in the chest, but he didn't budge. "You're the one I want to kill most."

"I'm working out your sexual fantasy."

She gasped. "Get. Out. Now. Or I'll destroy the rest of your drum kit."

He knelt. Head bowed, he said, "I'm sorry. Even sorrier I was a nice guy and let you torture us for weeks. I should have forced you to admit how you felt about me in the barn."

"I admit nothing." Suddenly, she felt like Marie Antoinette facing the guillotine.

Seth was still on his knees. "I'll get a makeover. You can dye my hair blond, throw out all my plaid shirts, whatever it takes for you to give us a shot."

Her throat tightened. "I don't want you to have a makeover."

He caught her hands, his blue eyes utterly sincere. "You know what I love about you? You're beautiful."

"That's not love, Seth, it's lust." She tried to free her hands. He raised them to his lips.

"Beautiful, Dimity, all the way through."

The sad, lonely, yearning part of her that she hid away for safekeeping slipped its shackles and stretched toward the light. Her eyes filled with angry tears. "Dammit, don't say that. Not unless you mean it."

"I do mean it. You're bluster and fury and always the first to help the people you care about. You don't suffer fools, but once you admit someone to your inner circle, you let them get away with murder. Maybe that's why you resist letting people get close. Even when you think yourself weak, you're the strongest person I know."

"You want me to tell you I love you. Fine, I love you." She broke his hold and flung away from him. "But I'm not happy about it. You effectively tricked me into it…using Mel and your niceness as some kind of Trojan horse."

He was trying to hide a smile as he got to his feet.

"You won't be so happy when I screw this up," she said scathingly. "Because I will."

"So will I, screwing up is a normal part of relationships."

She opened her mouth to argue, and he cut her off. "Don't bother giving me that bullshit about being missing the intimacy gene, and only being good at business. I won't buy it, and you need to return that bunch of goods to the store that sold it to you, because you're not bringing it into our marriage."

"What?" She stopped breathing. The beckoning light was bright now, almost too bright. Was she dying?

"Did I miss that part?" Seth said casually. "We're skipping the months where every time we fight like regular couples you decide you're hopeless at intimacy and try to break up with me. I'm not fucking going through this misery again. If we have a legally binding contract, you're more likely to think twice."

She sucked in air. "You can't be serious." The lack of oxygen had made her dizzy.

"I'm completely serious. No one works harder than you once you've made a commitment. But you won't have to work hard. We fit, Dimity, as colleagues, as friends, as lovers—right down to each having a parent who drives us crazy. You march to the beat of your own drum. Who better to keep time than your own personal drummer boy?"

Another breath, and another. She wanted so badly to *live*. She recalled her awe when Zee had started spilling his guts to Elizabeth. *So that's how you jump off a cliff.* Closed her eyes.

"I surrender." Her whisper was barely audible.

And because Seth was a nice guy he didn't ask her to repeat it, simply gathered her into his arms, where she belonged, and kissed her like a badass. Why hadn't she realized he was as complicated as she was? Because people were never one thing, but many.

Elizabeth's book was about a rock god making all the mistakes in his poignant attempts to become human, attempting his toughest reinvention of all—working from the inside out. That was what had made her cry, because she couldn't follow Zee on that journey. It took the kind of courage she simply didn't have.

I was wrong. I do have the courage to be loved.

A great relief welled up inside her. "I love you and I'm ju—ju—just so happy." She began to sob, and Seth murmured soft nonsense as he kissed every one of the tears away, not asking why she was crying because he got it. He got *her*.

She tensed as she heard the other guys returning, horribly conscious that she was disheveled, thoroughly kissed and bawling. Frantically, she clutched Seth's plaid shirt. "Don't let anyone see me like this."

His arms tightened, and she felt his smile against her hair as he kicked the door closed. "Honey B, I've got your back."

♪ ♫ ♩

Thanks for reading **FALL**, the third in my *Rock Solid Romance* series. Have you read the other books in the series? Find out more on my website at www.karinabliss.com.

Rise

Acclaimed literary biographer Elizabeth Winston writes about long-dead heroes.

So bad-boy rock icon Zander Freedman couldn't possibly tempt her to write his memoir.

Except the man is a mass of fascinating contradictions—manipulative, honest, gifted, charismatic and morally ambiguous. In short, everything she seeks in a biography subject. When in her life will she get another chance to work with a living legend?

But saying yes to one temptation soon leads to another. Suddenly she's having heated fantasies about her subject, fantasies this blue-eyed devil is only too willing to stoke. She thought self-control was in her DNA; after all, she grew up a minister's daughter.

She thought wrong.

Play

Rock star Jared Walker is within reach of career glory…but his marriage is in the pits. Determined to save it, he talks his wife into holiday dates with only one rule: they must pretend they are strangers. But when he discovers what Kayla *really* wants for Christmas, will he be able to give it to her?

PLAY is a 30,000 novella and is one of five stories in YOU HAD ME AT CHRISTMAS, a holiday anthology with Molly O'Keefe, Stephanie Doyle, Jennifer Lohmann and Laura Florand.

About the Author

New Zealander Karina Bliss's debut won a Romantic Book of the Year award in Australia and in 2016 she finaled for the fourth time with **RISE**—the first of her Rock Solid series, which digs into the private and family lives of rock stars.

Her fifteen romance novels have also received numerous accolades (Desert Island Keeper, 'Best Of' lists, RT Top Pick, Sizzling Book Club Chat) on reader sites like Dear Author, Smart Bitches and All About Romance. She lives north of Auckland with her husband and son.

I love hearing from readers. You can contact me by:

Emailing karina@karinabliss.com

Tweeting @BlissKarina

Visiting Facebook at: https://www.facebook.com/KarinaBlissAuthor

Sign up to my newsletter here for release updates:
www.karinabliss.com.

ACKNOWLEDGMENTS

I'd like to thank Janine Bliss, Janine Fisher, Abby Gaines, Sarah Mayberry, and Molly O'Keefe for their fabulous feedback, as well as advisor & marketer Sharyn Barratt.

Special thanks to editor Wanda Ottewell who held the torch when I was digging for the story.